BILLY'S WAR

Vincent Albert

BILLY'S WAR

VINCENT ATHERTON

Matador
Unit E2 Airfield Business Park,
Harrison Road, Market Harborough,
Leicestershire. LE16 7UL
Tel: 0116 2792299
Email: books@troubador.co.uk
Web: www.troubador.co.uk/matador
Twitter: @matadorbooks

ISBN 978 1803137 315

British Library Cataloguing In Publication Data.
A catalogue record for this book is available from the British Library.

Printed and bound in the UK by TJ Books Limited, Padstow, Cornwall
Typeset in 11pt Minion Pro by Troubador Publishing Ltd, Leicester, UK

Matador is an imprint of Troubador Publishing Ltd

Dedicated to the memory of William Atherton 1916 – 94

FOREWORD

I wrote "Billy's War" as the answer to my own question, "What did you do in the war, Dad?"

He always declined to answer, didn't want to talk about it. Then slowly, over the years, snippets crept out. He let bits of the story go, to me, my brothers and my sisters, not often in much detail. Many of those stories are filled out by my imagination and included in the book. It also has incidents included from historical research, assisted by his war records. The rest I just made up.

The novel is therefore a blend of fact and fiction, and while the characters included in the narrative are often based on real people, quite a few are just invented for dramatic purposes. So, incidents are described as they might have happened, rather than as historical fact. They are intended to be consistent with real history, rather than to actually be historic.

In 1948, after the period described in the book, he met Teresa Hart at Leigh Tennis Club. Hetty, had she actually been a real person, would have approved of the venue. They married in 1950 and had five children, of whom I am the cleverest and most important. Don't tell the others I said that, though!

He was always close to his youngest sister Celia (Auntie Celi). The dispute with Joe over his parent's house actually ran for twenty years, during which time they hardly spoke. Joe finally took the initiative to end it in 1968, when Billy was ill, with a recurrence of the amoebic dysentery he had acquired in Egypt.

William Atherton died in May 1994, a few weeks before the 50th anniversary of D-day.

The Israelis and Palestinians have yet to resolve their differences. I wish them both good luck.

AFTERWARDS

AMERICAN ZIONIST MOVEMENT, 40 WALL ST., MANHATTAN, NEW YORK

Bernard Brook,
Hoblarob Earldom,
The Tockarock Neck,
Georgetown County,
South Carolina

26th November 1947

Dear Bernard,

I hope you, Annie and the little streamlets are having a good time, up at the grand old house. I envy you those great views over the river and out across the bay. I loved my visit there; such lovely scenery and the weather was as warm as in Jerusalem.

Just want to update you on how things are running in NYC. Your guys did a great job in getting the vote delayed a few days, saved quite a bit of turis. I'm not saying we wouldn't have gotten a majority for the vote but not sure we'd have the two thirds they say is required for UN Resolution 181.

There's quite a bit schmoozing going on and the Department of State is also very good at twisting arms. That pressure brought

1

on President Truman produced good results. He was scared that support for the Democratic party might collapse, especially with the implications for future funding in New York. Most of the Caribbean and Latin American countries have now agreed to vote the right way. I expect Liberia and the Philippines to soon change over as well, as they also need US loans. Even some European countries might bend to any possibility of losing the Marshall Plan assistance and they're all anxious to persuade refugees to move out of their own territory. Even France is signalling it may vote for us now, after all those arguments about the rights of Palestinians! When their own funding came under threat it all changed.

Only that meshugener little island Great Britain is staying out of this, no one can understand their thinking. And their army still occupies my homeland. I know you like the British, especially your friend Winston Churchill, I do as well sometimes but you have to admit they do behave illogically.

Whatever happens with the vote at the UN the state of Israel will be created in the next few weeks. There might well be a war but our people are determined and well prepared for it. The money and armaments that are flowing from New York to Haifa will ensure that.

That British stuff reminds me of something. I got a diary sent to me from an English soldier, un acquaintance from Jerusalem. I can't say he's a friend, since he was part of the occupying forces, but I admit to liking him a little bit. I can't tell you how surprised I was to get it. I didn't think Billy would be capable of stringing three words together in writing, never mind this amazing diary. Obviously, he's not much of a movan, so it's no value as an historical account, there's far too many mistakes in it. For example, he habitually refers to Zionist freedom fighters as terrorists. What a schmuck!

That much is nonsense, but all the same, it's an eye witness account of how things look from a Gentile's view point. I enjoyed reading his ideas about me and especially his account of my trial.

In the end I guess he was useful both to me and our cause. Not sure if you'll get time to read it, but it's attached any way and if you don't find time to read it you can always get your maid to light the fire with it.

Afshr far itst,
    Hetty Borowska

Celle Airfield, near Hannover

April 15th 1945

A soft breeze plays over the green fields of Saxony and ruffles the hair of a small group of Englishmen. It even feels warm, as the sun tries to breaks through, giving every cloud a golden lining.

The last winter of the war has ended and the world is a better place. Not much better, of course, there's still a war on, the last little remnant. Thank heaven the grey clouds of the past months have dispersed. Dark days and the flat, sodden fields of Nijmegen, where we stayed too long, are forgotten and bright sunlight illuminates the half-timbered buildings of the town of Celle in the middle distance. Scarlet roofs and black timber against white plaster, a bit like the villages of the English Midlands. A glint of orange sunshine reflects from the surface of the River Aller, adding a little glitter. A pretty view on a sunny day; the land of my enemy is not hostile as I'd feared. Even the Wehrmacht, who put up such a desperate fight yesterday, have disappeared to lurk in the space beyond our view.

Beyond the perimeter of the airfield the trees cut us off from the world, low blobby hills in the middle-distance peep at us. They must be surprised to see sixteen Cromwell tanks and supporting lorries; gathered so far inside the Fatherland.

"Where's the bloody Jerries now? The yellah bastards ran away in the night. Not so bloody brave now, huh? We saw 'em off."

"Hey, hey. There's a few over there, Knocker, scuttling away in that half-track," yells Fido, his face flushed a blotchy red. He stands upright, pointing an accusing finger at a vehicle, driving away at a leisurely pace. The travellers must be confident that they're out of range.

A second or twos delay before Knocker sinks back into the tower of his tank and looses off a shot from the cannon. There's a bang, a brilliant flash of yellow and blue light and the near miss takes out a section of fence, throws up a cloud of dirt and demolishes several bushes. A second later the heavy crump batters our ears and the driver of the half-track accelerates around bend in a hurry, leaving a dense black cloud, slowly rising above the scorched forest. It scuttles away, like a frightened squirrel seeking to hide up a tree. It disappears round a bend and behind the trees. Or perhaps more like a rabbit.

There's a lot of laughter among the tank crews. Would any of us would be braver if we were outnumbered and out of ammo? It's a ridiculous idea but I'll keep it to myself; don't want to spoil the party. No one cares about being fair to Germans and every man, unwashed, in a grubby uniform and in need of a haircut, can sense victory. It's just an inch or two away but somehow out of reach. No one dares say it's over, it's been such a long haul that it seems too big and important to be happening, we barely believe it. The war that seemed to be unwinnable has been won, but this would be the worst time to die.

Even so, we're so confident that no one thinks of setting any trenches or defences. No need for sentries to keep us safe. All our careful habits are abandoned, we replace fear with complacency. Most important, the fire's lit and the boys are making a brew.

I light a cigarette and look round. For the first time in many days I can relax enough to take off my helmet. It's been driving me mad inside the cab, rubbing the tops of my ears red, banging on the roof or door spars. I've got the luxury to look around and take in a bit of flat, green countryside. Must be good farming land, why have the Saxons have left so much of it forested? Across the runway, red topped mediaeval houses glow and shimmer in the sunshine. The place has personality, probably a lot of history here.

More Cromwell tanks of the 11th Armoured Corps are arriving, moving in to secure the airstrip. I've supported these blokes across Europe from Normandy beaches deep into Germany. The Yanks have been left to take Hannover, they're said to be storming the city, house by house, right now. We hear the occasional distant bangs and booms from over there and a faint smell of cordite continually drifts across. Smudges of smoke rise on the horizon from time to time and then fade away again. There's not much to capture here, a grass field with a simple concrete strip and a few hangars. The sign says it's "Fliegerhorst Celle–Wietzenbruch".

We'd arrived just as the Luftwaffe was leaving. A solitary Juncker's 88 turning at the top of its climb and heading east through wispy remnants of cloud as we drove through the open gates. I guess that was its ground crew that Knocker had shot at. The hangars are littered with the burnt-out ruins of Junkers aircraft that the Germans destroyed as they retreated. The stench of the thin acrid smoke escapes in thin strips, fouling our nostrils, and the black bones of the airframes tell of defeat and ruin.

We've drunk our tea and are about to set up tent, when a jeep races over. The driver weaving madly, going too fast, throwing up dust and swerving to a handbrake halt. A pale, moonfaced man with a few strands of grey hair showing under a sweat stained peaked cap falls out. He wears the insignia of a Captain and the badge of Medical Officer, a doctor with a strong Scottish accent. "Got any medical orderlies?" he shouts above the tank engines. "Any K rations or vitaminised chocolate to spare?"

"What's up? What's gorrinter yer?" I ask with a touch of fear and foreboding. At close range his face looks grey with stress, deep lines etched across his forehead, his clothes are dirty and his shouting makes little sense. Now he stops, looks me in the eye for just an instance and draws a few breaths before starting again.

"Concentration camp up the road," he says, shakily lighting a cigarette. "It's dreadful – just dreadful." His shaking hand throw the cigarette away untouched. "I've never seen anything so hideous in my life. You just won't believe it 'til you see it – for God's sake come and help!" The tone rising until the last few words are almost lost in a mutter.

"Where is it?"

His hand trembles, seems unsteady on his feet, I think there's even a bead of sweat appearing on his brow. He is now going red in the face. "Over there," he points vaguely to the northwest. "It's called Bergen Belsen."

The tank crews, having stopped for their brew, ignore him, but the Jock medic is too agitated to stand still. He goes over to speak to, even shout at, a group of officers. Then they look as agitated as he does. Next thing, they are all running over, pointing at me, shouting at me, jumping into the back of my lorry, still squawking loudly from under the canvas cover.

"Get us over to that concentration camp place straight away, man. Alderton, you navigate," croaks an edgy Colonel in his newly acquired parrot's voice. This seems odd behaviour, my dirty old three tonner must be the most luxurious vehicle available to them. I suppose it's the only vehicle available.

This should only take a short time, this country has beautifully flat concrete roads. It'd be a pleasure to drive if it wasn't for scattered enemy forces. We'd intended to follow the medic but he's gone, long gone. Fast. His driving as agitated as his speech had been. There's just a faint mist of dust in the air that hints of his passage, drifting away over the fields.

2nd Lieutenant James Alderton is beside me, a fresh-faced young man with a happy smile. The Lieutenant is tall and slim, a bit underfed you might say, showing a thatch of dense red hair on the rare occasions he removes his cap. He's got a map and is happy dishing out directions. It's the first map I've seen since we left England, guess only officers get one. We stop at each crossroads, while he decides where to go, trying to recognise landmarks. I'm not confident in his navigational abilities but I'm enjoying his discomfort under the strain.

Now we're at a cross road in the middle of broad, flat green fields. I don't recognise any of the features on the map but Alderton says it is left and he's taking responsibility. So, we go left. We drive a couple of miles and come to a small village with a church which is definitely not where we're intending to go. He can find a church with a distinctive spire on his map. But it's the wrong way, perhaps into bandit country. This place holds small groups of desperate enemy forces who might appear around any or every corner. I reverse as gently and quietly as possible, so the guys in back don't notice and go back to take the right turn we'd ignored earlier. Get it right this time, Lieutenant, please! James Alderton's ever-present smile has gone missing; his eyes stare at the chart and a furrow creases his forehead.

Several miles of bright, pleasant sunlit pasture go by before we're approaching a large camp with a high fence and barbed wire all around it, peering at it through another rowan and birch wood. There's a faint but distinctly unpleasant smell of rot in the air. No doubt the new warmth of spring has something to do with it.

Eventually we can see enough through the trees to clearly make out a camp. I stop my Bedford a hundred yards away from the gates to take it in. The stench is much stronger, really affecting us now. I don't want to get any closer and so just stare through wire fence. When I glance across to Lieutenant Alderton he's sweating and gaping as well. He's open mouthed, his nose wrinkled. As I watch his face distorts into a grimace.

There are pits of dead and rotting corpses around the perimeter in open sight of the road, mostly naked, emaciated women. These are open pits filled with dead people with taut, blackened faces, their whole bodies discoloured and mis-shaped. The rotting human flesh is the source of the smell. I've never seen anything like this, never wanted to see it and hope I'll never see anything like it again.

Despite the Scottish Medic's hysterical warning I'm not ready for this, not prepared for the poisonous odours. An icy hand that's already gripped my heart is now compressing my lungs too and it's hard to breathe. I just gasp and pant. This is bloody ridiculous.

A wooden fence, topped with barbed wire, is interrupted by an occasional square guard tower. These are abandoned but machine guns still in place, sagging loosely rather than guarding their positions. They tell us something about the people who ruled this place. Not a nice story.

The Officers are irritated by my reluctance to enter the grounds, but they've had little sight of what's before me. Once inside the massive iron gates we drive a half mile along a sandy track to another wire fence, enclosing an inner compound. Beyond it, the wooden fences are painted white – short, stout and regular – well maintained. There are flower beds, neat and well pruned, elegant white marble kerbstones lining the drive. Beyond them are smart, well maintained wooden shacks which made up the administrative block.

In the compound nearby a group of ragged, emaciated skeletons are moving around in a loose, uncoordinated parade. So thin that I can see bones protruding through their skin, they seem little more than living sacks of bones with haggard yellowish, almost green, faces and vacant eyes. Men wear striped pyjamas or just rags, while the women wear striped flannel gowns or just old and dirty clothing. It's quite a cool day but many are nearly naked and all without shoes, just wearing socks, stockings or barefooted.

I pull up here and see that we're not first to have arrived. A noisy, excited troop of British soldiers are throwing opened tins of smoked ham into the compounds. There's a scramble among those who can walk trying to grab food but the majority just lie on the ground and some of them mew pitifully. There are thousands of sick and starving prisoners, shut in the overcrowded and dirty fenced compounds.

I stop the vehicle here and the Officers tumble out the back, one of them falling face first into the dirt from the rear of the stationery vehicle in his haste to see what's happening. We're not greeted, we're not welcomed, we're not even noticed until an army Medic runs over; hustles us away and shouts angrily, in a fury of self-righteousness rage. I am too troubled to hear what he said, I'm still staring at these people. The Doctor pushes me so hard that I stagger, fall over, and then sit down on the dust. "Get off, you idiot! Stay away," he screams at me. "They're all infected with typhus and dysentery. It's a bloody epidemic here. We can't release them without infecting ourselves and everyone else. Keep them in the bloody cages, at least 'til we've running water to clean 'em up."

Having delivered his frenzied messages, he turns, becomes red faced, looks at the row of silent officers and moves away without a backward glance, into the nearest hut. Obviously, having taken out his rage on the lowest ranking soldier available, some urgent task now needs his immediate attention.

Those inmates who are aware of events, have realised that the German guards are gone and pull at the fencing near to the food store. Some have a little strength and the fencing is close to coming down. A troop of agitated soldiers rush over there and raise their rifles. Everyone here seems to do things at a running pace. We all think that everything needs to be done immediately. The officer shouts at the inmates to get away from wiring.

A sharp volley of shots rings out. The mob stops and there's a troubled silence; my eyes searching their ranks to assess the damage. No one hit? The volley must have been aimed over their heads. With order restored, I join the other Brit soldiers bringing out any food we find lying in the store and throwing them into the cages. Some prisoners are fighting each other, without huge strength but with considerable venom. Many inside the cages, that other universe just a few feet away, are motionless; others able to move their arms but without the energy to walk. A few more are helped by those who are able to get the food. Most are just left to lie unaided. Yet others are walking around with blank faces. They just simply ignore food and everything else that's happening.

One of our medical orderlies staggers out of the bedraggled, grey, wooden barrack huts that line the far edge of the site. Holding his head, hands shaking and his eyes staring wildly. Despite the horror of the cages he seems to be even more sickened by what he has seen in there. I'm afraid he's about to scream.

"What is it mate? What's in there?" Even as I ask, I regret it; I don't wanna know. My intestines are screwing up in anticipation of another horror.

"It's filthy and they're all heaving with lice. These people are too weak to move and there's no sanitation. Their shit is everywhere, they're covered in it." I get a lungful of the stink of ripening crap but still look in. It's a mistake, a vision of the Beelzebub's den.

There is a mass of human excrement, floors covered and walls heavily smeared with it. The people in top bunks can't get out and have just dumped it anywhere below them. This place is full of flies and hordes of large beetles are crawling around floor. Rather beautiful beetles with a petrol green shell, sparkling blue as sunlight plays on their backs through an open door. This must be a sort of heaven for beetles, a land of contentment and plenty.

The same medical officer who reproached us before re-appears, bursting into the hut, waving his arms and screaming again with renewed vigour. "Get away, get away from there. I've told you there's nothing you can do for them yet. We need water to clean 'em up. Until then you only spread disease from being in contact with 'em."

Nothing I can do will remove the scent of human excrement in my nostrils, the sounds of pitiful suffering in my ears and the images of inhumanity burnt onto my mind. The dripping of body fluids from the bunks that line the hut thunder and echo in my ears.

Why am I so affected by this? The past few days have been good to me, the first few days that I've not come under fire for nearly a year. It's good that the shooting has stopped, I will be alive at the end of this day, a strange unfamiliar feeling. It should be good; it should be a celebration. Instead, I'm losing my mind, in a way that constant gunfire never achieved. What's wrong with me?

I look around and find I'm at the entrance to the camp. Beside me is the sign that identifies it. A name I'd never heard of before this morning but one I will remember most of my remaining life, and even more in my sleep.

*

After an hour of inspection, the officers have had all they can stomach and need me to drive them back to the airfield. I'm glad to go. This time the Lieutenant guides me back to the airfield without getting lost, but without smiling either. Neither of us speak on the way back, except for a few tersely muttered directions.

The Officers are anxious to get on the radio. I don't catch all of their conversation, but the Brigadier is clearly asking for as much medical support as can be spared. I can hear a particularly agitated demand for all the resources of the British Army to be deployed here. 'Do that IM-MEDIATELY. I said im-bloody-mediately.' His radio mike is slammed down and Brigadier stomps off red faced. If I didn't know him better, I'd think he's got tears in his eyes.

I wander back to sit with my pals, just in time to share a brew with them. They're sitting around and all as jolly as they were this morning. Cracking jokes and relaxing, trying to get a suntan, just like they're on holiday. They've even found some biscuits to go with tea, a real treat. Knocker pours me a mug and thrusts it into my hand.

"Well, look who's back. Been having a nice drive around the countryside have we, Billy lad?"

I sit and stare at Knocker in silence until he shrugs his shoulders and goes back to chat with the jolly boys. I sip my tea, unable to believe he's acting as though nowt's happened. I'm unable and unwilling to explain what I've seen. He lights a cigarette and looks away from me, studying the countryside and facing away as though the world is the same place as it was this morning.

BERGEN-BELSEN

16TH APRIL 1945

This time we're moving quickly and confidently through flat and forested countryside in bright Spring sunshine. The trouble with that is we get there quicker. It was easy to find the route but my hand still trembles a little as first stench of the camp reaches me. I don't stop this time, just drive straight past the iron gates, now permanently open.

And, as we enter a quieter camp, there are indications that the Army presence has started to make a difference. There's a new warning sign for a start: 'Dust spreads Typhus' it tells me. I brake, change down a gear so as to slow down and the wheels throw up a small fog which wafts onto the grass besides the track.

I'm soon driving past a group of women in SS uniforms working under the stolid gaze of angry British soldiers. They are digging a huge pit beside a pile of bodies, stacked five or six high. These frumpy frauleins are carrying bodies from cages, they look healthy and strong. The fences are still there but all the inhabitants we saw there yesterday are gone, apart from the dead who still litter the earth.

Sappers are swarming all over the site; trying to restore water, toilets and electrical power. They're working everywhere on the site and say it's all expected to be operating sometime today. That's what they always say.

On the fresh green fields, beyond the boundary of the camp, are tents where survivors are gathered. People being washed in buckets of cold water and dusted with powder. Nearby a group of soldiers are boiling cauldrons of soup, mostly turnips. There is a stack besides the stoves; plus a few onions and a handful of dried beans. There's a bit of bread being handed out too but it's rationed to just a broken chunk for each person.

I help by peeling turnips. At least I think I'm helping but get corrected very quickly. "Don't be a damn chump," my new pal Jimmy shouts at me. "We can't waste the peel. This isn't the bloody Ritz you know, we've gorra stop 'em from starving. Everything goes into the pot."

My turnip peel soup does not go down well with the unhappy camp people, many of them vomit it up. It seems that even watery turnip is too rich for their digestive systems in current condition.

One lady dressed in rags, head covered by a cloth square, does drink some and then takes one of my hands in hers and holds it tightly against her brown, wrinkled face. It feels like a collection of thin bones. Although there's no warmth in her hands, I hear plenty in her voice. I don't know why she is saying, "jenk wee yah, jenk wee yah," but I think I can sense a little of what she means. They all start chanting this through their tears: "jenk wee yah, jenk wee yah, jenk wee yah". She looks up at me, directly into my eyes, her whole body shaking. Crying and laughing, she holds tight to my hand. I cry and laugh too, perhaps a bit more crying. Is it really gratitude or just relief?

I'm looking at her. I don't get much option as I can't move away while she hangs on so tightly. There's still a lot of suffering in that look but she believes that I'm her saviour. It's more responsibility than I want and as soon as her grip weakens, I slip it and walk unsteadily away.

Jimmy Alderton has become a sort of a mate, very chatty for an officer. The tall red-headed guy with a grammar school education must feel a bit distant from the other officers, maybe because of his working-class back ground. He's become my only source of real information and a pretty good one. There are goods to be delivered to Belsen; the RAF have been flying in supplies. Large sacks of 'flour' marked as Bengal Famine Mix, a new one to me.

"The sacks contain a special mix of ground rice and sugar which was designed for victims of a famine in India in the '30s. It should be easier for these folk to digest and keeping people alive is a priority; they're gonna need good sustenance to fight off those diseases that are running through the camp."

It's an opportunity for me to tell Fido what is happening, he always used to get the gossip before me. A short, lean man with black hair and porcelain white skin, Fido seems to have lost his usual sense of humour today. He listens a little impatiently. I know that he's been affected by what's happening here and wants to get on with something. I guess it's his way of coping.

My new job is making up the famine mix. It looks like wallpaper paste, but let's call it gruel. Just rice flour mixed with water in the pot that had the thin soup in it yesterday. Today, me and Fido have helpers, quite a few helpers. Fido is with an elderly lady, in a long skirt and a head scarf and several gaps in her black teeth. I reckon she looks like a gypsy and I wonder if she is telling Fido's future. That might explain his melancholy look, I think he'd prefer not to know.

I'm accompanied by a rather pretty young man with stuttering English spoken in a heavy European accent. He's tall but very slender and has dark hair and a bright smile which makes him really different in this place of misery. His most striking features, however, are his eyes; a pale bright blue as though they have a light shining out from them.

"Hello," he twitters in a high pitch, that makes him seem even younger. "My name Jeno Riker. I want help feed my friends here.

15

We suffered together and I want stop their suffering. Thank you to English Army for making us free."

"No need to thank me Jeno, I'm only doing my duty. You deserve to be free, what happened to you guys was all crap, just pure evil."

"We hate fucking Nazis, you let me kill them now."

I'm not getting into that discussion. "You look a bit better than the others, Jeno. How've you done that?

"My brother Gyuszi and me was good at stealing from guards. Our job to look after animal on farm. We found scraps fed to pig. We eat many of food for feed pig. But my brother has some illness now, camp fever."

"That's really shit mate. I'm sorry and we'll help him as much as we can."

There's another round of stirring the pot and then Jeno tastes it for me. He pulls a face. "Not so nice. Needs some little spice, I want paprika, and maybe a little salt too."

That makes me smile, a rare smile. "You're a fussy little bastard. You're just being bloody ridiculous now, Jeno. It's not the bleeding Ritz, you know. Anyway, tell me where d'you come from?"

"I grew up in the Budapest. Before war our family good times. My father successful banker and I, tailor. The bad treatment of Jews starts before Germans come. My father sacked from job and then so I. Then we were much bad times. We sold everything and soon we went rich to poor." Jeno looks at me, his blue eyes defying me to interrupt but I've nowt to say.

"We knew dangers come when Nazis take over the Hungaria and so we applied go the New York. We waited long time for permissions from USA and permissions never come. Our country occupied and too late, we can't get out the Hungaria."

Another glance. I'm stirring the pot a little more vigorously now and feeling a bit of a cold chill. Maybe, it's the breeze that's got up. If that is a breeze.

"We ordered to live at ghetto for Jews but tried avoid. We

moved around the Budapest. My father's old friends from Bank took us, with much great risk. Last October we moved to house of the Szalasis. We thought they friends too. The mistake. They hand us to SS. When I go back the Budapest, I will make call on Szalasis. I something to say there, I got something to do with them."

Now I have another look at him, his face is twisted in a pained anger. Maybe he's not as cheerful and harmless as I thought. There's obviously a lot going on under the surface and the light in his eyes shines stronger than ever and now with a fierce red tinge to it, a little unnerving. It suggests he's getting out of control.

"Take a moment Jeno. I can see this is tricky for you, no need to carry on if it distresses you."

He ignores me, as though he heard nothing. "My family taken the Auschwitz but then my brother Gyuszi and me brought this place as labour slaves to work farm. I much afraid for rest of my family, they stay in the Auschwitz. I also afraid Gyuszi, he much ill. He over there, in blanket. He die soon, unless make him stronger."

Jeno's hand is trembling and he won't look me in the eye. He's struggling to his feet but his energy has gone. When he finally looks up at me, his eyes are full of tears and he immediately looks away. I put my arm around him and say: "Come on mate. Let's get this gruel made and Goosy can be the first person we bring it to. We'll feed him up and make him stronger."

He tries to smile back but it comes out looking more like a grimace. He can't manage to get through his tears for the moment, the blue light disappearing momentarily. He buries his head in his hands and sobs. I let him cry, a hand on his shoulder and stir the gruel as it comes to the boil.

Soon the gruel is ready and there are lots of hungry mouths; we take it out to the field. There's a scramble of people holding out bowls for a portion of steaming paste. Once I've given out enough for that first group, I try to haul Jeno up onto his feet but he flops like bag of rags; the smile is lost, his energy evaporated.

I hold him up, make him stand and walk because we're off to

find and feed his brother. Just as he had said, Goosy is in a tent under care of the Medics, very pale and asleep and lying on a camp bed under a stack of old grey blankets. Jeno kneels besides him, holding him and whispering into his ear. There's no movement of any sort.

Jeno holds his brother and gently brings his frail frame forward to the bowl to feed him but the body lies limp in his arms. Jeno puts a spoon full of the gruel and smears it onto the thin blue lips. There's still no response. He's muttering something to Goosy and rocking him.

I need to move away, need to leave now. I can't bear to watch when Jeno realises that there is not going to be a response. Outside the tent I stand for a moment and wait for the wail of anguish. Then I keep on going.

Fido has been watching all of this and he puts a hand on my shoulder but says nowt. After a moment we all move further away and stand at the top of the slight rise. Jimmy Alderton comes close to me too, facing away from the camp. There's silence apart from bird song, which is amazingly loud and a stillness only interrupted by the gentle swaying of the trees. The buttercups and red campions make a brave show of colour amidst the grass and give off a faint but pleasing scent. We all stare down the slope at the woods and the woods are full of sound, the wind among the needles of the pine branches, the chitter of insects and the cries of small woodland creatures, as well as bird-song; and from time to time a stronger gust of wind makes the branches of cedars and firs move against each other and groan like a cello.

The weather is quite nice today. It was really sunny earlier this morning but has got just a bit cloudier this afternoon. We might even get a spot of rain later.

179 Chapel St., Leigh, Lancs

2nd August 1945

The blue and cream Leigh Corporation bus, number 26, that brought me from Manchester goes on down Chapel Street, past a long row of red brick pubs, shops and houses, towards the town centre. Under the steel sky it looks exactly as grey as it was when I'd left. We'd had both a lady bus driver and lady conductor; I've never seen that before. Now I'm alone in the most familiar place in the world, in front of the very same terraced house that I grew up in. It looks smaller than I remember but the brick is brighter red.

I've enjoyed the journey. It's been fun all the way from Calais. The mood of the nation is giddily upbeat, celebration and good humour abound and everyone in uniform is a hero. Lots of guys shook my hand as I walked across London to Euston station. Several girls I'd never met before came upto me, hugged me and one even kissed me. Folk shook my hand or patted me on the back as I walked down the train and the people I sat with in the carriage all congratulated me on my victory in Europe. I'm starting to believe that I've beaten Adolf Hitler single-handedly, he must've been pretty scared when he heard I was on my way. And I never even got to Berlin!

Time and time again I hear the same phrases repeated: "it

makes you proud to be British", "we showed those Jerries" and "good times are just around the corner". I hope that last one is right; we need better times.

Now I'm actually home my feelings are in disarray, I'm either happy or sad, confident or anxious. Maybe all of them at same time, maybe none of them at all. Above all, I don't know whether to expect welcome or rejection from my own folks and my brother. We parted on bad terms but things should be different now. I hope.

The brown front door of our house is shut against me and I have to knock to be let in. I've never done that before, always had my own key. That key got lost when I was hiding in a ditch under artillery fire, somewhere in the north of Belgium, or maybe it was south of Netherlands. Who knows? Who cares? It's been two full years since I was back here and the dull paint on front door seems even duller and a few pieces are flaking off. It's even threatening to rain. Apart from the missing key, nowt has changed.

This has always been the most ordinary of places, a brick terraced house in an inconspicuous row. The vast amber bulk of Butt's Mill towers over it and its chimneys are filling the air with the smoke, smell and even taste of burning coal. Behind it I can see the winding gear of one of many collieries that are scattered across the surrounding landscape. Nothing of interest ever happened in this house, although there's often much activity all around. Nowt is happening again today, but it's happening fast enough to make my heart beat at twice its normal rate. Thud, thud, thud in my ears.

The door swings slowly open, just a crack, emitting the faint sound of tinny radio music and revealing a nervous, little old man peering suspiciously at me over his half-moon glasses. It takes me a few seconds to recognise my Dad. His hair is almost as grey as his moustache, his skin a similar pasty shade of off-white, emphasised by the contrast with dark areas around his eyes. This red, black colouring seems to be running down the deep wrinkles on his face. He's much slimmer than I remember and bending forwards.

I do recognise that blue striped shirt though, he used to wear it with his suit in the office of the family business. It was new, clean and well ironed then. He was important in those days, always smart and very confident in all his business dealings. Now it's crumpled, faded and he has his braces over it, supporting a well-worn pair of grey trousers. His face folds in puzzlement, then lights up with a great smile. He comes out onto the pavement to hug me and I drop my kitbag to give him a great big hug back. He shakes my hand and shouts to the kitchen.

"Billy! It's our Billy! Home from the war, Alice. Welcome home, son. So good to see you. You must have been through hell but you're here now. Safe and sound, and the war's over."

I've had our differences with him but they're forgotten. A rush of relief pulses through me, cleansing my soul and filling me with joy and a new affection for the stubborn, cantankerous old git.

"So good to see you, Dad. Great to be home, great to be alive. A bit of a surprise too. I didn't think I'd ever see this house again." I quickly wipe away shameful tears that momentarily fill the corner of my eye and hope he doesn't notice that, the wavering in my voice or the tremble in my hand.

We go into the snug at the back of the house and the music gets a little less tinny and a lot louder. Dad collapses into his armchair and has a fit of coughing. He pulls out a cigarette from a pack on the sideboard and lights it, sucking at it as though he thinks it'll ease his cough. Then he leans over slowly and turns off the radio while I watch in silence, noting everything around me. For the first time the dark decor of this room seems appropriate. The dark brown of the sofa is as sombre as I feel; the red, green and blue floral carpet shrieks with silent anxiety and the drawn curtains don't cover up our strained relationships. The glowing fag hangs off his lower lip and a little ash falls from it into the carpet.

My Mum calls from kitchen. "Who is it, Joe?" She hadn't heard his shouting from the front door when he'd bawled it at top of his voice. Or maybe she's got used to ignoring him? Her pale round face appears around door.

She stares at me for a moment. Then jumps up in the air, holds her hands to her mouth, shrieks with pleasure and grabs hold of me in a crushing embrace. An alarmingly energetic performance for an elderly lady with an unknown muscular disorder. Her excitement is so much that her slippers fall off. Blue ones. They must be new, well second hand new. The ones I remember, with bright red heels, and little silver buckles, that used to jingle as she moved, have gone. No doubt they've fallen to pieces. I missed that momentous event while I was driving across France under fire, crawling through soggy Belgian ditches or sleeping in an icy Dutch field.

She is thinner too and her hair has gone completely white. That frightens me a bit. She's still wearing the same pink, threadbare dressing gown, although it's a bit late in day to be wearing bedclothes. This is definitely still the same one she's worn for many years; I'll always remember her in this dressing gown.

"Billy! You're here at last, and I'd no idea you were coming. Thank God, you're safe. I've been so frightened when we heard of all that fighting in Europe."

I'm laughing too and place a chaste kiss on her cheek, sealing the finish of a long painful chapter for our family. Our arguments are all finished, our differences are over now. I hope.

"Let's have a cup of tea, Alice."

Mum ignores him and replies to me, though I haven't said anything. "We can have some tea if you like Billy, we've run out of real milk but there's some powder. Is it all right like that? You know it's difficult, everything being rationed. But you look really well, you've grown bigger. Must be all that bully beef they give you soldier boys. But why didn't you tell us you were coming?"

"I did. I wrote as soon as I knew but we only got three days' notice ourselves. It's a special embarkation leave. I'll bet you get the letter in the next few days."

"What d'ye mean? Embarkation leave?"

"I'm going to be flown to Burma next week. We're going to fight the Japanese. That war isn't over yet."

There's an awkward pause and they both stare at me in horror.

"No, no. You can't be. That's bloody ridiculous. We've only just got you back. You can't be going back to war." She puts her head in her hands and starts to cry silently. At least, I think she's crying.

"Well, I am. I don't get a choice. Sorry."

"No. You're out of the Army, the war's over."

This ragged conversation causes a period of quiet reflection, as we sip an extremely weak cup of greyish tea with powdered milk and chat about how my parents have coped with rationing and having very little money. They don't ask about my experiences in the war and I don't offer to tell them. We exchange a few sentences about the weather in Europe, what the countryside looks like and the relative merits of French and British architecture. None of which is of much interest to any of us.

In return they tell me what's happened in Leigh. Seems that anyone not in uniform has been getting a hard time. Few reasons or excuses for not fighting get believed, even the Bevin boys get a hard time. And a lot of men's jobs have been turned over to women, driving buses for instance.

As the afternoon slips away into early evening the front door opens silently and my younger sister Celia arrives home from the Mill. She, Betty and Vinty are the siblings I'd always been close too. My other brother and sisters are much older than us and since both Gertie and Nash got married, I've seen very little of them. Now little Vinty has gone too, he's an Air Traffic controller for the RAF, somewhere in the East of England.

Celia's got a floor supervisor job at Leigh Spinners. She greets my Dad and asks why he's grinning. Then spots me sitting in the big chair, still in my uniform, a big smile on my face too.

"Billy, oh Billy. It's our Billy." She stares at me and puts her hand over her mouth and seems frozen to the spot. A look if… well, what is it a look of? Horror, fright, shock maybe?

"You're home, you're home. Safe. I thought you'd die. So many times I nearly died myself when the post came, fearing it could be from the War Office. But you're back at last, safe and well. Thanks be to God. Don't ever go away again."

Her hug meant more to me than I can explain but she does not smile, she does not cry out with joy. She just falls into the armchair on top of me. Then she holds me close and cries, sobbing deeply and gulping air in between gasps. She's clinging to me and I feel her tiny body shuddering. I was determined not to weep; soldiers don't do that. But a damp spot still appears against my face among the red and blue roses in floral pattern of Celi's frock.

"It's lovely to be home, to see you again, my darling little sister."

I think I'll let my Dad tell her that I'm going off to fight the Japanese in a few days.

THE GEORGE AND DRAGON, LEIGH

3RD AUGUST 1945

The Friday market is in full swing as I go for a walk around town. Even with rationing it's possible to buy a few extra bits to eat. Those rabbits look especially tempting, if only I could find the money for one.

It seems sensible to wear my uniform since it's all I have that fits. The clothes I wore before the war are still here but they're too small. Besides it's nice to be the centre of attention, now that a man in uniform is every one's hero. It's a bit of a thrill to bump into those old friends who stayed behind. Everyone says they wish that they could say they could've gone and done their bit too. Now it's all over it must seem like it was all glory, no muck or bullets, and everyone wants a part of that.

Here's Jimmy Unsworth, all ruddy cheeks and goodwill, coming for a chat and pumping my sore hand. His trousers have nearly worn through and he seems to have been wearing his striped shirt for quite a while. Here's the slender frame of Geoff Dodds, who I haven't seen since we left school. He wants to slap me on the back, as though we've always been very best of pals. In fact, I do remember him as a nice bloke, all those years ago, if I remember him at all.

I'm fighting my way through a whole range of occasional friends, distant relatives and odd acquaintances when suddenly one of them turns into Don. Someone I know well. His hair has acquired a lot of pale grey and his skin has gained a strange, orange dappled effect. It seems the safe war he obtained for himself has not suited him very well. He speaks much more quietly than I remember too.

"So good to see you, mate. Let me buy you a pint in the George and Dragon. You deserve it after all you've been through."

"Thanks Don. That's really good of you but I can't afford to buy you one back."

"Don't worry about that, pal, it's a privilege to welcome back the returning hero," he smiles a bit self-consciously. He offers me a cigarette and we both pull on them as we stroll over to the George and Dragon, the oldest pub in Leigh. You can tell that from the black and white timbered frontage, all of it in very poor condition these days. The paint has not been renewed for many years and much has peeled off. Quite a lot of the beams have woodworm and rotting timbers sag out from front of building.

Inside the pub is full of smoke, clouds of it trailing from a low yellow stained ceiling. It's difficult to see from one end of the low bar to the other. Full of hot, sweaty bodies in the summer heat, many leaning on the bar and creating chaos and blockage. But most of all it's full of noise. A clamour of bustling, happy men, losing all their worries into the bottom of a glass for an hour or two on a Saturday lunch time. Not a single woman in sight anywhere. No doubt this is what the inferno will look like if I go to hell when I die. It's a good argument for behaving yerself.

Don seems to know the workings of this underworld, greeting his many acquaintances amid a lot of back slapping and witty banter, all shouted at top of their voices. He's very proud to show me off to his mates.

"This is Billy, just back from Germany. He's fought his way across Europe from the D-Day beaches all the way to Berlin."

I've never seen Berlin but Don's not concerned about

unimportant detail. A bit of added drama is his major interest. And it works too, because soon I'm surrounded by half drunken men, slapping me on the back, breathing beery fumes into my face and wanting full details about what Berlin looks like after the bombing, what Adolf Hitler said before he died and how many Jerries I've killed. They also want to know whether Hitler wore red underpants with little black swastikas all over them and just how grussen were Lilly Marlene's busten.

It's tricky to fob them off good humouredly. I can tell them a bit about how to fix a gear box on a Bedford and something about the liberation of Antwerp. But they're not interested in mechanics and have little idea what or where Belgium is, never mind any kind of twerp, so I can tell it's all a bit of a disappointment. Next time I'll have a better story ready, about wrestling SS officers single-handed, glad-handing cheering Russians at the front of the Reichstag and dancing down Unter den Linden with a frolicking fraulein.

Finally, I find a story they do like. It's all about Adolf Hitler's testicular limitations, the similarity of Heinrich Himmler's condition and the terrible plight of Josef Goebbels. It goes down very well, particularly when it's all set to music and everyone can join in.

Finally, we make it safely into a corner with a couple of pints of frothy brown beer, and collapse into the comfort of a soft, old green leather bench. It's seen a lot of beer drunk and maybe even more spilt over the decades, to stain it that interesting patchwork of black, green and brown. The place also has its own collection of interesting, difficult to define, odours.

"Did you have a good war, Billy?"

"No mate, it was crap. I hated every second. What's it been like for you?"

He pondered for quite a while and then sucked his breath in through his teeth before replying. "I shouldn't complain really. I've had it quite cushy compared with what you've been through. But there's been a lot of work and not much money. And there's always someone pointing the finger and asking why I'm not in uniform. It's not been much fun, looking back. I think I'd have been happier fighting."

"To be honest, I'm surprised you didn't get called up any way."

He looks at me sideways. A long look, narrowing his eyes and there's a long silence. I take a swig of the ale and savour the bitterness as I wait for him to reply.

"Well," he said. Another silence. "Well, you must know how it works."

"Don. I've no idea how anything works. What the bloody hell are you talking about?"

Another long look, more narrowing of his eyes and there's another long silence. "Officially, I've got slipped discs that make me unfit for war service."

"So, what have you really got, officially or unofficially?"

"I've got your Dad helping me. He fixed up for me to stay at home and sit out the war."

"What? That's bloody ridiculous. What the hell has it got to do with my Dad?"

"He's an important bloke in this town, always has been, what with owning his own business and that. The Grand Knight in our branch of the Knights of St. Columba can arrange most things, if you need his help. He got me the medical certificate and a job in the Drawing Office at Callender's Cables. I'm a draughtsman there."

"Knights of St Columba? How does that work then? What is it?"

"It's how us Catholics stick together, just like the Prods do with the Free Masons. We look after our own, with jobs and other favours. Those bastard Prods have been keeping us out of work for centuries. This is our way of looking after our own. You must understand it a bit. After all, you went with me to Liverpool in September 1939 when we tried to join the Merchant Navy to escape draft."

I laughed a short nervous chortle as I trawl the dark depths of my distant memories. "Yes, I remember that day. We were so bleeding stupid. It was a bad thing to have tried to do and thank God the Merchant Navy had more frigging sense than to take us."

"Was a fun day though, do you remember all that happened? We had a real laugh."

"Yeah. How could I forget? Not much to be proud of really but maybe a bit of fun."

"How do you fancy doing another trip to Liverpool, tomorrow? We might even have some fun again."

"That sounds good to me, Don. All right, we're going to Liverpool."

"Sup up then, I'll get you another."

Leigh to Liverpool

4th August 1945

Our train jolted forward so hard it rattled my teeth, not my best feature any way, as we left Leigh's tiny and dilapidated station. Our coach and then the two others behind it chugged into motion with a clunking of chains. Steam shot past the window, followed by the stench of burning tar from the asthmatic old locomotive. It panted in protest against pulling the passengers and the carriages reciprocated, constantly creaking in complaint. A symphony of incidental smells and sounds.

We were delighted to escape the windswept platform after running to get out of the summer rain and into the cool calm of the carriage. It was just like our first trip, taken in September 1939, the first week of war. I remember that I'd been complaining by this point, having stubbed my toe getting onto the train and had to limp to my seat. Once in my seat, I'd been condemned to being called Hopalong for rest of the day. Don had thought that hilarious, but we found so much fun back in those care free days. The mood's a bit more solemn today.

We'd also been off for a day trip and there'd been three of us that day. My cousin Charlie had been with us as well. We'd intended to go first to Liverpool and then perhaps on to somewhere even more exciting: South Africa, Australia, India, or anywhere else in the Empire. We'd wanted to see the world and escape the war. All three of us were feeling good that day all those years ago: a day off and a chance to find our destinies. After we'd had a full week of discussing the coming war, so we were using Saturday to do something about it: Charlie would volunteer to join Royal Navy, he wanted to confront the enemy. Don and I preferred to try a shipping company so we would do our bit and still get to travel, without risking our lives doing any actual fighting.

My dad had had no idea what I was doing. I thought it'd be great to get back to work on Monday and hand in my resignation. What a shock he would've got.

This time the journey seems just the same, except there's two of us now. No one has heard from Charlie since he disappeared after that weekend. In the George and Dragon someone suggested he'd been blown to bits on The Hood when it was sunk by Bismarck but another thought he'd been invalided out of the Navy and was now living in Tyldesley. There was a bit of a debate about which was worse.

The train struggles on, almost as feebly as Don's jokes. It goes steadily but always noisily onwards, calling at many small towns on the way: into Newton-le-Willows, then past the sugar works at Earlestown and through the industrial wastelands of St. Helens with its glassworks and great smoking chimneys. Many, many coal mines dot the route, the wheels on their winding gear whirling energetically, just like at home in Leigh, bringing black, shiny coal up from the depths. Most of all, they contribute miles and miles of grey and black slag heaps covering most of the landscape.

Eventually we manage to wheeze our way through the deep red sandstone cuttings at Edge Hill into the tunnel and then suddenly emerge into Lime Street. The old loco's energy is spent but he's hissing contentedly as though he's fulfilled by his efforts. Or just knackered, maybe. We descend from carriage and move quickly away from the platform, just as we'd done in 1939.

Today the station is much busier, really full of movement. So many men in uniform arriving, women in uniform too, mostly dark blue. Some going away, probably home on leave, while others are returning to their ships. Many of those dressed in civvies are bound for the docks as well.

My mind went back to the previous arrival six years earlier. Outside Lime Street station we'd been surprised by evidence of the war which had already appeared there, nowt had changed in Leigh by that point. Lots of the buildings already had criss-crossed tape patterns on the windows and I noticed people carrying gas mask boxes, just like newspaper pictures from the Great War. A single grey barrage balloon, like a low flying elephant, flew from a steel cable attached to a Morris van. Now the tape was gone but there was still a barrage balloon, lying deflated on the ground, accompanied by its six flattened companions. Their task was just about to begin then and today they're finished, flaccid and useless. I know how they feel.

I'd been struck by the grandeur of Liverpool's architecture in those times. Although I'd read a guide book before I'd arrived, about the city and particularly its centre, the real thing had been much more impressive. First there were the bright lights of advertisements, decorating the buildings facing the station. Across the road was a collection of classical buildings, with the Walker Gallery at its heart. There were statues of Michelangelo and Raphael around the entrance, just as the book described. I hadn't seen this sort of stuff before; we didn't have any of it in Leigh. The Corporation Baths was grandest building I'd seen then. Now I've got memories of Amiens, Ghent and Antwerp as well, once fabulous places, though all badly damaged by fighting when I saw them.

Today a column in the middle of the square has signs round it proclaiming "Victory over Germany 1945" and telling us to "Give thanks by saving", the whole thing backed by red, white and blue stripes. I just wish I'd some money to save. Green trams of

Liverpool Corporation trundle back and forwards across the edge of the square, along Lime Street itself, adding to the noise and energy of place. There's a lot to look at and time to take it all in.

There'd been little time to linger and admire in 1939. The Royal Navy recruitment office had been in a marquee on the square right beside us, so Charlie left us there. Don had been anxious to press on down Victoria Street towards Pier Head. He'd been told all the maritime offices were there. Now we went down that same route, retracing our steps and visiting our memories. Neither of us had much to say, our heads full of thoughts of what might've been.

The city is greatly changed. Vast areas of rubble have replaced most of the Victorian architecture, largely in great blocks of brick and stone rubble, with just an occasional building still standing. Even those are badly damaged, often with walls missing and floors sagging out over empty space left behind. The Blitz had been very effective here and very little has been re-built in the year since it ended. The city is lying in ruins but life is going on all around, as though those vast piles of rubble aren't here.

I recall that as we'd neared the waterfront, a car on the rickety structure of the overhead railway passed above us, it stayed in my memory because it had rattled even more than the steam train. There're no trains on it today, too many gaps in the track remain from the bombing, although repairs are said to be underway. Even more impressive architecture had greeted us as we'd found our way past the railway to the river front; the Liver Building with its weird green birds loomed above. How had that survived? I remember the local story that one Liver Bird is male, looking inland to see if the pubs are open, whilst the other is female, looking out to sea to see if there are any handsome sailors coming up river.

Besides the river, there's a flat back lorry with the remains of an American fighter aircraft. Looks like a wreck has been pulled out of the river. I recognise it as a Thunderbolt. We all got to be experts on aircraft recognition in Normandy, especially American ones. The saying was that when the Luftwaffe went over the Allies took cover, when the RAF went over the Germans took cover but when the Yanks went over, every one took cover.

The wind sweeps along the river and Don and I look over to Wallasey. The sandy brown river ripples wildly in the breeze, the tide is fully in and a whole herd of white horses ride its surface. Across the water are docks and grand old offices in grey stone. Little grey clouds scud over the water and resemble the barrage balloons that had previously appeared over Birkenhead docks. A tired old freighter wanders its weary way along the water. And there are another two battered old ships moving along the river, belching out black acrid fumes in the same dirty fashion and leaving a smudged trail in the air behind them. An occasional whiff of the black filth reaches us and makes our eyes water.

Across the river the Royal Daffodil is manoeuvring to face into the tide as it approaches the jetty, throwing up a lot of white water. Smoke and steam belches from its funnel speaking of the forces it's fighting. I hadn't noticed it on our previous visit but perhaps it was moored up, maybe here on the Liverpool side.

Back then Don had asked a passer-by where to go to join the Merchant Navy and he'd directed us, in what we'd thought was a strange sort of voice, to the footbridge over Canning Half Tide Dock and the Dockmaster's offices beyond. Today that scouse accent is familiar, I heard it many times in the Army. Once at the Office he'd asked again, very politely, how to join the Merchant Navy.

The Dockmaster had laughed. "Nor 'ere mate. Mebbe try der White Star offices ober der."

We'd walked back under the railway, besides James Street station, and across Strand Street. There, we found our way to the distinctive red and white striped brick of Albion house which carried the sign of Cunard-White Star Line. As we had entered a bulky doorman in a navy-blue uniform had blocked our way.

"Wot's up la'? Wot do youse lads want 'ere?"

"We wanna job on a ship. We wanna be sailors."

"Oh, youse do, do yeh? Try de Cunard Building ober dere. Dey'll know wot to do with the likes of youse woolly backs." He chortled and turned his back on us.

We'd trudged off again, feeling a little discouraged but still confident of finding the right place, although anxious it might be several more "ober deres" away.

The rooms in the Cunard Buildings were huge and intimidating. We're stood outside today but on that previous trip we'd entered the great hall decorated with elaborate Greek or Roman plaques. As no one had been there to talk to we'd moved on into a vast white room, with gilded plaster portraying bald eagles and every other part of the wall covered by carved dark wood panels. It was pretty grand! We'd wandered into the area reserved, according to sign, for First-Class passengers only.

"Oy, youse two. What do you think youse are doing in 'ere?" A loud voice had echoed through the grand space, violating its sanctity.

A blue coated official had bustled purposefully towards us. Don had suggested that perhaps he was going to offer us tea, cucumber sandwiches and a delicate slice of seed cake in an attempt to sell us first Class tickets for a transatlantic crossing. Or perhaps not.

"Well then, what do *you* want?" I can almost hear his angry voice again, echoing around the vast, empty space.

"We're looking to join the merchant navy, to become sailors," Don had said.

"Oh yer, what kind of sailors? What skills 'ave youse got, what experience?"

"I dunno, just sailors. What kinds are there?"

"So, what're youse all about then? Coming 'ere with no idea what sailors are. If I didn't know better, I'd think youse were trying to dodge service with the army. We've 'ad 'undreds of your sort 'ere since Monday."

I'd looked at Don, it'd been his idea. Don looked at the floor and the official had looked straight at us both. His cheeks had glowed and turned a colour similar to beetroot. It was only a matter of time before steam came out of his ears and his eyes popped out of his head.

"Right, youse pair of bleedin' losers! Fuck off then, fuck right off, right now and don't come back. Nor 'ere, nor anywhere round 'ere. We don't want your sort around this place."

There'd been no point in arguing with beetroot man, so we took revenge by not buying any First-Class tickets. Don and I needed a new plan. Maybe we were not going to be white gloved waiters on the Queen Mary. How about becoming a pair of coal covered stokers on an old tramp freighter?

We'd gone on to reach the working docks, just a few hundred yards away, at the offices of Blue Funnel line. We walked there again today. Just as in 1939, there is movement everywhere, men walking, men running and lorries being driven. But maybe even busier, more crowded. Clouds of steam and smoke had come from the cranes as they'd swung and rotated, filling the air with smoke and sulphur. One was being moved along the dockside, rattling awkwardly as it shuffled its ill-fitting wheels along rails.

An amazing number of unhappy men had clattered past us in worn out boots or clogs, cloth caps pulled low over their heads and with badly stained and sweaty clothing. So many voices, all taking at once, so they merged into a hubble of sound. Occasional laughter broke through but mostly an anonymous rumble. It had felt soothingly familiar. They were working men just like me, and it seems they're still here.

Standing here, I remember how I felt six years ago. Like I'm an ant, surrounded by millions of worker ants. All of us in a hurry to carry out our tasks. They all seem to know what they were doing, but I haven't a clue. We share the need to run and hurry about but I leave the shouting to them.

The docks are full of ships again. Not entirely back to normal, several of the cranes are missing and even pieces of the dockside. The remaining men are working even harder. Liverpool docks are running at speed, full of ships from India, South Africa, Australia, Canada and USA. Those that had once struggled to beat U-boats now have a clear, safe passage through to the oceans of the world.

Several lorries had been unloading sacks of coal, the drivers carrying the sacks protected themselves with a sheep's pelt on their back. Voices of the horde of dockers and drivers had merged with mechanical sounds to contribute to a rich broth of sights, noise and smells. I'd strode confidently across to the main door for Blue Funnel Line, but found it closed against me. Well, I'd hammered on it any way. It didn't help me at all, no one answered and there'd been no sign of life. I'd looked towards the next shipping line: British India Steam Navigation Company. That'd been closed too.

Today I can see those same doors and they're all locked again, but now it seems they are locked for ever. They look abandoned. Little wonder, the buildings behind them are totally bombed out, the rooves gone and blackened by smoke.

Last time I was here bundles of freight had been lifted by crane from the "City of Benares" which had been moored alongside, its red funnel had white and black rings round the top. All along the docks freight had moved but few offices were open. I'd had time to observe the activity in the dock itself; and remember how "Capitão Magalhães" had left the dockside, creeping towards an open lock to go straight into the river beyond. A tiny bow wave had indicated its movement, otherwise immeasurably slow. The lively red, yellow and green livery of Linha Portuguêsa had made her stand out from the rest. It had looked strong and purposeful and spoke of hot and exotic places, maybe that's why it's burnt onto my memory. Countries where bananas grew and dusky maidens wore grass skirts; I'd wanted to be part of it then but now I gave thanks that I hadn't. I might not be here.

I can see something of the remnants of the Battle of Atlantic, with sleek grey hulls of two cruisers moored in the place that the "City of Benares" had vacated long ago. They look wonderfully well-kept and superbly elegant in contrast to the ragged mayhem of the dockside, with its twisted wrecked cranes and the burnt-out warehouses. Nevertheless, they are leftovers from a past time. So vital to the welfare of nation a few months ago, they are now left empty against the dock wall, while some bureaucrat in the Admiralty figures out how to use them in peace time. Maybe they'll be scrapped, but not yet. No one can really make themselves believe that it really is peace. There's even talk of a new war with the Russians that might be just beginning.

I remembered how the sun had come out in 1939 but it could only cheer me up sufficiently to buy a sandwich. I'd declined plates of lobscouse offered to dockers for three pence. My fighting spirit had evaporated for a minute and even meat and potato couldn't have restored it. Well, it's not the bloody Ritz is it? This needed something stronger; tea, docker's tea. We'd needed a lengthy session of tea drinking, as we'd debated the confused condition of our world, with feet propped up on the seats, looking up at clouds.

*

"Why're we joining the merchant navy Don? I don't remember wanting to be a sailor. I can't swim and might be sea sick."

"It's a great way to serve our country, do our duty and stay away from the fighting."

"Actually, I don't mind fighting; I'd just prefer not to die."

"Yeah maybe, but there's some risk in everything during war. Being in America would be fun, wouldn't it? As well as keeping us safe."

"Could be but being a stoker in the bowels of a tramp steamer under submarine attack doesn't appeal to me. It all seemed right when I thought we were going on Queen Mary."

"We can't all go first class, mate. Sounds like you've lost your get up and go?"

Today, darkened remains of the kiosk are still here but sadly broken down, boarded up, no sign of its former vigour and worst of all, there's no tea available.

A little further along row of warehouses, I'd seen the office of Ellerman Lines in '39, with its door open. This could have been it, the chance to get a job! Obviously, they *were* working on Saturday and it should've been our next call but Don was right. My enthusiasm had sunk, my intentions had been torpedoed and having been swamped by the tidal waves of tea I'd abandoned ship. Even Don's enthusiasm for the bordellos of New York and Rio de Janeiro didn't seem to inspire me.

So, we'd started back towards Lime Street instead. I remember how it had been harder work than we'd expected, streets which had been nice and flat when we walked towards Pier Head had developed a steep upward slope as we returned. We got breathless and very warm in the sunshine as we'd climbed back to station. Now the climb seems pretty easy to me, though Don seems to find it hard. This Don is noticeably much quieter and calmer than Don of six years ago. I wonder what experiences have caused him to lose so much of his youthful energy and confidence. We stop to light cigarettes before walking along puffing away at them.

We'd met Charlie at top of the street back then, just as agreed, for a quick pint in the Crown before we caught the train home. He'd been shouting at us before we'd even seen him, jumping around and waving his Royal Navy papers.

"I convinced the recruitment team to appoint me as a Leading Seaman with the prospect of becoming a Petty Officer," he told us.

"That's great mate, well done." I'd replied.

"I've to join a new training camp: HMS King Alfred, in just over a weeks' time and already have a one-way rail warrant to take me down to Hove next Saturday."

Then he'd become Popeye in Don's banter. Which I'd thought

was great because Hopalong was forgotten about. The pub was full of men with ruddy complexions, many accompanied by pale, shadowy women, standing glasses in hand. We could barely see them through the haze. There was a strong buzz of lively conversation around smoke-filled room with another yellow ceiling.

Of course, we were very curious to revisit the Crown to see if it was still the same cheerful place that we remembered. Don bought a couple of pints and we sat quietly in the very spot where we'd been six years before. Those memories kept flooding back. No need for Don or me to say anything.

"Three pints of bitter, luv," Don had given his order to the bar maid, who'd just scowled back. As she'd turned her back, he stuck his tongue out at her. I'd looked around the room and it seemed easy to catch the eye of pretty girls. They were all smiling at *me,* lots of attractive young faces with eager eyes. I'd enjoyed being in this pub.

After a bit of discussion about how day had gone, it'd been my round. As I'd got to bar a lively young lady had arrived at same time and leant on bar next to me, looking up at me with a broad grin. She was a slender brunette, a bit older than me, one of those who'd been beaming at me. She'd bright red lips around that grin and brass ear rings dangled around her face. Her pink blouse was unbuttoned at the top, revealing a little of the inner woman and she was wobbly on her red high heeled shoes. I'd noticed black stockings on her slender, shapely legs and especially the sickly-sweet smell, flavoured by sugary roses, that arrived just before she did.

"Hello sweetie! Are you buying a drink for me too?" That look had given me a warm feeling and I grinned back, looked into her dark, damp eyes and got lost there for a moment. Her perfume caught in my nostrils; I'd never got close enough to smell it on a woman before. My head had swum with excitement. She'd looked very pleased at the effect she was having on me.

"Hi, I'm Daisy."

I looked into her smiling face and time stopped to let me catch up with it.

"'Ello darling, I'm Bill. Love your big, dangly ear rings, Daisy. What d'you want to drink?"

"Port and lemon, please dearie," she'd said holding onto my arm as I carried beer back to Don and Charlie. They also had ladies with them now! I was introduced to Rosie and Lou; Daisy seemed to know them already. Everyone was smiling although perhaps I shouldn't have been. I got to pay for two more port and lemons. After we'd all had a sip at our drinks we'd settled down for a jolly chat.

A little later we'd piled out of the pub, even jollier than when we'd arrived, our arms linked with girls and had found our way to a chippy, on the corner of Skelhorne Street and Hilbre Street, then up onto Copperas Hill, six pence for fish and chips with lashings of vinegar. They'd tasted good to a hungry man and hungry women seemed to enjoy them too.

As newspaper wrappers were discarded Don and Rosie had started cuddling on the street, Charlie and Lou had already disappeared down an alley and Daisy pressed herself against me. She felt soft and warm and my head swam with a mixture of confusion and pleasure.

"Come on Billy, give me five bob and I'll show you a bit of fun. You boys need a bit of comfort on a Saturday night and I wanna help. You're a nice boy."

"Five bob? I 'aven't got five bob for that kind of fun. That's bloody ridiculous. Besides what you're suggesting is a sin."

She'd laughed aloud and her eyes had flashed with a blue light, the sound sweet and soft. "Sin! We all need to be sinful; don't you know we sinners have all the fun." Her lips pressed on mine and I felt her breasts flattening against me. That was quite a feeling, my head filled with cotton wool but my body stiffened.

I held her back. This was not right. Then my arms were around her but only to show appreciation for her smiles and friendliness. She was kissing me. Her delicate fingers were working lightly on me, teasing me, persuading me to let her just a little closer. Very close. I remembered gasping, the first time I'd been touched like this. Maybe she was right about sin? It felt nice and warm and after all, no harm was coming to anyone.

In the end we'd kissed and cuddled a bit, but no more. Well, not much more. Certainly not enough to give her five bob. But eventually, under the pressure of her hectoring, I *had* reluctantly given her two half-crowns though. Just for the sake of friendship as she said; I hadn't wanted to fall out with such a fragrant new friend after such a nice evening.

But the next thing I'd known Daisy had gone. I saw her going off down the hill arm in arm with Rosie and Lou, all of them laughing loudly. I'd noticed Don was nearby and soon Charlie shuffled out from the alley, re-adjusting his shirt as he came. We had retired to Crown and reflected on an interesting evening. We had needed to go back there anyway; it was Charlie's round. But it had all seemed a bit flat after the girls left.

We'd finally staggered across square to Lime Street station where the last train home had been stood puffing and wheezing. That day was over and as we'd stumbled along, it was time to consider its results. Don's idea about joining the merchant navy had just been plain daft. Thank goodness, I'd realised that before I got carried along with it. I could've been facing a life of seasickness and torpedoes.

I'd learnt a bit about life in Liverpool too. An expensive lesson, since that five bob had been hard earned and easily lost. Charlie had succeeded in escaping from the Tweed Street Works but I'd failed. Soon he'd be leaving to have the adventures I'd hoped for. I was returning to suffer my Dad's self-importance and Uncle Iggy's whinging. Now, I was going to have to face all this without any consolation from my mate. Thank goodness Celi was on my side, she'd be even more important to me now.

Most importantly though, my head had been full of questions about Daisy. Who was she? Where had she come from? Why'd she just walked off like that, without another word? And, most of all, how do I see her again? I'd really liked her and wanted her company again.

*

Now I empty the last of my pint and turn and look around the room, then at Don. He smiles back. That memory seems to please him too. We look around this room, hoping to catch the eye of pretty girls. There are plenty of them here, but none are looking at us. There is certainly no sign of any one as young and pretty as Daisy. Where is she now? I'd love to know how her life has turned out. Is she even still alive? This place seems much duller than the same pub before the war. I don't feel at home here now.

We put down our glasses and quietly leave to get the train home. There'll be no adventure this time but there's plenty of time before our train so we decide to have a walk up Skelhorne Street to see if the chippy's still there. But it isn't. Just a huge pile of bricks.

As we stand there two men in black capes, wearing skull caps above huge black beards turn into the street and walk towards us. Don recoils and shudders at the sight of them.

"What's the matter, Don?"

"You wanna keep away from this sort of people, they'll be black marketers. They profit from the war but contribute nowt to it."

"You mean the Jews? You think all Jews are the same, none contributed? I can tell you that they did. Maybe not these actual guys but a whole lot of Jews in Europe did. They were even more involved in the war than we were, they certainly suffered a lot more. I made a good friend with Jeno, one of the Jewish boys I met in Germany. I'd have kept in touch but he had no address, he was just a wanderer."

But there's no way of changing his mind. He has no reason other than ill-informed gossip, as far as I can tell, but Don's sure about what he believes. Two gentlemen pass me by and I say "good day" to them. One of them looks at me, rather suspiciously and growls, but neither reply and they walk on. Nor do they look back or around, just straight ahead.

I feel strangely troubled by the incident, so trivial it shouldn't matter. I've shown warm feeling to these gentlemen, contradicting my friend's reaction, yet it's not been recognised. There seems to be a huge residue of bad feelings towards Jewish people and back from them, which I don't understand. What's the reason behind Don's comments. "These sort of people." These are not just his feelings, others seem to share his opinions, yet I can't find any reason for it. What is it all about?

Finally, what does it tell me about my friend? Don used to be a naturally warm and happy man. Now that seems to be covered by a sulky animosity towards everyone, even including himself. I thought I'd had a difficult war but it seems to have been more depressing for him.

As we settle into the grimy seats in our third-class carriage Don looks up and asks:

"What do you think of Liverpool now Billy? A few changes, eh?"

"Yeah, Liverpool's had a tough war, bomb damage is bloody awful. Should've overwhelmed 'em but they kept going through it all. I admire their strength and courage."

"What would've happened if we'd joined Merchant Navy in September '39 do you think?"

"Well, who knows, really. Our lives would've been very different. I guess we'd have seen lots of places. Gibraltar, Egypt, India. Maybe even the US. I think we could've had a lot of fun. Problem is we'd have had a good chance of being sunk and drowned in freezing waters. Not a good way to die. But from what I saw in the Army dying is not a lot of fun, however you go. I bet we'd both be dead by now."

"Good thing we never got in then. The trip wasn't anything like as lively this time, was it?"

"No mate. Maybe we didn't go with the same purpose as last

time or perhaps we're just missing Charlie. It doesn't help to have no money either."

"I thought it would be Daisy that you missed most," he said with a grin.

"Yeah, I did. Daisy was fun, even if there wasn't never any future in it. Didn't you ever meet any one, Don?"

"Ah!" he said quietly. "I was engaged once. To a girl from Warrington called Edith, she was pretty."

"Really? She sounds lovely, what ever happened to her?"

"She went off with one of those Yankee flyers from Burtonwood," he said, with his bottom lip curling up, distorting his features. "Last time I heard she was going to live in Chicago."

He gives a sigh and this conversation dies out into an awkward silence that lasts all the way back to Leigh. The decrepit old train finally trundles into the depressing old station. Then as we walk down the ramp to leave the station, I shake his hand. "Good bye mate, I hope everything turns out well for you."

"Thanks Billy. And the same to you. I think you'll need some luck fighting them Japs, they're supposed to be a nasty lot." And he turns and disappears under the railway arch, onto East Bond Street and past the Railway Hotel. I stand looking at his back, wondering if we'll ever meet again. And if we don't, do I care? This man looks like my old pal, but inside he seems altogether changed. The bright, lively, laughing pre-war Don has been replaced by a shrivelled up, dreary and detached Don.

But it's thoughts of Japanese brutality, the discomforts of Army life and diseases of jungle warfare that linger in my head as I walk slowly back, in the dark, to 179 Chapel Street. The street lights are still not restored to anything like their pre-war strength. Leigh Corporation have no money to spend.

After all, there is still a war on. Somewhere.

Our house

5th August 1945

"Neah then, our Billy. Good to see thi' safe and well," said Joe, smiling as I shook his hand. I'm privileged that he's made a special trip all the way from Wilkinson Street to see me, after church. We've not been here together since we were kids. Or at least I was a kid, since he was already a teenager by then.

A shadow passed over me as I remembered those times. I'd always felt in awe of my talented and confident older brother. He knew everything and had strong opinions that reflected that superior knowledge. I'd always been reluctant to comment in case my ideas were swatted away, dismissed with the contempt they obviously deserved. In comparison, my arguments with Chalky and Fido have been glorious, funny and delightful.

On the other hand, I never got bullied at school, despite being the smallest boy in the class. My older brother looked out for me. We look after our own, was always the philosophy.

We've been to the eleven o' clock mass too, high mass with the choir belting out old Latin hymns, wrapping us in a cloak of glorious, rich but indecipherable sound in the grandeur of the colours of the church. The stained glass shed its red, green and gold hues onto fourteen rich paintings of the Stations of the Cross, spread around the whole church. We understood nothing of the words, we just imagined it was praising God. Then we walked back together, exchanging pleasantries about the weather and the condition of St. Joe's church. We both agree it's in need of a bit of repair and restoration and hope there'll soon be some funds available to get it updated.

"Good to see you too, Joe," I said, trying to smile pleasantly, as though I like him and remember him fondly. "It's been quite a while but I've always had your letters to keep me in touch. Any way how's your life been? How are Agnes and the baby?"

"They're both doing well, thanks Bill."

He offers me a cigarette, an expensive brand from a shiny, silver case with a gilt embossed monogram. I take it and wait as he strikes a match on his shiny, silver vesta case and take a light. The sudden burst of sulphur assails my nostrils, disappearing in an instant and replaced by the comfortable aroma of burning tobacco. We both sit down on the old couch and take a big draw on our fags, watching the tip glow bright red and burn. It feels good, calming and mellow, unlike my emotions.

I look around at the best sitting room. We were never allowed in here as kids, except perhaps when a grand visitor came to see us. But it doesn't look anything like as posh as I'd remembered. All the furniture is old and the upholstery is well worn, with signs of decades of accumulated, trivial damage all around. The dark brown curtains frame a view of Chapel Street with Butts Mill looming above the houses opposite, the midday sun above, attempting to break through a thick bank of high cloud, but failing. Badly.

Joseph Atherton has been an important name in our family for generations, the name given to the firstborn son. My eldest brother is Joseph, my father is Joe Atherton, as my grandfather was before him. Perhaps my great grandfather before him too, for all I know. The name conveys status, not just in our family, but in the whole local community. It suggests intelligence, confidence and wealth.

The source of our wealth was the family business; the Atherton Brothers. Although in reality there was only one brother that ever mattered at a time, it had been handed down through the generations. My grandfather had built it up, changing it from a local blacksmith to a wheelwright in the 1880s and then moving it from Hindley into the newly built Tweed Street works in Leigh, during 1899. In my father's time it has boomed and finally bust. The big boom came while building large wooden spoked wheels for the Royal Artillery during the First War. Our wheels have seen action on the Somme, at Ypres, Passchendaele and all the great battles, allowing the guns to defy the deep mud. The importance of the business to the war effort gave my Dad exemption from being drafted into the armed forces and I know he valued that privilege greatly. It may well have kept him alive.

After that war business had declined sharply, despite a brief upturn while Chat Moss was drained in the 1920's. So, Joe changed the Atherton Brother's business once again. This time from wheelwrights into a coach body building business, using our skills in wood and iron, to produce a small lorry, the chassis and engine being bought in. The recent war killed all of that, as mass production in Luton and Birmingham put us out of business.

My brother obviously knew the importance of his name and the position it indicated. He is the eldest of six children. It seems that my parents had their children in threes. First Joe, Gertie and Nash (Ignatius), then a gap of ten years before I was born, swiftly followed by Betty, Vincent and Cecelia. Joe had felt like a second father to the younger ones and took on the role of disciplinarian with some enthusiasm. I was beaten for small instances of bad behaviour with the leather strap he kept for this purpose. It left a deep impression on us all.

"You look well, nice suit, Joe. Is it new?"

"Yeh, I was lucky to pick it up cheap from a friend who knows people over in Leeds."

"A bit of good business, not easy to get new clothes these days."

"We're doing fairly well. Aggie can stay at home and look after little Sheila while I'm out at work. But it's just normal stuff, we're not rich by any means."

"I heard Dad got you a job at Cable Works, what is it that you do?"

He seems to shudder at the suggestion. "I'm in charge of doing the weekly wages, it's quite a bit of responsibility. And no, mi Dad had nowt to do with it. I can look after myself without any influence from the Knights of St Columba." He drew another breath from his cigarette and looked along it, into my eyes.

"I'd always expected you to come into the family business."

"Well, it's a good job I didn't, now it's gone bust. Dad only just cleared his debts when he sold the Tweed Street works to County Motors. He felt like he'd lost everything. The family heritage gone. It's left him and Mum with nowt to live on after he paid everyone else off. But that's the kinda bloke he is, puts everyone else ahead of his self."

"No need to tell me. I know better than anyone what's happened. After all, I'd worked there since I left school. I'd never known anything else, that closure cost me my job and I would've either been out of work or, more likely, I'd have had to go down pit if I hadn't joined the Army."

"It wasn't his fault that no one wants to buy those lorries. Look, it's all very sad but never mind about that now. I need to have a serious talk to you, about some family matters that's important now."

"Oh! What matters?"

"Your support for our parents, in particular."

"What? What about it? You know I'm giving 'em money."

"Well, there's two things about it. Firstly, it's not enough, they're really struggling. Secondly, it shouldn't come with conditions. You're the single son and it's your duty to support them. They raised you when you were a child in need of help."

"What are you talking about?"

"I think you know." He looks at me again, a dark stare. Perhaps slightly angry.

"No, I haven't a clue what you're going on about."

"I'm told that you've extracted a promise from my Dad that he'll leave you the house when he dies."

"No. He offered that, I never asked for anything. But it is fair enough, though."

"I don't think it's fair at all, not fair on Dad but especially not fair on me, Nash and the others. We've as much right to an inheritance as you."

"I don't think inheritance is a right. It's Dad's property and he can leave it to any one he wants to. Whatever he decides to do with it is fair, as long as he meets the promises he's made."

"It's normal for the oldest son to inherit, not the junior. Haven't you heard of primogeniture?"

I laugh at him. "Who do you think we are? Some branch of the aristocracy? We're just ordinary folks with nowt burra terraced house to argue over."

"There's a matter of principle to consider."

"Look, if it's bothering you, I'll make you a proposal. We'll split the contributions to Mum and Dad down the middle and the inheritance as well. How about that for a fair deal?"

"No, that's not fair. You're a single chap and I'm married with a wife and daughter to support."

"I understand that but, if you can't contribute then you shouldn't expect anything in exchange. That's fair."

"I don't think that's funny, young William. You're ignoring everything I've said."

"That's because I don't agree with you. I made a deal with Dad and it's really none of your business."

"I thought you were a Christian; don't you believe in courtesy and fair play?"

"I am, I do and that's why I'm rejecting your one-sided proposal."

"What'd yer mean by that? Who do yer think yer talking to, anyway?"

He stands up abruptly and moves across to the sofa where I sit, standing directly above me. I stand up too, look him directly in the eye. His eyes narrow, his eye brows crumple and he comes forward. I stand still, not moving, directly in front of him. We stand there for a moment, glaring into each other's eyes. I notice that he's bigger than me.

He seems surprised at my reaction. His mouth falls open, obviously to say summat further, but no words come. The compliant young brother is not agreeing with him anymore, is no longer intimidated. I've grown up in many ways, the horrors of the war have steeled my nerve.

I'm no longer the baby of the family, not the seven stone I'd weighed when I joined up. The wartime Army hadn't fed its men extravagantly but it was still a far better, richer diet than I'd have had here during the lean times of the thirties. I've put on weight steadily and am a good two stone heavier. There's a lot to be said for the health-giving qualities of spam, bully beef and tinned pilchards. But he's still bigger than me.

Joe looks at me sideways, I can see thoughts running around in his head. Maybe he's wondering if he can still use the leather strap he used to enjoy so much. But that thought don't last long. He moves away, turns his back on me, and paces up and down. Then he looks at me again, seems to want to say something, but stops himself.

The clouds outside seemed to lighten a little, my eyes suddenly drawn beyond the curtains, now a light shade of brown, onto Chapel Street and the Mill. The thick bank of high cloud has faded and parted, revealing a pale version of insipid sunshine. The room is flooded with orange light.

Joe looks at me once more, before kicking the sofa and walking out in silence.

RAF Lyneham

August 14th 1945

Well! Who should walk in but my mate Chalky White, old misery guts his self. Haven't seen him in months and never expected to see him ever again.

"What the bloody hell are you doin' here mate?" I want to know. "I thought the bullet you took near Utrecht had got you a nice rest, yer lazy slacker."

"The bleedin' MO's ruled me fit to return to duty," he spits bitterly. "Warra dick'ead." It seems Chalky's learnt to lay on the misery extra thick.

"What about that hole it left in yer leg?"

"That one's healed, filled in. What about that hole between yer ears Billy?"

"Why don't you wind yer neck in, mate? Major's about to tell us where we're goin'. Good t'see yer, by the way, yer miserable old bastard."

Fido's here too, so the three of us who have fought Hitler to a standstill in Europe are a team again. Ready to take on the high Emperor Wotsits-ito. I snuggle into the middle seat between my two pals. Look out Japs, you've no chance now.

A tall, fresh faced and earnest young man strolls to the front of a whitewashed conference room and positions himself behind table. Major Algernon Breck is perfectly groomed, standing straight and tall in his beautifully pressed Officer's uniform. Stopping to look around the room, he stands up straight to address the troops in a quiet but assertive voice, heavily accented from the playing fields of Eton.

"The war in Burma is going very well gentlemen, we are pushing the Japanese out of that country. They have retreated as far as Rangoon. That is where we will be going, to chase them all the way back to Tokyo."

This is my first meeting with him and I like his confident, understated manner. He might just be on the side of the ordinary soldier. We've not been briefed like this since we left Tilbury on June 4th last year, so I'm chuffed to know what's going on. The only way we ever knew who was winning in Europe was by listening to the gossip. That big liberation celebration in Antwerp was reassuring and we heard of a few other celebrations. Eventually we'd heard the announcement of the German surrender but only after we'd pushed so deep into the Fatherland that victory was obvious anyway. Since early August I've been at home, so I could read newspapers and have been better informed for a while.

"They're in dire need of drivers in Burma to keep the supply routes open. You're very fortunate to be flown there, it normally takes weeks by boat. You'll fly to Calcutta to pick up new lorries and then drive down from there to Rangoon. They are Bedford three tonners just as you were driving in Europe. You'll find the jungle roads a bit more difficult though. Calcutta is too far for one flight so you'll make a couple of stops in Jerusalem and Bombay. There are a few hours to recover at each stop while the aircraft are refuelled. The first two legs are around twelve hours flying time but it's a bit less across India.

Enjoy the trip men and good luck to us all!"

There's a weary whimper of a cheer.

It is my first ever flight. Excitement overwhelms my fear of going into a new war for a while. Those tales of malaria and Japanese fighting abilities can be forgotten for the moment.

My home leave is over. Eleven days at home was enough for me any way, although it was lovely to see my Mum and Celi again. Dad seemed happy to see me alive and still in one piece. Joe had put in that one brief appearance but even he managed a grumble on my behalf. "The war's over. The Germans are beaten, our homes are safe. Why do they need to find another war for you to fight? It's bloody ridiculous."

Bloody ridiculous is an expression we're all using in the conference room. Hitler threatened our country, our homes, our families and everything we hold dear. Hirohito just threatens our Empire and no working man from Lancashire wants to die for that.

Obviously, our leaders think otherwise. Even this new Labour government want to continue the war in the Far East but, of course, Clement Attlee doesn't need to do the fighting his self. They're sending Chalky, Fido and me over there, to fight and perhaps to die instead. We really just want to go home now; we've seen enough bloody people die.

Maybe I shouldn't have voted for Attlee, since I thought he'd get me out of this damned army. Getting out of uniform and back to my own life is the only thing I want. Now it's the bleeding Japanese that're holding me up. Newspapers are suggesting it will be another year, or even two, before they're also forced to surrender, so they get quite a good chance to kill me first.

Would Winston Churchill have given me a better chance of staying at home if I'd voted for him? Norra hope. He'd have been even more determined to save the Empire, after all it's his class that benefit from it.

I stare at the peeling paint of this weary room for another two hours and decide that it might originally have been white. By the time the spotty WAAF Corporal calls us to board the plane I've counted three broken light bulbs, four cracked light shades and ten window panes that need replacing. Fifteen lino flooring squares are peeling up round their edges too. Not sure I've got all the cobwebs though, they're more difficult to spot. There's a breeze running through the place and Fido makes a point of standing in it to cool down. Good job it's summer, this place would be freezing in February.

We pass the time with an arm-wrestling competition. I beat Chalky and take a couple of ciggies off him but immediately lose them again to Fido. Spud won't join in, windy bugger. I could've easily beaten him. I light a cigarette now, as there'll be several hours in the air when it's not allowed.

The B24 Liberator is well designed for its job: dropping bombs. Now it's being called upon to do an entirely different job. We're in for a long and uncomfortable journey, travelling halfway across the world in a rattling cage up in the frozen air of high atmosphere. They've put seats in but we're warned that breathing may be difficult. That's bad news for me, I've always been fond of breathing.

They've got us into place nice and early, perhaps to give us extra time to get used to boredom. The seats are very small but I can fit into them quite well, it's much more difficult for taller men. I call them seats, but it's really an arrangement of steel tube with a bit of brown canvass stretched across them.

The engines finally burst into life and we're ready for a twelve-hour flight. Most've been falling asleep since we've been inside the aircraft but now there's no chance with the deafening racket and vibrations from the engine. Anyway, I want to see everything and enjoy every second.

Our cabin is like a narrow, short tube with a few seats across its width. There are rows of tiny square windows on either side but they let little light in. There's a couple of bulbs glowing orange on the ceiling and casting a weird shade into this cramped space. Once inside, we're all expected to stay strapped in our seats.

I've got a bottle of water, having been advised to sip from

it regularly through journey. I've a greatcoat to wear over my battledress, with extra layers of underclothes underneath. The tropical gear we were issued with is still in my sack along with two blankets I've been given. No wonder we're finding it warm.

The aircraft's manoeuvring on the ground is nerve wracking, the lads are all straining to look out of the tiny windows. Then it turns onto runway and soon we see the ground rushing past. I'm not sure this thing is going to get off the ground though and the way it lumbers along convinces me that we'll crash into the perimeter fence. If we do crash it'll be at high speed, this thing is really starting to move. There's very little runway left as the plane staggers up through thin cloud and slowly drags itself up towards vast empty blue sky. The plane is wallowing, the engines are straining at full stretch and could fail at any moment.

As the aircraft struggles into the air, I can see the ground beneath dropping away and a set of shiny lines which mark the route of a railway. They seem smaller that a toy railway set and it's difficult to believe they are real. Toy lorries and cars are driving along pencil lines across the landscape.

Then I see that I was right to worry. Something's terribly wrong; the wings are bending up and down, almost like they're flapping to get us airborne. Looks like they might break at any moment. I watch them in horror. Isn't anyone else watching? Can't anyone see there's a problem? Is it just me? I'm breaking out into a real sweat in the excess of clothing I'm wearing.

*

The overwhelming noise of the engines is itself overwhelmed by a failure of my senses. My hearing is dulled by thin air and a loss of body heat and I've drifted in and out of consciousness for several hours as the plane has droned onwards. Now I'm fully awake again but too cold and tired to either think or move and breathing is still a strain.

I can see below, through the window, if I lean right forward. There'd often been clouds beneath as we set off us but we've flown into night. Vast areas of darkened ground pass beneath us, with just an occasional light or group of lights standing out brightly. I guess it's southern Europe but I've no idea what country. Italy? Greece? Denmark?

I've a dull ache in my ears, Chalky is complaining of a stomach upset as well as a headache and Fido says he has a feeling of dizziness. We're all exhausted but no one can sleep. Each of us has had a ration pack for many hours but no one wants to eat any of that dried up crap. Just an occasional swig of water.

Chalky rolls into a bundle, groans, falls off his seat and lies in the aisle. Everyone looks alarmed. I get to him first but Sergeant Cox is our first aider and has a metal canister. He fixes a face mask over Chalky's mouth who instantly breathes more easily. After a minute he regains his feet. Sitting down again next to me he still looks very pale.

The Sergeant takes away the face mask to see Fido and Spud rolling around in the aisle and groaning too. "All right you jokers, you can cut it out now," he grins. "No one else gets oxygen."

"Aaw! Give us a squirt, Corp."

"Oh yeah? Which end d'yer want me to stick the tube in then?"

Ten hours into the flight I finally feel able to break open a tin of bully beef and eat it with one of the crackers. I even offer some to Chalky who's sitting next to me and looking in need of something to brighten him up.

"Bugger off and leave me alone," he grunts. Perhaps boiled beef is not the very thing he needs to cheer him up, after all.

My view through the window changes; even in the near dark I know we're over the sea. It's flat and featureless apart from a sole nameless steamer struggling towards an anonymous port. The engine note has also changed, lower, quieter and smoother, the aircraft feels lighter, less strained and is getting lower. We cross a coastline, into a new land. I can see a lot more now that the sun has started to put its first pale golden light onto the landscape below. There are hills and fields, even a few square houses scattered around.

A head appears from the pilot's cabin. "Get yerselves strapped in yer seats and ready for landing. We're approaching Jerusalem." The head disappears again and the door closes with a harsh snap.

Bitter cold has given way to warmth and then, as the noises change, to heat, solid heat. It hits us long before we reach ground. I'm sweating bucketful's, trying to discard layers of clothing while still strapped into my seat. The whole aircraft is now full of uncomfortable, wriggling soldiers.

The aircraft hits the runway with a shudder and bounces back into the air again before a good solid jolt starts us trundling along foreign ground. The engines roar as the craft slows towards the end of the runway. A timid cheer breaks out among the relieved but exhausted passengers. We taxi across to the tower, having arrived in the Holy Land. Despite my exhaustion, excitement tingles in my brain, a place I've heard so much about but never thought I'd see. I wish we could stay here, rather than go on to fight in Burma.

I never want to get onto another plane ever again.

*

Worra relief to get off that bloody aircraft and walk around. The ache in my legs gets a little easier, the dull thudding in my ears has stopped and oxygen rich air makes me feel light headed. I've discarded my coat and stripped down to my underpants, as have all of the lads before we hastily put on our tropical dress. We must look unusually scruffy, even for soldiers. Most of us light a cigarette, several have started sweating from the need for nicotine and we look around at the new scenery.

The hospitality of the RAF is underwhelming, they obviously do fighters and bombers pretty well, but troop transport? That's clearly of no interest. There's an old aircraft hangar where we'll sleep on the ground, with just the few blankets we brought from the aircraft. There's a big urn of horribly stewed tea, but no milk and some flat bread with slimy yellow savoury paste. It's oily and horrible, with a lot of strong garlic to poison our breath. This is certainly not the bloody Ritz. It is abso-bloody-lutely ridiculous. What wouldn't I give for a nice tin of sardines in tomato sauce now?

None of us can sleep as it is full daylight now. Chalky and I wander around the building and out onto the airfield to smoke yet another cig. It's some sort of a chance to look around. The surrounding land looks pale; parched and dried out by the sun. Everything's straw coloured, except for a few dark scrubby bushes. A collection of white buildings sits beyond the airfield boundary. The architecture's very foreign, pointed towers and grey stone everywhere and it all says we're far from home. The only familiar building is a concrete airfield tower. Further away we can make out shapes in a pale cream mountain range as the morning sun casts an eerie white light onto this strange new world.

Somewhere out of sight, a man is wailing a strange chant into morning air. It seems to be coming from a slim pointed tower. This is a strange, alien place full of weird people. Thank God, I'm with my mates.

There's a hell of a lot of buzzing goin' on too. Everywhere there are flying insects and unknown creatures scurry around on the floor and into the corners of hangar. Those big black mosquitoes've already found us and are enjoying a right jolly feast. All of us have angry red blisters all over our arms and legs. It's bloody ridiculous. Sooner we're out of here, the better. Back in the hangar I toss and turn in a blanket for an hour or two, stare at a huge spider scurrying around room for a bit. I can't stand this and stamp on it, only to find out it's a scorpion. Was that a really dangerous thing to have done?

I finally settle and get a few hours shallow sleep before waking, still feeling drained and ill. The strengthening sun produces heat of a new intensity, and I'm rolling around in discomfort. This must be what hell will be like; thank heavens it's just a short stop here before we go onto India.

But the short stop has already built up to hours, heat risen further and the day stretches out before us. Maybe they've forgotten we're here? No point in looking forward to lunch, it's sure to be another horrible foreign thing. I can't wait to get back on the plane.

Eventually Major Breck appears from the Officer's Quarters, looking fresh from his shower and stands tall in his Officer's uniform, freshly laundered and beautifully pressed. He looks like he's enjoying himself.

He strolls to the front, bristling with self-importance. This guy must have had a good war, he's done well to become a Major so young. He would have waited years to achieve such a rank in peace time, despite the Eton and Oxford education. There were plenty of blokes just like him as Lieutenants and Captains in the European war but mostly they got themselves killed instead of making Major. Breck is a survivor. I admire him for that and respect him for the very sensible way he's conducted himself.

We're all glad to see him; since this means we will soon be on the plane. What a relief. Whatever Bombay and Calcutta are like they have to be better than this bleedin' hell hole.

"You can stand down men," he says brightly. "The flight to Bombay has been cancelled."

"What do you mean, it's cancelled?" a high-pitched voice comes from Fido, somewhere behind me. This might get ugly, we're all in bad shape and seriously pissed off.

Breck spins around angrily, looking for dissenting voice and shouts, "That's it. I've told you everything I know; the flight has been cancelled. Now stop asking such damn fool questions."

"But where're we goin', what's happening to us?"

"Where will we stay? What'll we eat? Why can't we just go home?"

That snooty toff just stares directly at us, snarling the last words we want to hear through his gritted teeth and directly into our faces: "There's been a change of plan; you're staying here." Then the serpent turns around and slithers back towards the same hole he's just slid out of.

It's just bloody ridiculous way we're always treated by those snotty pricks.

ATAROT AIRFIELD, JERUSALEM

AUGUST 16TH 1945

Major Breck is assembling us for a new briefing, it's badly needed. Morale has collapsed, there's a lot of bad-tempered bickering and confusion has taken over. The intense heat, well over a hundred degrees, is taking its toll on everyone. Most of us are scratching at the mosquito bites we've acquired overnight. We've found our tropical dress but short pants and lots of pale white knees have done nowt to restore good humour. A mutiny isn't far away.

Sergeant Cox fusses, getting us to stand in line, until we're all gathered around the officer who stands at ease, his legs apart and his baton gripped behind his back. Through the hangar door we can see mountains behind him glowing a brilliant yellow and buildings clustered over them shimmer in the heat. He's got a great backdrop and this speech had better be just as good.

He seems to know this and hesitates briefly before he starts, in an unusually high-pitched tone, "Whilst we were in the air the Japanese Supreme Council delivered its surrender to Allied Command. It will not now be necessary for us to carry on to Burma. The war is over. That's the reason our flight to Calcutta was cancelled."

A ripple of gasps runs through the soldiers and the Major smiles at the effect of his words. The crisis seems to have been averted already. He lets the effect last, lingering a minute before he speaks again.

"A provisional decision has been made that we will join the forces of the British Mandate, here in Palestine. Then, in good time, a process will be put in place to return you to your civilian lives. Until then you will be transferred to temporary accommodation within the British Army HQ at the King David Hotel in the centre of Jerusalem. I'm sure you will find that much more comfortable than here at the airfield."

The Major looks as smooth as ever, the confusion of yesterday has gone. But I guess he didn't sleep on the ground without any change of clothes or need to wash in a bucket like we did. There's a distinct whiff of sweaty, grimy Tommy around his audience.

"This is a great day. I am sure you will all join with me in rejoicing over our wonderful and complete victory which has saved so many lives. Perhaps even our own. God save the King."

The rejoicing takes the form of stunned silence before a few men clap briefly, there's even a bedraggled cheer before a confused silence descends on the group. No one asks what happens next, or what will happen to me, they're left as the great unacknowledged questions hanging in the air.

He turns and leaves quickly while the better mood survives. We stumble away, confused but happy, well sort of happy. None of us knows what to do or where to go, except as far out of the scalding sunlight as we can get. That's means back into the stench and gloom of the stuffy hangar. No one has a clue what to say or think. This news has come right out of a far corner of pale blue sky and given us a good hard smack in the gob.

I'm one of a group of clammy men with exhausted red eyes, walking aimlessly and chain-smoking ciggies in the murk of an uncomfortable silence. Each one gives me his blandest, blankest look before looking away. Eventually Chalky gave a voice to just one of big questions running around our heads: "Why would the Japs suddenly just give up like that?"

"I guess it must be something to do with those atom bombs they were talking about in newspapers," I said to anyone listening. "They said that it'd destroyed entire cities with just one bomb. I read that one had been dropped on a Japanese city just last week. Hirohito, I think it was called."

"What bloody difference would one bomb make?" asked Fido. Someone had been listening.

"I imagine it's a really huge bomb, the size of a house. They said it was something called nuclear fission. But I don't really know what that is."

"New clear fishing? Atom bombs? This is just bollocks, you stupid mongrel, you're just using words that don't make any sense. Are you makin' up all this to take the piss?"

A calm voice is obviously needed, "Seems these atom-bombs are special ones that can blow up a whole city at one go. I don't know how they can do that. Anyway, something has frightened the bastards into surrendering. Let's just be happy, it's probably saved our lives and we won't need to fight in the jungle."

"Why did it have to happen when we're here? If only they'd dropped it one feckin' day sooner we would be stranded in England. Even bleedin' Wiltshire would be better than this bastard flea pit."

"Yeah and one day later we'd be in Bombay. Two days later we'd be in Calcutta and three days later we'd be half way to Rangoon. Let's be happy we avoided all that crap. Non-stop diarrhoea and the sweats. Anyway, what's this Palestine Mandate thingy we're joining?"

"No idea," says Fido, squirming as he scratches an insect bite on his backside. "But this could be a nice place to spend the winter. At least it'll be warm and there's no fighting here. Cheer up lads, we're alive. We've survived the bloody war."

"Can I go home then?"

A vision of Joe's face comes into my head and maybe going home doesn't feel so great any more.

A group of shabby, old trucks, painted grey, have turned up and we're all bundled into the back of one. All of us are packed in nice, tight and cosy but most of all, hot. They take us on a long ride into the city of Jerusalem, passing endless strange and unfamiliar white stone buildings along a hot and very dusty road. A very long road of many potholes. Those idiots hanging around the back get a great view of the new country and might well soon get a very close view, at least of the road surface if they don't hold on tight.

When we get there, Jerusalem city centre is actually rather grand. I'm impressed. The grandest place of all, the King David Hotel, is located at the end of a long avenue and is definitely a step up on the aircraft hangar. For a start, there is only the very faintest smell of shit, piss and sweat.

On arrival we parade before the Garrison C.O. who welcomes us by telling us all that we're scruffy, our brasses are unpolished, our uniforms are dirty and unpressed; in fact, we're a disgrace to the British Army, get ourselves sorted out sharpish. And this before we've even been allocated a place to sleep.

We're not actually going to be in the hotel and are sent by a tall, hot Sergeant-Major, into an army camp on the south side of the main building. He has beads of sweat running down his face, disappearing into a damp patch under his collar. There's a tent for every four blokes and a block house with wash basins and a shower. It's not luxury but it is better than we had during the invasion of Europe and best of all, no one is shooting at us.

Over the surrounding walls we can see a tall and impressive, square tower of Jerusalem YMCA. This is an impressive old building, built in the white or gold limestone which seems to be the typical building material of this ancient town.

I make a bee-line for the block house and get straight under a shower, the first time I've ever used one of these funny American contraptions. I tinker with the taps trying to get it warm but soon realises that there is only any water in the cold tap. Even that doesn't really live up to its description but the tepid water feels ok on my back. A bar of coal tar soap restores a healthy pink glow to my parched skin. Mostly because it's full of grit. My shaving cuts burn so I take a look in mirror for reassurance but the reflection in the mirror fails to deliver. Whose thin, anxious face is that? He looks pretty knackered and unhappy.

As the camp is linked to the hotel by a side entrance Fido, Chalky and I can take a walk into main building. We've seen a few new countries this year but nowt like this. It's time to explore.

"We're in centre of the Holy Land, one of the world's most famous places. There's going to be a lot to see here and we're sure to get plenty of time off. There's no one to fight."

"Yep, you're right Billy boy. The war's over."

"Say it again."

"The war is over. And we won," adds Fido. I think there's a tear forming in his eye, the soft sod. He looks pretty knackered too, that seems to be spreading too. We've all got it.

The King David Hotel is an extraordinary and magnificent building with pink quartz exteriors. It looks like a palace from a bible story, belonging to King Herod, Solomon or David even. There are spacious private gardens that enclose green lawns, tennis courts and a swimming pool. Also, a tropical garden under the outdoor restaurant on terrace. Inside it has dazzling public rooms decorated with gold motifs. Wow! I'm a very long way from Chapel Street.

Chalky, Fido and Spud are staring into the bar where tall, slim and athletic black waiters in tight fitting, immaculate red jackets are serving British Officers with tea, coffee or pink gin. The gentlemen have pith helmets besides their seats and their ladies carry white parasols, now neatly folded. It's a vision into another world. A pretty weird one but I wish I could be in that version of the pantomime; it looks nicer than the farce we're involved in.

I grab the chance a few minutes chat with a lady on reception.

Her badge tells me that her name's Hetty and she's dressed in the white blouse and black skirt of the hotel uniform. To my eye she has something of a resemblance to Ava Gardner. I like the idea of meeting a film star.

"Hello. Have you just arrived, soldier?"

"Yes, Hetty. We didn't expect to be here though. We were supposed to be going to Burma so I don't know much about Jerusalem."

Without further prompting she gives me a well-practised speech. "A short walk from here will take you to the Old City, which is divided into four quarters: the Armenian, Christian, Jewish and Muslim. Each quarter has a rich history that dates back thousands of years. The Wailing Wall is the most sacred place for Jewish people and the Dome of the Rock is one of the top sites in the Muslim faith. In the Christian Quarter, Jesus's final steps can be followed by walking through the Via Dolorosa. The route ends at the Church of the Holy Sepulchre where Jesus was crucified. We can also see a lot from here, as the Hotel overlooks the city from an elevated site: walls, minarets and domes are all visible."

I'm spellbound. Her soft, lilting voice has had an amazing effect on me. I hear most of her talk but I watch Hetty closely and I'll remember her appearance much longer than any of her words. Coming here could really prove to be a blessing in disguise for a working-class lad; how else would I ever get to see a place like this? Meet a girl like Hetty?

I look at the view she is indicating through the window, anticipating that it will look like a Hollywood set. In a way it does but the set is peppered by barbed wire around roadblocks and pillboxes with an occasional tank emphasising that British Army control this city. It seems much better prepared for military defence than any of the cities that I saw in Germany. Yet that all seems so normal to Hetty that it might be invisible. I guess they're not really needed any more, since the war ended yesterday, so no one need worry about all those guns.

"It's great to be in a peaceful place, we expected to be going to another war zone."

"There is a kind of a war going on here. Not a shooting war with cannons and bombers like you've been through in Europe, of course, but there's a lot of bad feeling between Arabs and Jews. The Palestinians resent the way we've been coming in slowly over a few years."

"We? You mean you're Jewish?"

"Yes, I came here from Warsaw as a child in 1925; when Jewish immigration into Israel was controlled by the Zionist Executive. Before the British took those rights away from us. There were many of us who came from Poland that year. They called us "the Capitalists" as my parents had enough money to buy a little hotel, which they still run."

I'd never have known she's Polish from her English. It's almost perfect, though now she's told me I *can* hear a slight European accent. She fits naturally into the civilised and pleasing atmosphere of the King David Hotel. A slim, shapely girl with brown eyes, black hair and rouged cheeks. She has a smile for every one and is falling over herself to be helpful. And after Belsen, I feel a great sympathy with Jews, especially since Jeno became such a close friend. I remember him with great warmth.

It just feels right that they should have a homeland. And this seems the right place, just like the Bible. I wish I could have stayed in contact with Jeno, but as soon as his brother was buried, he disappeared. He seemed suddenly, stressed and anxious and so I guess he went home to Budapest, he'd said he had some things to sort out there. Some business to sort out with the Charlies, if I remember it right.

Reception and the bar in KDH are a place where the Officers hang out. I guess that driver/mechanics might be expected to keep away but I'm not going without being told. The entrance area is, however, patrolled by a unit of Royal Scots Guards.

"Hey yoo! What are yoo doing here?" growls the sergeant

leaning into my face and breathing his smoky breath into my nostrils.

"Just finding my feet Sarge. We've only just arrived here and are looking over the place."

"Well, get your feet oot of here, before the boot on my foot assists your skinny arse oot."

He jerks his thumb at Chalky and Fido too. I'd forgotten they're still here.

A few minutes later I'm back in my tent staring at Fido and I realise that I'd rather be looking at Hetty. She has greater appeal to me than he does and I don't think it's *just* his bad breath and yellow teeth. Life has given me a new challenge: finding a way to spend my time going back into the hotel and chatting her up. For now, there is nowt to do but lie on my bed. It's very hot and I'm the only one still awake.

*

The tent flap opens and the familiar tones of Sergeant Cox's jolly voice jolt me out of my stupor, disturbing a dream of a return visit to Hetty in reception and various ways of impressing her. He gives me a big grin and says:

"Wakey, wakey, Billy boy. There's a message from Major Breck: Other ranks are not permitted inside the Hotel building from now on, except on official business."

His head disappears and I hear heavy footsteps pounding the grass until they reach next tent.

"Message from Major Breck…"

Now this really is bloody ridiculous.

A bench at the King David Hotel

1st September 1945

Hot air, full of humidity that suggests Autumn is coming, hangs heavily, pressing down hard on any one unfortunate enough to be below it. There's a fine view down to the tennis courts from up here on this bench, in the shade of a high terrace, constructed of great stone blocks. I'm very sheltered here against the wall, as cool as anywhere can be in this oven of a country. It's a great place for a quiet smoke.

It would be an even better view if those two chubby, damp officers would give up on their attempts at slow-motion tennis. Their white shorts reveal stumpy legs which barely move as the ball crosses the court. There's a lot of double faults but almost every serve is an ace and any return is a winner. As soon as I wish for it, they oblige and disappear into the pavilion, taking their dripping bodies away but leaving their heavy breathing behind. They have heard my thoughts my extra sensory powers must be improving. The sun smiles at that idea and makes an extra effort to fry me alive. I feel an insect on my arm, just in time to squash it as it bites me, leaving a bloody smear on my limb.

The lads in camp told me this garden was designed a decade ago by rich Egyptians and they intended it to be a refuge from the heat, a place that hides its occupants under shade of palm trees. Purple flowers on the bougainvillea bushes are starting to fade but their dark green fleshy leaves are flourishing. I'm the only beneficiary of this complex and expensive landscape and can devote myself to enjoying it. There's nowt I can think of that could add to my enjoyment more than the tin of pilchards in tomato sauce I've recently liberated. I've also acquired the temporary use of a silver fork with letters KDH stamped proudly on it. I know it's not the bloody Ritz but it's nearly as bloody good.

"Hello soldier."

A soft, lilting and strangely familiar voice interrupts my trance. A trace of European accent promises a new, altogether more alluring, presence which instantly replaces pilchards in my thoughts. It's just an enchanting piece of magic. I lick the tomato sauce off my lips and wait for the background music to start, surely this is a scene from a film.

"Hello Hetty."

Her curly, shoulder length black hair, looks a little more like Ava Gardner this morning. I have my own film star smiling down on me.

"You remember my name, that's nice. What's yours?"

"Billy. And I'm very pleased to see you." I say, fully aware that my grin and the glow in my cheeks have already given her a clue about my reaction. I try to look into her eyes rather than at her slim, youthful body.

"It's my lunch break, can I sit with you?"

"Of course. I'll share my view with you."

"How kind, it's a very nice view."

I feel better when she sits, it's less obvious that she's taller than I am. She sits nice and close too, her knees pointing across the bench towards me, as she smooths her skirt. I catch the slight scent of her perfume. Her eye contact is strong, almost aggressive and takes me by surprise. She seems a more self-confident woman here than at reception.

She looks straight into my eyes, and I can see how green her eyes are in this light, they'd seemed blue inside the hotel. A deep emerald green, like the sea would be, if the sea was perfect. Or perhaps the fierce green eyes of a cat eyeing up a mouse before it pounces and bites deep into its bones and flesh.

"You're watching the tennis courts? Are you a tennis player, soldier?"

I laugh aloud. "No, that's not my kind of game. I'm just a driver. That's a game for officers."

"Ah! There seem to be a lot of funny rules in the British Army. Only officers can do this, and go to this place, other ranks do that and go somewhere else. As though you're frightened of each other. It's obvious you need to be separated from each other all the time, I've no idea why."

"How do you like working for the British Army?"

"Not much. It makes me unpopular among the Yishuv, they call me *that one* and won't talk to me."

"Why would they do that? So petty."

"I'm not staying here in Israel. When my papers come, I'll be off to New York. My uncle lives there and he's trying to get me in. Many of us really want to go there but it's difficult to get permission from the US Government."

"Why wouldn't you stay here, isn't this homeland of your people?"

"Palestine is very troubled; the Arabs plan to kill us all when the British leave. They're already doing what they can to attack us."

"Why? The war's over."

Now she laughs. "Which war is over? We have our own new war here. The Arabs think it's their land and have killed many of our people in the past. It was far worse before the World War. Many innocent people were killed in massacres. We'll fight them again if we need to."

"They may have a point; they've lived here for thousands of years."

"No! No! No! It isn't their country; we were here before them. We've also bought land off them, marshy land that they could never farm and they'd abandoned as unsuitable for farming. My people drained the swamps to build kibbutzim. It is promised to us, by God and also by the British Government, don't you know about the Balfour Declaration?" The happy smile has transformed into a stern grimace, her green eyes focussed on a distant point. I'm not sure where she's gone or even if she remembers that I'm still with her.

I shudder. "Sorry, I didn't mean to upset you."

I need a moment to think. To look at her again. This is a very complicated and clever lady, so different here than on the first occasion we met. I've unlocked a depth of emotion in her, on a subject I hadn't even known was sensitive. There she was in the role of a helpful and pleasing receptionist but here, in the garden, she's thoughtful and passionate behind that pretty face. And she knows a lot more about Palestine, its people and past than I do. And who is this Balfour chap? I hope he's declared that volunteer soldiers should all be de-mobbed and go home soon.

"And what do *you* want, soldier? What are you doing in *my* country?" Her mood lightens once more. She beams as she looks at me. It's as though she has mentally returned to the garden and now can see me again. Her broad smile pushes me back into the bench as I'm hit by a shock wave of new energy. A smile flickers onto my cheeks in return as I look at her and I form a mental list in my head of what I would want from her, do with her if, if… well, if I might believe she could be interested in me.

"I want to go home." I saying, making a big effort to ignore my mental list. "The war I joined up for is over."

"If it's a war you want, there's another one here for you."

"Well, it's a bloody confusing war and I don't wanna be any part of it. I don't know who's right or who's wrong. I don't even know which side I'm on. I'd much rather just go home." It all blurts out, without my intending it. A little out of control.

"You don't think we Jews should live here? You don't think we're right?" Her voice is suddenly very quiet and the serious eyes are back. This time they are entirely focused on me.

"Well, if I must think about it, I'm sure you Jews need a homeland. God knows you deserve it after all stuff I saw happening in Germany. I saw some of that that first hand."

Hetty looks at me, a long meaningful look, goes silent and then stands up. "Yes, well I should go back to my work. Thank you for your company and good luck in Jerusalem, soldier. Maybe you deserve it and you may well need it."

She glances briefly at me and leaves without a further word. The cat has lost interest in playing with its mouse. Maybe there's bigger prey to be had.

I watch her sway along the length of the gravel path, the tight skirt compressing her movements but expanding my interest. She leans forward, her outline visible as an 'S' moving in female form, then continues up steps, onto restaurant terrace and disappears into pink quartz of hotel building through rotating doors. Despite my efforts to will her to look round and glance coyly back at me there is not a moment's hesitation; not a backward glance.

The sun feels a little cooler.

There is, however, movement in the bushes at the end of gravel path. Two grinning, sunburnt faces appear: Chalky and Fido. The last people in the world I wanted to witness my meeting with Hetty.

"Hi Billy boy, been having a good time with the nice lady, have we? The lads will be pleased to know about this," Fido smirks. They run off gleefully clutching their berets in their hands and giggling aloud like little schoolgirls. They look bloody ridiculous, they sound bloody ridiculous and above all, they're behaving in a bloody ridiculous way.

But now, at last, I've got time to enjoy pilchards. The tomato sauce tastes even better now it's warmed up but it's just as good at splashing over my uniform top. Once I've licked the tin out, carefully avoiding cutting my tongue, I look at the recently captured silver fork I've been using. But it's not silver, it's a fake. Under close scrutiny the back of the handle confesses to be SHEFFIELD STEEL. I fling it down onto the path. Imposter.

This is only delaying the inevitable though. I finally *have* to go back to camp to face the music from the masses assembled to greet me. What fun they are having. And what songs they are singing.

"Wha hey, here he is! The five foot four Casanova."

"Romeo! Romeo! Wherefore art thou Romeo!"

The boys have formed a line in front of tents along both sides of track, so I've no option to walk between cheering men; the biggest round of applause I've ever had. They slap me on the back, ruffle my hair and trip me up. They're also shaking my hand as they laugh. These lads know how to have fun. I can hear their comments.

"Wadyer mean Clark Gable? Ridiculous. He's more like Charlie bloody Chaplin."

*

By evening the bench has acquired magical properties. It's already associated with the twin miracles of Hetty's smile and pilchardy tomato sauce; a temple to all the pleasures. I must visit it again to sample these memories and to escape the unceasing banter of the brainless pillocks in the camp. My foot unintentionally kicks a small metal object in the dark, which scuttles along the gravel to escape onto the grass verge. I let it hide there.

In the gloom, my view down to the tennis court is much reduced and my focus turns from an empty tennis court to the bright lights of the terrace, shimmering above me in the heat. It was silent and still at lunch time, but now it's decorated with strings of red, white and blue lamps emitting a thin watery glow in the last mellow strands of sunlight. The officers and their elegant ladies are gathering for green, red or yellow cocktails before their grand dinner begins. Down here I'm reduced to a shadow under the wall, watching them rejoice in the sunlit uplands of the main restaurant. We're all loving the warm, moist evening air as does my only company, a number of large black mosquitoes, who also think it's dinner time.

It'd be nice to be an officer but I know I'd never fit in with such grand folk. I've no need of a rich sauce on my dinner, having already sampled the joy of spam fritters and boiled potatoes in our mess tent. There are other delights here for me and hearing a swing band play from so close by is a real treat. This is no thin five-piece affair but a terrace filling array of braying oboes, trombones and saxophones, complemented by a solitary drummer. He's making it his personal mission to play louder than all the others combined but they all notice and respond to the challenge.

It's been a long time since I enjoyed lively music. I can sit here unobserved as they run through "*Chattanooga choo choo*", "*In the mood* "and "*I got rhythm*". After staying unseen so successfully, I feel confident enough to take a risk by lighting a cigarette. The tiny glow marks my presence in the dark, but no one's looking and my secret remains intact.

The bar's working at full pace dispensing rounds of cocktails, the African waiters circling the tables to dispense them. The buzz of voices blends with strong tone of the busy instruments and the cacophony floats over the dark and anonymous space in which I secretly lurk, slightly afraid of discovery, but still confident in my disguise. Stout men and light-footed girls come and go like moths among the whisperings and music; the champagne, cocktails and stars.

The lights glow a little brighter as the sun merges with the horizon, before giving a final surge of orange light. Then it is twilight for a few minutes. Darkness, when it comes, is welcome, it suits my mood. I want to disappear into darkness and remain the unknown, silent observer. I don't belong in the bright, colourful, floodlit universe but delight in seeing into these new wonders from my dark blue underworld.

Smoke tastes pleasingly bitter in my throat and the crescent moon looks reassuringly sympathetic, even to a Christian soldier. It seems to get rid of some of the biting insects for a short time, though they leave the sores they had made earlier. When I lean back into the bench and close my eyes, my mind detaches from my body and floats off into darkness, swaying to the rhythm of the band and soaring up to join the myriad stars twinkling in heaven above me. When the music stops it's a shock to open my eyes, see dark sky and feel the solid, parched earth of Jerusalem beneath my feet again.

As the evening draws on, the band is joined by a slender, blonde soprano in a long, glittering ball gown, who gives us *We'll meet again* and other Vera Lynn classics in a strangely accented English. I wonder where they've found such a creature from among the dark-haired people of this region.

Finally, deep into the evening, there's an announcement requesting revellers to take their partners for the last dance. A slow dance to *A nightingale sang in Berkeley Square*. I wish I had a partner for this last dance but silent solitude and non-participation is the price a private soldier has to pay for clandestine entrance to this other world.

I throw my last cig down onto the gravel and step on it, grinding it out, and take my leave. As I walk away my view of the terrace opens up and I can see more of the dancers. The area is full of primary colours and bare shoulders, with hair elaborately shorn into complex fashions. My attention is immediately drawn to just one dark haired young lady, who looks fabulous in a dazzling white evening dress with sparkling diamond earrings and necklace. She has impeccable make up, her red lips visibly glowing even from this distance. They complement her black shoulder length hair and she really does seem to be Ava Gardner.

She moves with grace like an elegant hawk, circling her dance partner before seizing a cocktail and throwing it down her throat, her head tilted backwards. Does she need more courage? She already looks happy and confidant. Then she clings closely to her companion, a tall man in a white dinner jacket who has his back to me. He sweeps her elegantly around in the rhythm and must be amusing her with clever and witty remarks as she holds her head high, laughs aloud and looks gloriously happy as the singer continues:

> *I may be right, I may be wrong,*
> *But I'm perfectly willing to swear*
> *That when you turned and smiled at me*
> *A nightingale sang in Berkeley Square.*

Then they swing around and I recognise her partner. It's that bastard Breck.

The mail arrives in Jerusalem

2nd October 1945

Sergeant Cox barges in, interrupting my thoughts. I start up a little irritated but forgive him immediately because of the reason he came. He's instantly the most popular man in camp; the one distributing mail from home. "One for you Fido, *five* for you Chalky. Dirty little bastard, how many women have you got?"

"They're all from my sisters, Sarge."

Loud laughter.

"Two for you Romeo. You must be upto summat too." He thrusts the two envelopes into my grasping fist, crumpling both as he dashes onward.

I recognise this writing immediately, it's from my brother Joe. Why doesn't my mother ever write, or Celi? The other bears an unfamiliar stamp: "Republique Francaise" it says. I tear that one open as fast as I can. A very faint whiff of eau de cologne reaches me from the pastel pink paper and rolls over me like a tidal wave. No one ever puts scent on writing paper, what is this? Who do I know in France?

As I read the opening words, I can hear an almost forgotten voice again, softly speaking in broken English:

34 Rue des deux Eglises,
Amiens
France 8

12 Aout '45

Mon petit soldat,
   I hope you are safe in the Palestine and can see the holy places. We hear many the bad things that will trouble you there but I wish you the good chances. Here in Amiens everything is peaceful and better. They build Amiens again in the old style. Almost like the old city in the nice times before the wars came.
   I remember the evening I you met. It was the beautiful moment in the bad time. I like the way you drive me, my familley away from danger in your petty camion. My father is much better now but he still walks with a lump. You are so courage when the cannon was firing. We are safe because you. I want you hold my hand again, look me in the eyes and give me chocolat like the before and comfort me with your calm voices. I think that often.
   I hope you will me write soon. I hope you will me come see some time when the British Army you let go. I go learning the English now to know something for you so we can be chatting together, like you say.
   Je me souviens souvent de toi, et toujours avec emotion.

Ta cherie,
   Margaux

Bloody hell, Margaux, that little froggy bird! She still remembers me. I'd forgotten all about her. Posted in August! It's a letter of few words but it's enough to send a warm flush sweeping through me. I can see her; the soft brown eyes, broad smile and crazy make up, her long chestnut hair up in a tight bun. The memory was faded but its flooding back. I also see her mother, giving Margaux another of many disapproving looks and passing more comments in a harsh, garbled language that I couldn't understand. Kurt seemed to be mentioned a lot but I have no idea what a kurt is.

In my memory she wraps her arms around me and kisses me passionately in the way she never did. I sense her tiny body trembling in my arms, which it also never did, and I know now that I must find a way to go back to Picardy; it's obviously not just roses that bloom there.

Margaux was quite a character. I only knew her a few hours but she is burnt onto my memory. When I first saw her, she didn't look so wonderful, crawling out of the ruins of a freshly shelled farmhouse covered in white dust. More like a tatty little weasel. I'd been rushing to get new supplies of ammo for the two tanks I accompanied, acting as forward artillery, when the building I was approaching disintegrated in a yellow flash and a cloud of smoke. I never heard any sound as splinters of rock sprayed around me, shattering the windscreen and shredding the canvas cover of my lorry. It was a struggle to keep it on the road.

I had to stop and see if there were any survivors, pull them out of the wreckage. Sure enough, two dirty faces appeared, and I dragged the women clear. Once they had wiped their faces on my only spare shirt, I could make out that one was young and pretty and the other one was her mother.

More noises came from below the building rubble, though I had difficulty in hearing. I found an old man trying to push stones off himself. The poor old sod was terribly bruised and evidently in a lot of pain. I doubt he would have got out on his own; those stones were nice regular square building blocks and bloody heavy. I nearly ruptured myself lifting them off him. He also wiped himself down on my once clean shirt, slowly. He moved very gingerly than the women, had a lot of visible bruising and was genuinely in some distress. Bravely, he seemed to want to disguise it.

The daughter was almost hysterical at sight of her father's

injuries and I needed to calm her down, holding her hand speaking slowly and soothingly to her. I doubt if she could understand any of my words, but my tone might have helped. I even gave her one of the precious bars of Hershey's chocolate that I'd liberated earlier and hoarded in the cab. I didn't have one for her mother who reacted with obvious bad grace.

After that, I got them all into the back of the lorry and took the whole family back to the safety of the ammunition dump, driving slowly though still bumping all the way. There was a medic there who took charge of her father and seemed quite concerned about his condition. I wanted to stop with her but my lorry was already being re-loaded with shells to be taken back to my tanks and the yardmen were calling impatiently for it to be moved on.

Before I left her, she hugged me and asked my name, giving me a peck on the cheek. I remember how much she was shaking, even at this point. By now she'd wiped away all of the dust and I could see how young she really was. Sad, soft brown eyes with moist edges looked right through me and it was quite a wrench to turn and leave. She promised to write to me, in her halting attempt at English, but I'd no real expectation that she could even if she tried. But I was waiting and hoping for this letter and now, when I'd given up and forgotten her, here it is.

How could she have found me? It's just addressed to me c/o the British Army in Palestine. The Post Office boys have done great to track me down. I dash off a reply to Margaux, quickly, easily and with great pleasure, gushing out my delight at being in contact again.

Then I look at the letter from Joe and the prospect of going home doesn't feel comfortable any more.

The gardens of the KDH

Oct 3rd 1945

I took a walk out to my favourite bench under the terrace in the Hotel gardens earlier this morning and am still sitting here. I'm completely alone, the restaurant and tennis courts are silent. No one comes down from reception to sit beside me, no matter how hard I will her to come. It's empty, shaded and calm. I'm alone with just my thoughts as company, apart from the biting insects that are always following me.

A couple of hours are taken up with yesterday's letters, first re-reading the one from Margaux. The fact that she remembered me is flattering. That she is keeping in touch is exciting. I read the letter again, quickly, easily and joyfully.

Then slowly and carefully, I read Joe's letter.

4 Platt St.,
Leigh,
Lancs

17th Sept 1945

Dear Bill,

I hope you are safe and we hear that you have nice, warm weather in Palestine. It must be lovely to be there, just like a glorious holiday, I'm sure you are enjoying sights of the Holy Land. I envy you being able to travel and see such wonderful places. I'm sure you're happy to be in a nice safe place too, the threat of war being removed now. I have always wanted to see the glories of the Empire but I have such heavy obligations to my wife and daughter. I envy you all those wonderful chances you have had in life.

It's good that you are supporting our parents but I don't think you know the real extent of the problems they are facing back here in Leigh. Everything is very expensive these days and it's simply not possible for them to feed and clothe themselves on the small amount you are sending. I'm not sure what you think my mother can buy for a shilling a week. They are on the verge of starving to death.

I know you don't mind me letting you know about it. You'll be sure to understand that it's all for the best.

Warm regards,
Joe.

Of course, I don't want my parents to end up in poverty but I am the only one who could help? Surely Celi is contributing something? I know that Joe is supporting a wife and small child but can't he help them a bit, if their conditions is really this bad?

When I first told my Dad that I was joining the Army, back in July '42, he took it really badly and we had a big argument. He'd said then that they were depending on me to support them after our family business had gone bust. He'd lost his job and I would have lost mine too.

I'd agreed to give them half of my Army wages. In return, he promised that I'd inherit the house. So perhaps, Joe had a point. It would be tough right now to give them all my wages but in long run I will get something really significant out of it. It's going to be a big sacrifice but I write him a brief note telling him that I will send them all seven shillings from my wages from now on. In fact, that's everything I earn. From now on I might get a few cigs from charity parcels and nowt else.

When I get back to the camp, I feel shocked and hurt, struck by Joe's ingratitude and lack of appreciation of my circumstances, but also worried about my parents being in such a bad state. Fido can see something is wrong.

"What's up, mate? Something bad happening at home?"

"My folk are 'aving a bad time, they can't make ends meet. I already send them some money but now I'll have to send it all."

"That's very tough on a private's pay, mate. We got only get two bob to start with."

Right, I need to do what I can but why does it all fall on me? Why can't Joe or Nash or Celi help? I suppose it's because they promised me the house. Joe obviously resents the promise of my inheritance.

I plod wearily over to Paymaster's office, hoping he won't be in. He's notoriously hard to find. But, of course, he is in, this time.

"What can I do for you, Private Atherton?"

"I need to assign my wages to my parents."

"Let's have a look at your card. Ah yes, I see you already assign them a shilling a week. How much do you want to assign now?"

"The whole two shillings."

"Are you sure? You won't be able to get yourself anything now.

No chocolate, not a bottle of beer, no cigarettes. Nothing. That seems like a big sacrifice for anyone."

"Thanks, but I've gotta do it, send it all to them."

"Of course, if you say so Private Atherton, I'll make the arrangements. Sign here, please."

British Army camp, KDH

4th November 1945

A strong wind whistles through the trees, around the YMCA tower and over the walls of the KDH to ruffle up all of the tents in camp and the rain is coming down in stair rods. The field inside the pale stone walls of the hotel is swamped, we're all in danger of seeing our homes demolished in the gale. We all retreat into the messroom, a big sturdy structure, for a bit of respite. The Holy Land has become a wholly miserable land.

We three musketeers, gather around a table in the mess, in the safety of an actual stone structure, each holding a cup of NAAFI tea. I lick the tomato sauce off my lips, saved earlier from a sneaky tin of pilchards. We look around at the changed scenery as the breeze rearranges the camp. A feral cat whines from the swaying branches of a large cedar tree, apparently unable to get down and appealing for a rescue none of us fancy making.

I stare at the fading, stained colour of dreary canvass and deduce, through a piece of sheering cunning, that it might originally have been white. Before I finish my cuppa, I've counted three cracked light shades, two broken light bulbs and six side panels that need replacing. Not sure I've got all the spiders though.

The other two are glancing around as well, quick jerky movements. No words pass between us. Most of us light up cigarettes, several have started sweating from the need for nicotine.

So, here I am among a group of clammy men with exhausted red eyes, talking aimlessly and chain-smoking ciggies in the murk of an uncomfortable gloom. Each one gives me a bland, empty stare before looking away to spot anything of interest that might appear through the door. There's rarely any means of entertainment provided anywhere in this camp, though Jerusalem is said to have many distractions for the brave and wealthy. An ordinary soldier has to make do with plainer stuff, we do occasionally have a film show, right here in this messroom. Last Friday evening, it's always Friday evening, they showed Bing Crosby in "Going my way". The week before it was "Casablanca".

We know all the film stars well but none of them has appeared in person yet. It is, however, less than three months since we arrived, so it's too soon to write off a grand entrance by George Formby. He may be heading here right now, to entertain with his little ukulele in his hand. Or perhaps a guest appearance by Charlie Chaplin? Personally, I'm hoping for Greer Garson, or Ingrid Bergson.

The rain has stopped and a small group of soldiers has gathered around the tree in the centre of our courtyard. The animal's plight providing the only point of interest on a day of extraordinary tedium. One of the starts to climb towards it but the animal climbs further up, keeping away from its rescuer and getting stranded even higher.

I suggest that we pass the time with an arm-wrestling competition. I beat Chalky last time and took a couple of ciggies off him but need to avoid a replay with Fido, whose wiry arms are too well adopted for this kinda sport. I light a cigarette now, avoiding the need to offer them around to the others.

"Let's have a game of cards", yells Fido in a fit of enthusiasm. "I'll take all your money off yer, you load of losers."

"OK mate, keep your hair on. I know there's not much

excitement here but it's not worth having a heart attack over," says chuckling Chalky.

"You won't get rich taking all my money, Fido. I ain't got none." is my contribution.

"Well, we can play for matches. Who's got any?"

I produce a box of Captain Webb's; Fido has Bryant and May but Chalky takes pride of place when he produces an extra-large box of Swan Vestas.

"Oy," says Mr White, "this ain't fair. I got the best matches, you only got cheap uns."

A calm voice is obviously needed. "How about this for an idea," I say cheerfully, "stop talking bullshit and let's get on with the game!"

"OK, don't get bossy, Billy lad. Just because you got the reception lady doesn't mean your important now. You might be the five foot four Casanova but you're not the boss yet."

I stare back staring at Chalky, mentally comparing him with Hetty. She's definitely got the greater appeal; not matter how much he flashes his yellow teeth in that toothy grin. Is he trying to flutter his eye lashes at me? I'm looking for the glamour that will brighten this place up but short pants and brown knees do nowt to make the place memorable.

"Whose deal is it? Shall we turn over cards to decide?"

I got a four of hearts. Chalky the ten of clubs, so Fido won with a Queen of Diamonds. He's already pleased with himself. "See. Told you I'm the winner. Not hard, with you lot though." He scratches his balls, quite methodically, before dealing the cards out, seven to each of us. Whatever is causing his itch will now be available to all of us. That's the philosophy of the camp; whatever we have, we share.

I hold the cards very gingerly, just by their corners. "You don't wanna play poker, Billy, if you're going to pull that kinda face when you see your hand."

"I can't really call this a hand; it looks more like a foot to me."

"Well, if you're looking through a face like Billy's, nothing would look good."

"Ho, bloody ho. You're such a wit. I thought that was Tommy Trinder for a moment."

"You're look more like Arthur Askey yourself, but only in height. Your jokes are as funny as Boris Karloff's."

"Hey, I can tell great jokes!"

"Right, let's hear one."

"A man walks into a doctor's and says; Doctor, doctor. I've got all of the toes from my left foot on my right foot and all the toes from my left foot on my right foot. The doctor looks at it and says; Wow! That's the worst case of myxomatosis I've ever seen."

A spate of mewing comes from the audience, very much like a feral cat in distress. We all feel a little more sympathy for it now.

"Oh well, if you're telling Doctor, doctor jokes, I've definitely got you beaten: A man walks into a doctor's and says; Doctor, doctor, I have terrible dreams. Sometimes I dream I'm a wigwam, sometimes I dream I'm a tepee. Sit down and relax, says the doctor, take it easy. You're obviously being too tense."

"Nah! I can do better than that. A man walks into a doctor's and says; Doctor, doctor, I keep imagining I'm a billiard ball. The doctor stands up from behind his desk and shouts – how dare you burst into my surgery like that, get to the end of the queue!"

"Hey, that's so funny, Billy. Laugh? I thought I'd never start."

Fido plays an ace of hearts. Let's see you beat that, you smart asses. Your card playing is more like comedy, than your joke telling.

A sudden draught blow across the messroom and scatters all the cards to the far corners of the room. Out in the yard more pathetic mewing comes from the cedar tree, now swaying vigorously.

"Right!" says Fido, striding out towards the courtyard. "I'm going to sort out this bloody cat, once and for all."

From the shelter of the mess, we watch him trying to shake the cedar tree which is huge and has probably been there since King Solomon ruled here. The cat doesn't seem to notice. Chalky goes out to join him as he obviously needs help, probably from a psychiatrist.

"My moneys on the cat", I say, to no one in particular, although a small group have now gathered to observe the battle of wits between Fido and Chalky and the cat in the tree. No one takes me up on the wager. I wait for the background music to start, surely this is a scene from a fantasy, or perhaps more like a farce.

I look around and can confirm the conclusion I came to months ago, when I arrived here. The world has gone mad. I volunteered to join the Army to fight Hitler and he's been dead a year and a half now. It was my own choice to defend my country and our people. I shouldn't be here, in the Palestine Mandate, that was never part of my choice. It couldn't be, I'd never heard of it. The strong wind whistles through the trees, around the YMCA tower reminds me that I've had enough of the Army. I want to go home now.

Fido and Chalky have returned from outdoors, the crowd has got bored and moved away from the window and behind them the cat is moving casually away from the tree, unnoticed and holding a small creature in its mouth, perhaps a mouse or even a baby squirrel.

Day dreams at the King David Hotel

10th January 1946

This morning's breakfast is a true feast, we always eat well in Palestine. There are two flavours of jam, lots of bread and I can have as many boiled eggs as I can eat. Back home there is still severe rationing.

As many boiled eggs as I can eat! When can anyone have said that? When was there ever such a time of such plenty? Not in wartime, never in the thirties. In fact, not in the whole of my life in England. I can only remember it happening once before. A memorable occasion in Picardy after D-Day, when our rations ran out but we found ourselves in a barn full of roosting chickens.

That was a rare quiet moment. The beginning of October '44 was a period of particularly heavy fighting as the 11th Armoured Corps pushed hard through Northern France towards Belgium. I was attached to a tank Regiment, the Black Bulls, at the time and spent my days driving furiously across fields, down narrow lanes between two tanks in forward positions and onto the ammo dump a few miles behind lines. My boys were acting as light artillery and I often lost them in the open fields and woods as they followed whenever the German infantry retreated. They fired shells off so fast that I could hardly get them a new supply of shells before they ran out again. Back and forth all day, as fast as I could drive through unfamiliar scenery to the dump, which itself kept moving location as the front line advanced. It was as though it was designed to confuse a simple driver but I kept finding them.

All of that day we had been under constant return fire from the retreating Wehrmacht, who looked to make a stand or counter attack at every opportunity. It was devastating for the local population and most of the towns and villages were laid waste as we passed through. We were seldom welcomed by those we liberated. Just a handful cheered for their freedom as we'd entered Amiens, the remainder of bystanders staring sullenly as we passed through the wreckage that had once been their town. Older people had seen all of this before in the previous war but that didn't help them take it well.

Just beyond Amiens, we'd stopped. The intensity of fighting had dropped during the evening as both sides had fought ourselves into a stalemate of exhaustion. Finally, the guns were silent for a short time. Our tank crews drew up beside a large barn, using it to conceal themselves from hostile gaze. The building was obviously ancient, made of the grey stone that is such a feature of this area. In places it had been repaired in timber, now painted black, and the original straw roof had been mostly replaced with wrinkly tin in a garish scarlet. Our guys gathered for a smoke and chat besides the building, before venturing into the barn to catch a chicken or gather eggs.

Inside the barn were a great number of straw bales, heaped high as we entered from small rear door, but much lower at front before large main doors. Chickens were roosting among bales so there were eggs scattered all throughout building. No one could catch any of chickens but I was too fast for the eggs. Not one escaped.

We came into the open area at the far end, beyond the stacked hay. What a shock! The floor was already covered by young men, all wearing grey uniforms. Germans. We all jumped at the sight; taking cover, sensing danger. But no danger appeared. Nothing moved. Just silence.

I looked again into that area of the barn. The grey men lay around on hay bales and on the floor, not one moving or having anything to say. An unnatural calm and silence hung in the air and the draught blowing through barn doors was the only breath being drawn. For the first time I noticed a faint smell of stale meat.

Fido went slowly over to one and prodded him to see if he'd respond. He's often the bravest, or most reckless, stupid one. As I'd expected there was no reaction. He pushed him over to look at his face. But his body rolled off the hay stack and fell onto its back on floor. Its eyes stared blankly up. The waxy pallor of his skin betrayed the condition of the victim.

We counted twenty-two dead Germans. They must have died quite soon before we arrived, certainly no more than a day earlier, but I think less. Each had his hands wired together behind his back and a small, neat bullet hole in right temple with a larger exit wound on left. There was a lot of blood, some of it dried black around the edge of the wound, some of it across the victim's face and onto their uniform but most of it piled up red and tacky on the hay.

These were young men of a similar age to ourselves. Apart from their uniforms they looked just like us. It was difficult not to sympathise with them, though we tried hard to hate them. They were our enemies; they'd probably been shooting at us earlier that day but now they were just victims of the war.

When we'd seen all of that, we asked ourselves what to do about them, but no one wanted any part of this scene. We all turned our backs, left them; then sat down and lit a small fire outside, pretending they weren't there. Then we boiled the eggs and ate them for our supper. I had four delightful white eggs. Four!

*

Later we found an Officer and reported what we'd found. The Captain, I forget his name now, conducted an urgent and very brief inquiry next day. He rapidly concluded that they had fallen into hands of a group of French Resistance who'd shot them in revenge for the oppressions carried out during the occupation. That's what he put in his report. I don't think he called for any evidence other than a quick look at the scene.

It seemed a bloody ridiculous verdict to those of us who were there. This was the first time we had heard of any activity by the Resistance in this area. I doubt if it even existed. We just knew that 47 Commando were operating ahead of us in German lines. A tough and very dangerous job and there were stories that any Commandoes captured were being summarily shot by the Germans by the personal command of Adolf Hitler himself. Commandoes are hard men and it looked to me like they didn't take that idea very well.

Those dead boys inhabited my night time dreams for many months afterwards, right across Belgium, then on into The Netherlands and even to Germany itself. I was always afraid that we'd find some more pale, waxy bodies. Or become one of them. When I left Hannover last August I thought I'd left them all behind, back in the Fatherland where they belonged. It had seemed the right and fitting end.

So, this morning is first time I've met these ghosts again. The first time that they've found me in Palestine. And now I know that there's no release, they'll follow me everywhere I go. For the rest of my life they'll come to seek their revenge on me. They've discovered a route into my thoughts through the medium of boiled eggs, perhaps for many more breakfast times to come.

I prefer jam today and take a little of both types. I even risk taking some horrid stale bread, famous for its weevils, rather than eat the delicious boiled eggs with bright yellow yolks that everyone else is devouring with such relish.

This is definitely not the bloody Ritz.

Jerusalem to Ismailia

March 2nd 1946

"Welcome to the Sharon Desert, Billy. If you thought Jerusalem was hot, now you're going to know what hot really is," says Fido from the driver's seat. For once, I'm the passenger and it's not my favourite job.

We'd been hanging around waiting for ever at the KDH before they finally let us depart. And I hate waiting. The sun burnt down and there was nothing to interest any of us, except the odours of fried onion and potato coming from the mess tent combining with petrol from the fuelling of our vehicles.

The journey's going to be tough. The desert will be terrible, I've been warned that it's likely to be uncomfortable and hot, but even the little towns on the way will have some problems. Everywhere we'll be pestered by Arab youths selling eggsy bread, doubtful drinks, or stealing something, anything, but especially a rifle if they can get hold of one.

While I'm stood, smoking a cig, around a Corporal from another Regiment comes across for a chat. Difficult to know exactly what Regiment as most of the identifying marks seem to have taped over.

"Hi there, Driver. I hear you're just off to Ismailia."

"Sure, we are mate. What's it to you?"

"I promised to send my mate a few crates of beer, it's a lot more difficult to get beer in Egypt, it being entirely Muslim and all. Could you help out and take them over for me?"

"Yeah, no probs. Always happy to help. Is there a beer or two for me in it?"

"Of course. How about a crate of beer each, 240 Senior Service cigs and ten bob apiece to carry this lot over the border to Ismailia?"

"Blimey, there must be a lorra beer for that."

"Well actually, there's 400 crates. But that should be easy for you in a lorry. You go over there empty any way."

"Well, ten bob's not enough then. We want a quid each," Fido's quick to blurt out.

"Right, it's agreed."

I hesitate. It's illegal, a breach of military regulations, a real risk. But Fido is immediately sold on the prospect of making a quid.

"Come on, Billy. A quid's ten week's wages. More than that for you, you don't get any wages."

In just another twenty minutes we've been over to the YMCA tower and collected a huge stack of Stella light beer to cart across the desert. Strapped down securely under a black tarpaulin it doesn't look like that much. We get the beer and cigarettes now, with the promise of being paid a pound each at the other end. Delivery to Graham, in the Suez Canal office.

Now, after all that inactivity, it's a relief to be moving, part of a convoy of twelve nearly identical three-ton Bedfords. Even in this heat it seems better than doing nowt. There's a journey to make and our orders are clear; to Ismailia and collect goods for camp; food, medical supplies and ammunition. I've never been to Egypt before.

"Right Fido, carry straight on to the pyramids. You've just been promoted to Pharaoh, 2nd class."

"More like a Beeraoh, with this cargo."

Once we're clear of Jerusalem we are obviously in desert, a

filthy, dead place that even mosquitoes have abandoned. It's not long before we know why, as we're struck by a sandstorm which comes with little warning.

The first sign is a small, obscure, dark cloud on the horizon, which gradually gets closer, taking on a reddish tinge as it moves. When it nears us, I can see that it is not a normal cloud, it moves ever nearer along the ground. Finally, it envelopes the convoy and invades our cab, filling it with fine dust and infiltrating every orifice in my body. There's no place to escape and no ways of improving things. The windows of the cab are already tightly shut. Despite the heat my face is covered by a tea towel, brought especially for this purpose but fine sand still gets into my eyes, nose, ears and throat. I had been warned of the wind, it's called the Khamsin. It's a feature of Spring here and blows mostly from the north-west.

I can see very little through the dust and watering eyes, so a collision is just bound to happen. It seems just a matter of time. But as evening falls, we're all still moving and completely intact. I have to congratulate Fido; he's doing a great job and has got us all way across the border into Egypt. There was no incident at the border, nor even any checks, as both sides are in the hands of British soldiers. We just get waved through. No scrutiny of what we carry, thank God.

"No problem mate," Fido tells me. "Someday you'll might get to be as good as me. It's just a matter of good looks and talent. Think of it like that though, you've got no bleeding chance."

"Your jokes are so weak, just bloody ridiculous, mate."

The heat here is even more terrible than in Jerusalem and there's nowhere to escape it. Nowt we can do to feel more comfortable. I wonder why do we have to travel in daytime like this?

As the evening arrives, the sun sets in a matter of just a few minutes and darkness surrounds us, just the feeble efforts of our headlights show the road ahead. It is still hot but as fiercest heat cools; the wind falls away and then our convoy stops. It's more comfortable now but driving in the dark is more dangerous. I get the job of brewing tea and have to make it with boiling water drained from the engine radiator. I don't recommend it, there's a smoky after taste, something like Earl Grey. But the dense, cloyingly sweet taste of condensed milk covers most of it up, anyway.

The road ahead is unclear and journey is very slow. It will take another full twenty-four hours to reach Ismailia and I get my turn as we set off again. Despite the difficulty of darkness, I drive through the night and there is no wind. So, in a way it's easier. Fido dozes, jolting around in the seat next to me. Although it's calmer, dust still gets into my mouth and eyes. Hours and hours, I just drive onwards, seeking out the badly marked road and trying to avoid hitting the vehicles in front as they appear in the beam of my headlights. Just as the sun rises, I find myself staring at a tiny, very distant ship floating above the sand and moving slowly northwards. As we move towards it, it sits upon a narrow green line which emerges across desert ahead. There's just a green line for thirty minutes before it resolves itself into trees and bushes.

There is a grey, yellow haze on the horizon and the rising sun, instead of its normal blazing ball looks more like a lump of yellow soap at the bottom of a dirty sink. There is still no breeze, not even the usual faint cold air that is usual in the desert climate at dawn, but every now and then I notice faint scurrying in the sand and tiny little dust devils dance and wriggle among the scrub bushes. Then there are puffs of hot wind that scorch my skin and these grow and get more regular until at eight o'clock the wind is at full blast again.

Eventually I can see a glimmer of light on water, a wide stretch of the Suez Canal and the once distant ship is close to us, now floating on the water rather than mid-air. A city appears across the water, at a point where the canal enters a lake. Minaret towers standing up like eccentric pencils pointing up to heaven out of flat landscape. Some are very tall and others low, some are slender and others broad. They are often alone but sometimes gathered in groups, of up to four towers. Now there is water everywhere around us and more trees than I've seen since I left England. This is Ismailia, our destination, the so-called City of Beauty and Enchantment.

A large sign proclaims this "The Suez Canal", very helpful. I'd wondered what it was. I'm intrigued by the large conical buildings punctured by a pattern of holes and inhabited by large flocks of pigeons.

I follow the lead vehicle across rickety pontoons and upto the Suez Canal Company's offices, where steel piling makes a sharp division between dockside and water. By a stroke of luck, I've ended up as the last in line. Getting over to see Graham in the office is easy. He's already waiting for us with two Arab workmen and the beer disappears into a shed besides the office in five minutes. The easiest quid, I ever made, if you'd don't consider the risk of a month in the clink.

We're scheduled to arrive at the docks and the NAAFI are expecting us. They have a meal ready for us, hot coffee and meat pies and are a bit disgruntled when we arrive so far behind the others. How good the pies taste after spending all that energy unloading. We haven't had this type of grub for ages and we sleep for remainder of day. Mosquito nets are vital here; I make one little slip, move net and nasty little bloodsuckers are all over me. I thought I'd got used to them in Jerusalem but these are really huge and even more numerous.

The first symptoms start during night and instantly get me out of bed and on the move. An unpleasant gurgling has started inside me, threatening to drain out through my body. Fortunately, the latrines are close by.

The heat is stronger than ever, sweat covers my body and runs down my face and onto my back. This room keeps moving around and my eyes are boiling over. The floor is also moving under my legs and it's inevitable that I fall. I feel weak and my body seems to be strangely slimy, wrapped in sticky blanket. Then there's that horrid smell. But most of all there's sweat and heat and a bubbling and gurgling that I can feel going on inside me. I wonder if this is the enchantment of Ismailia, it's definitely got no beauty attached to it.

The MO washes my face and gives my eyes a good examination. I'm told to rest. There are loads of people around me here, all talking at once though I can't see them. No one is in focus. They're all part of a hot swirling blend of blurred bodies, high pitched voices and disjointed buildings. Lying on the floor I can just pick out a few bits of the buzz of conversation from swirling outside world.

The little prick's shit himself, it's all over the shop. Gerra blanket o'er 'im."

"Jeez, he stinks to high heaven. Gerrim outa here. For God's sake, gerrim outa here before he infects us all."

I'm flung onto a stretcher and bounced around for a while, hoping for the nightmare to stop. Even when I vomit over the side, my insides continue to gurgle and boil. I feel the warmth of a new trickle flowing down between my legs. I can't hear what stretcher bearers are saying any more, it just sounds a swarm of angry hornets.

My God, they're right. The stench really is awful and the orange-yellow slime covers everything. It's horrible. This is really bloody ridiculous. Bloody, bloody, bloody ridiculous.

*

There's a small hospital here, alongside the canal and they put me in the smallest ward there, along with three other blokes from our group who I think all have the same thing.

The Doc seems calm, but calls for a specialist to be flown down from Cairo. I thought all the doctors here would be specialists in dysentery. They have enough cases to fill this entire ward but it appears that they see something different and worse in me.

Fido comes to say farewell, he's going to have to go back without our lorry as there's no co-driver available. He's very quiet for Fido.

When he says goodbye, he looks at me through watery eyes and then turns suddenly and strides off without a backward glance.

Once outside he addresses the Ward Sister and his loud voice carries his crass thoughts back to me.

"He looks in a bad way Sister. What are his chances?"

I strain to hear her reply. Her voice is softer and quieter but it sounds like: "About 50/50. Some men make it through but a lot don't. We'll try to keep him drinking water, often they die of dehydration. But try not to worry, he's in good hands here."

"I wish you good luck, thanks for what you're doing for him. I hope I'll see him again but I'll not bank on it."

He expects me to die. How dare he write me off and just disappear like that? I'm not going to bloody die. I've been through too much in this bastard war to just peg out from the shits.

I drink a lot of water. The pills that Cairo doctor gave me seem to help too. Visits to latrines are a just little less frequent. And the smell is not quite as sickening as before.

Any way if I do die, at least I'll die rich, I have a quid in my pocket.

Ismailia, Egypt

March 12th 1946

I'm spending my convalescence visiting places around Ismailia, but my favourite place is the flower gardens alongside the canal. It reminds me of the garden below the restaurant terrace at KDH, even though there aren't any tennis courts. More importantly, there's no swing band and, of course, no Hetty. Just trees, wind, dust and water. The only sounds are the gush of the breeze, lapping of the waves and occasional bird song. It's a form of beauty and also of solitude. Still searching for the enchantment though.

There's a steady improvement but I've had difficulty in finding things to eat that don't create symptoms. I'm eating relatively little as a result and have lost even more weight. The mirror's not normally a friend but it's become a real ordeal to look at myself now. My eyes seem to have shrunk into their sockets and the skin on my face is drawn tight.

I've usually got the place entirely to myself apart from Arab gardeners who are obviously avoiding me. Their job seems mostly to water plants every evening, there's certainly not much weeding required as they simply don't water anything they haven't planted. They take no notice of me, even if I speak to them. I suppose they don't understand any English or prefer to act as though they don't. Occasionally, one of the other patients from the Army hospital gets here too, only then do I get to chat to another human being. At least it's easy to get cigarettes here, they hand them out free to all the patients. I guess they think its calming. I don't yet need to start on the Senior Service, which are still stashed in my kit bag, under my bed. I don't feel like drinking beer either but that's hidden in a lorry.

It's only a great place to sit in the morning because there's few mosquitoes then. At dawn I can smoke a few of the cigarettes that I scrounge, on a seat under the shade of palm trees. Days last a long time here but fortunately there are English and Indian newspapers and magazines. Not too far out of date either. There's also a couple of Australian sports magazines covering rugby league, just like we play at home and I'm soon an expert on Aussie rules football. This little place has better contact with the outside world than the great city of Jerusalem. There's plenty of good English food as well, which, in the main, I'm really happy about, though I avoid the meat pies.

Nearby, the sand hills have a number of snakes that bury themselves in holes, occasionally leaving discarded skins behind. So many small lizards dart about that they sometimes get trodden on. I've taken a liking to chameleons and collect them to put on my mosquito nets. They feed on the clouds of flies there. I find them on mosmoha trees, blending into yellow and green of trees. The familiar flies find me too and I'm constantly bitten by huge black mosquitoes. My back is still a crowd of angry sores with yellow heads, where the bites have festered.

Time is measured by the passing of boats, and there are always boats passing. Some days they all head north in convoys of around ten or eleven vessels and the next day the convoys head south. Most are scruffy little freighters but on one visit to the garden, the liner 'Mauretania II' is passing through. This is an exciting event, surely the huge ship is just too big to be on such a narrow strip of water.

It glides slowly past, just a few feet from the bank and looming over us, the wash running up and over the edge of canal. Well-dressed, wealthy people wave to me from high above. I can just make out others playing deck quoits and sipping cocktails. They all seem young, healthy and happy. Just a few yards away but in a completely different world. A happy, healthy and affluent world. Today, I need some luxury of my own, I need to start on those beers.

I try to remember any times that I was young, healthy and happy too. Maybe the day I met Daisy in Liverpool. The home leave before I set off, supposedly for Burma. Definitely that evening I met Margaux in Amiens. Not a lot of happy memories though, definitely not enough.

I long for another letter from Margaux and very next day my wish is granted. Post has somehow been re-directed from Jerusalem to find me here.

34 Rue des deux Eglises,
Amiens
France 8

22 Fevrier '46

Mon petit soldat,

I am taking lessons in English so I can write to you and my teacher checks my work so I know you will understand it. She me tells that I make the progress good. Perhaps you can be the more happy with my writing now.

I hope you are well and keeping safe, I know that it will be a hot and sandy place and you might not always like it. I hear of some shootings there and hope you safe. I want to see it for the holy places and then I be near to Jesus in that land. I know you will be praying there and I also pray for you. I dream that someday you might visit to Amiens again and that we can meet to have our friendship made new. I remember you as quite the small but a good man and very handsome.

My life slow is here. The farm is good, we have a good crop last year with no war to interrupt our work. I think the Paris is prospering, since their restaurants want to buy all of our produce and not just potatoes. My father still complaints of pain from his broken bones but he can work in the fields and is the better each day.

Please send me some pictures of the place where you are now, I want to see what looks it like. And I long for your next letter, make it soon.

Au revoir, mon cher,
Margaux

Thank goodness she remembers me, it's great to have such a friend. I sit down to write my reply, gushing my gratitude and good wishes and include a postcard of the pyramids. Now I remember her as ravishing, a very charming and beautiful young lady. I must make sure I include that in my reply, if only I can somehow find the time to write.

I write back immediately.

Ismailia to Jerusalem

April 4th 1946

It took three weeks before the doctor says I can leave and an hour later I've got a new pal with me, Kenny Hindley. He's been released from hospital too and needs to get back to Jerusalem. All our belongings are packed and we're in the lorry ready to go. I've never met him before but he seems a jolly man, so we're chums already.

There's no co-driver, Kenny doesn't even have a driving license. I collect the only Bedford in the yard and we set off as soon as they let me out. We are always expected to be in groups in these times and always armed in Palestine. I've kept my rifle with me, it is by my side wherever I go. There is just one vehicle, strictly against military protocol as we're required to travel in convoys. Surely it doesn't matter in the desert, no one will attack me there. Just need to ensure there's enough rations and water for the trip.

I set off in late afternoon and drive through the night. No one notices me leave, there's no one interested. Even after I've spent so much time here, I'm just a number, another patient passing through. I think Ken thinks same thing, he glances back as we drive off and looks rather depressed. He's got little to say and seems deep in thought. As the dawn comes, I pull over and we try to sleep. There are fewer mosquitoes in the desert, but plenty of dust and heat. As always, the wind builds in a howling sand laden gale, this time from the south.

We're travelling through classic desert scenery with huge sand dunes moulded and sculpted by winds, their golden crests clashing with a clear blue sky. Fringes of sand grains blow over the high ridges revealing how colossal amounts of sand move across the landscape. Around the fringes of Ismailia Egyptian workers are engaged in an endless and pointless task of removing sand from the road.

After a couple of hours, I look up and see Ken staring at me, wide awake. The thermometer has gone up steadily until at midday it is hitting one hundred degrees. All this while, the gale has been roaring along carrying with it not only the dust and sand of the desert, but also the powdered clay from the wadi beds and the dried filth from villages and their camels.

"Neither of us can sleep in this atmosphere, mate. We might as well be moving again."

"That's fine with me Bill, it's your shout. After all, you're doing all the driving."

I am, despite being a bit bleary eyed. I'm not sure how I got to Rahat, it's not supposed to be on my route, but it's a charming old town full of grey stone buildings and brown men, shrubs and palm trees everywhere. There's also an old well here, with a stone wall, with a wooden bar across it and a very narrow shaft down to the water. Arab women all wear pretty native dresses and are drawing water, carrying pitchers on their heads. They all wear amber beads and offer to sell me some, as they say they keep illness away. Too late for that I tell them and squeeze the cheeks of my bum together for good luck.

They also offer to sell us Arab bread and fruit but we prefer to stick with our rations, we've been issued with. My digestion wouldn't cope with any exotic foreign stuff just now. Let's go with things we know. I can see these girls are very disappointed in the results of their sales efforts, but that's life.

"We should've got some of them beads before we went to Ismailia, if they can really keep off illness," says Ken with a wry grin.

"It's not likely, mate. I reckon you're just hoping to humour the local bints by buying their beads."

I look at him, weighing him up for first time. He is definitely younger than me and has perfect, smooth skin. Taller than I am, as everyone is, and heavier too, despite having suffered from same illness. His black hair is tussled, it looks like he hasn't combed it for a month or two and definitely hasn't had it cut. He'll get in trouble for that, when he's back under the eye of the Sergeant-Major. His skin is a deathly pale white, unusual in these climes. Clearly, he's been keeping out of sun and I guess that's why there was no sign of him in the gardens. He's a good-hearted bloke but clearly a little lost in this situation. I feel he's relying on me completely to see him safe back to the camp in Jerusalem. The responsibility lies a bit heavily on me, I'm not used to looking after anyone else and don't really like it.

"Not sure I believe that, but will you buy beads for your sweetheart, Kenny? Do you have a poppet to send them too?"

"No. I joined the Army pretty much straight from school. I'm one of six kids. They're Catholics and believe in that kind of large family. My Mum's Irish, though my Dad's English."

"Yes, it's a good Lancashire place name. Just like mine."

"How about you, Bill?"

My thoughts touch briefly on Hetty but quickly move on. "I met a pretty girl in France, but we're not sweethearts. Not yet any way." I don't want to tell him about my family and the failure of Dad's business.

While I'm stopped in the village, I re-assess where to go. There's a map in the cab, but I'm not used to maps and anxious to make progress, so I don't stop long. Once refreshed by the cool water from the well, we're off. I'm keeping up my habit of drinking water as often as I can. I sweat heavily in this heat but there's large orange groves quite near the road and we can take plenty of fruit. Rations had been issued to me to last forty-eight hours, but I always save what I can. Citric juices don't always sit well on my tender intestines though Ken seems to be enjoying them.

"We get such great food here. It's so different from the rationing back home."

"Yeah, I know a few of the guys post cases of Jaffa oranges back home. Their families can sell them for good prices. No one's seen an orange there since 1939."

The roads here are unmade and very rough. We pass a big hoarding saying "Welcome to Palestine, the land of fruit and sunshine." We both get bounced around more in the land of fruit and sunshine as it's also the land of crap roads. As I approach Jerusalem it is steep hills all way, so low gears and crawling slowly, steadily and noisily up the slope. I'm delighted to be moving up the valleys to the relative cool of the plateau. I pass through Hebron and into Bethlehem, with its multiple Christian churches and minarets, and come to the City. Now I'm happy to have another guy with me. The threat of being kidnapped by terrorists seems much more real here. Am I sweating so heavily just from heat?

There's a check point at Ramat Rachel, with soldiers armed with sten guns and rifles supporting the Palestinian police. Their sergeant bawls us out for being just two of us, says there were seven squaddies murdered by gangsters in Tel Aviv the day before yesterday. He's too busy to take much notice though and soon I'm soon through and driving into and through city. Not far now to my own base beside King David Hotel and a chance to report back. It's a good feeling, there's no place like home! Well, a sort of home, or at least a familiar place with a few good friends.

Kenny asks to be dropped off near the YMCA and we shake hands before he saunters off cheerfully. He almost bounces along the road as he goes off along the street. I expect I'll bump into him again some time.

At the end of a long, tough journey the place is silent on arrival, no one to report to. There's no one around. I slip quietly back into tent I occupied before I left for Ismailia, to find my bed occupied by another soldier.

Obviously, I hadn't been expected to come back.

Jerusalem, the Old City

Sunday 21st April 1946

The sun rises quickly here. One minute it's dark, but soon it's half-light, the real dawn still hiding behind an orange aura on the horizon. Beyond the buildings, white hills shine in fresh new light and above us dark blue sky is becoming paler. Then suddenly, as the edge of the sun peeps above horizon, it's almost full daylight. Full light but little heat at this point. It's a nice time of day to be around, before the heat builds up and long before the mosquitoes are awake.

Nowt else has changed. No one moves among the streets and minarets except for a single, silent line of twenty men in sandy coloured shorts and shirts that makes up our patrol. Then silence of the city is suddenly interrupted by a wailing from tower of the Dome of the Rock, echoed by similar wailing from other mosques in the area. The call is to awake the faithful and summon all of them to prayer. Now there's a sense of city stirring softly, surrounding us with silent shuffling.

There's no official curfew but sensible people don't walk the streets at this time of morning. Officially there isn't any war either, but people are still getting killed. We march with our rifles raised, safety catches are off and we're ready to defend ourselves. The Zionist terrorists Lehi, Irgun or any of the Arab Islamic groups might attack at any moment. Most of the recent trouble has been in the south of the country but there's rumours of renewed Irgun conspiracies to attack Mandate forces.

The Arab groups have been surprisingly quiet recently but their politicians are noisy, loudly protesting against Jewish immigration. None of the terrorists have any respect for Easter. It's far more likely they'll see it as an opportunity to try to catch us off guard.

Narrow streets inside the ancient walled area, so hot, so crowded and so noisy during day, are cool and silent now. Only the smells of rotting food and bad sewers remain, hanging in our nostrils, distinct from swirling dust. The pale limestone buildings are all locked up, windows shuttered. All the goods sold in the souk have been taken away and are behind black iron grates across the arched windows and doorways. Through the metalwork we can see piles of brightly coloured garments and carpets which will soon be on sale again as the Judaic and Islamic Sabbaths have both finished. Sergeant Cox's torch light picks out brilliant reds and golds on clothing but greens and blues seem to be more reluctant to be seen, hiding in the shadow.

The stone slabs of an ancient pavement have been worn smooth by countless centuries of feet of pilgrims of many faiths. Fido slips and clatters his rifle against the wall, causing a large group of sleepy pigeons to spring into an indignant flapping flight. Their squawks resonate around dormant buildings.

"Cut it out Dobson, yer dumb fucker. We'll 'ave every terrorist in Palestine knowing where we are." Sergeant whispers, just loud enough to let every terrorist in Palestine know where we are. Then he turns back to scrutinise the way ahead.

"Yeah, yer dumb fucker," chides Chalky with a grin, prodding Fido with butt end of his rifle. Fido stares back and growls, a low rumble in his throat.

As we reach the end of Chain Street Coxy peers furtively

around the corner. Only when he's satisfied there's no sign of an ambush do we advance, turning left to cross the road and following the Western Wall around Temple Mount. The wall itself hides the Dome of the Rock from our sight, though we soon catch a glimpse of it through Cotton Merchant's Gate. The Golden Dome gleams above multiple arches of bright blue tiled mosque. It looks like it has supernatural powers, just as Muslims believe it does. None of us goes near it, perhaps from respect for Islam, or perhaps in fear of being transported instantly to Mecca, as the prophet Mohammed was supposed to have been in the ancient legend.

On the opposite side of the road the Cotton Merchant's Market runs uphill before disappearing into a jumble of ancient houses built in white stone. The whole of the Old City has been constructed from this same rock. Here outside the Wall there's extra light but still little warmth.

Then a faint mechanical sound rattles between buildings. The only noise disturbing the peace of early morning. It sounds like a motor bike, the transport of choice for roaming gunmen. All of us crouch down beside the wall, forming a huddle as we look for the source of the noise. Some look forward, others back but I'm looking up the market to our left. No sign of it anywhere. Must be somewhere in the jumble of streets around us. Might be coming towards us but usually we get all excited like this and then the sounds just disappear.

Then we see them. Two black motor cycles coming up behind us. Sergeant Cox stands up and shouts "stop", his arms waving. They do stop. Quite a way from us. Both of bikers are wearing dirty Arab dress with head scarves wrapped around their faces. Then they turn both bikes revealing a pillion passenger carrying a machine gun. The gun is turned towards us.

"Right! Fire! Fire at them. Kill them," screams Cox and we all crouch and let off a shot or two at bikes. The only time I've ever fired a rifle in anger. Fido gets off his second before the gunman starts firing back with an automatic weapon. A rattle of bullets ricochets off stonework, just above our heads, showering us with chippings. We're sitting targets out here besides the Wall.

"Come on, take cover," Sergeant shouts, heading across the road, to gain shelter inside the market. We all follow but they're still firing at us. Chalky stumbles but is caught by Fido and I, who carry him to safety. He's trembling, can't speak any more, just gurgling, blood coming from his mouth. There's a huge red hole in his right side and he's bleeding profusely. The flesh is depressed around four distinct red holes and blood is flowing freely over his whole body. Fido and I are fighting each other in a scramble to get bandages out of my backpack. Fido rips off Chalky's tunic and I grab a handful of bandages to stuff into the open wounds. There's blood everywhere, including from his mouth as he gurgles a red froth. His eyes are staring straight at me, full of fright and alarm. We feel the horror together.

Fido wraps bandages right around body of the injured man, using the bundle of bloody rags, what's left of my bandages, and tightens a dressing over them. Chalky's bleeding seems to have lessened now but he's covered in a sticky red black mess. And he's silent.

Most of my mates are firing around the corner of the street. I look up and I can both see and hear motorbikes revving up, moving away amid a volley of rifle shots from our guys. One of motor cyclists jerks and twists, a man falls off the bike which then wobbles ferociously before it recovers and speeds off.

"Hah! Got 'im. Got the bastard," bawls Eddie Rowley, his fist punches the air. Others cheer, pat him on his back and laugh. "Well done, Eddie. Gerra nother one quick, gerrem!"

They turn to look at Fido and me labouring over Chalky. Our eyes meet and they're silent again.

"Will he be all right, Billy?"

"We dunno, Eddie. Looks bad."

The sergeant has moved himself away from us and is talking in an agitated manner into a radio. None of us can make out what he's saying, no matter how much we strain to hear.

It seems ages before the jangling bell on a British Army ambulance cuts through warming air of Old City. We *are* centre of attention from native population now, as though they've only just noticed. Despite our efforts to keep them away they've all come to stare. Some of these men in long gowns look towards the injured soldier, being looked after by the members of the patrol, but rather more stare at the still body of the terrorist, which is still lying in the street. An unattended bundle of blood-stained robes, centred on a dark pool, where it fell from the back of bike. No one seems to be helping him but it's likely that he's still alive and in great pain.

All along the market, traders are still setting their stalls out onto the street for a day's trade. Many already have their goods on display and are cajoling people to buy. I can hear haggling going on and already a few purchases being made. These people ignore the injured soldier and the body of a terrorist as though it's just someone else's problem.

The paramedics take a look at Fido's efforts at bandaging. They say it will do until they can get Chalky to hospital. He's put onto a stretcher and promptly lifted onto the ambulance which speeds away. We're left looking at each other.

All eyes turn to look for forgotten Sergeant Cox. He's sat in a doorway across the street his head in his hands, tears rolling down his cheeks. Corporal Williams sits down beside him to chat slowly and quietly.

But there's not much sympathy from the troops; "You're in the bloody Army, fer Godsake! People get hurt in wars. What d'y'expect?"

A few minutes later a second ambulance arrives and collects the gunman's body. Again, there seems to be no attention given to the possibility that he might be still alive and saved.

Now that Coxy has composed himself, he lines us up in two ranks and we march proudly back to our camp at the King David Hotel, straight upright, arms shouldered and arms swinging to make a statement of our defiance. The crowds of Jews and Arabs reply by ignoring us. Occasionally, through corner of my eye I think I can see groups of young men gathered together in dark corners turn to look at us and mutter.

When we get back to the camp, inside the walls of the Hotel gardens the NAAFI is serving breakfast. Of course, it's boiled eggs again today. No one except Eddie Rowley can eat them. He's still in a great mood. Fido and I sip a mug of stewed tea and I take my boots off, to soothe my aching feet. There's a raw, red callous on the sole of my feet where the boots don't fit properly.

"What the bloody hell's going on Fido? Why's someone just shot Chalky? It's just bloody madness."

"I dunno mate. Chalky never hurt any of 'em. I don't even know who it was that shot at us. Might be Jews, might be Arabs, they all seem to hate us. Just for being here."

"Well, now that's the thing. Why the bloody hell are we here? I joined up to fight Hitler and he's been dead a year. I wanna go home now. I don't care about Jews or Arabs; I just think this place is horrible. It's a hell hole, stinks of shit, is full of flies and people are trying to kill us."

"Not sure why you're asking me mate. You can read the papers, same as I can. I don't have a direct line to Clement Attlee."

"And that's another thing, I voted for a Labour Government to get us a new world after war. Now we're here protecting a piece of British Empire. That's the old world? And we still seem to be in a war of some bloody sort. I don't even understand who's side we're on."

"Palestine isn't supposed to be part of the Empire, Billy. It's just a bit of the old Ottoman Empire we got after the last war and are looking after until the League of Nations decides what to do with it. Meantime they've scrapped the League of Nations."

"God almighty. I thought it was just me that's confused but it's the whole bloody world."

"Yeah. Seems the whole world is confused. I'd like the Jews to have a place of their own. I thought the war in Europe was hell until I got to Belsen and saw what hell really was. I'd like the people we got out of that place to have a good place to live."

"Yeah! Seems right, but what about the Arabs? Don't they get a say how things are done in their own land?"

"Is it their land? I ain't got an effing clue, mate. I just want Chalky to be all right and for us all to go home."

There's a noise as a group of officers enters the tented area. Looks like our top brass are coming to see us and it's not often they come down from the safety and comfort of the hotel. Major Breck himself gathers us together and addresses the group.

"It's my sad duty to inform you that Private Alan White died from his wounds one hour ago at the Military hospital. Unfortunately, there was nothing the medics could do to help him by the time he got to hospital, he'd lost too much blood despite the valiant efforts of his comrades to keep him alive. Private White was a brave man who died in the service of his country and will be greatly missed. I know many of you were good friends with him and I want to offer you all my deepest condolences."

I look at Fido but he has his head bowed and I can't tell what he's thinking or feeling. I wait, staring at him but he just doesn't move. His eyes just look a bit moist as he swats another of the big black mosquitoes.

Major Breck turns to leave but then looks back at us and says, "but let me wish you a Happy Easter, everyone."

I hate that bastard.

Ballroom of the King David Hotel

June 27th 1946

Something big's about to happen. Everyone's been edgy for a day or so and all the Officers have looked grim faced for the last week. They all look anxious. There's talk of General Montgomery coming over to plan the next move against the Zionist terrorists.

I get just a glimpse of reception as we shuffle past, and desperately want to look in. Who's that dark-haired girl over there? Lift your head out of those papers, for heaven's sake, Hetty. And then she does, but it's not Hetty.

A new officer, who's been announced as Major James McAllan, has come to take charge of our group, replacing Breck. He's called us to assemble in one of the Hotel's ballrooms and is about to start. We're rapidly hustled into the room. It's a rare thing for a private soldier to see inside the inner sanctum of the KDH, normally reserved for officers, and it's certainly more impressive than the tented village we inhabit. It's even hotter when we get inside and soon, we're all glowing, sweating and seeping.

We're seated in neat rows of wooden chairs with our new commander standing at front. A quietly spoken and distinguished grey-haired man, he is quite a contrast to his predecessor. Shorter, older and with a tired look in his dull eyes. What they share is a public-school accent.

"You'll all be aware of the very serious situation facing us here, in Palestine. British soldiers and officers are being murdered on a regular basis. Good, honest Tommies and their officers who are only doing their duty, attempting to keep the peace between Arab and Jew. All of us now know someone who's given his life in the pursuit of peace."

Of course, I think of Chalky, but we all know who McAllan's thinking about, Breck was very much one of his own kind. His murder was the point at which it all started to really frighten us. Gossip says he was killed by a girl he picked up in a bar last week. She got him into the street and round the back of the bar. After that incident no one has been allowed out alone or unarmed. I carry a Lee-Enfield .303 over my shoulder almost every moment I'm out of the tent now. Worst still for some of the guys, we are all ordered to leave the local floozies alone.

The Major is at his most earnest, his baton gripped behind his back, exactly as Majors have always been before him. If we don't already know how important he is, then he certainly knows.

Breck's passing has had a huge effect on all of us. It shocked us in a way that even Chalky's demise didn't, despite that fact that I loved Chalky and despised Breck. At least our pal died a proper soldier's death, killed in action, something we understand and accept. It has a considerable honour in it. But Breck has been taken out in a really underhand, devious way, which offends every sense of fair play. What's more, they got him despite the best protection the British Army can muster.

"You'll also know of the extensive bombings by terrorists that took place two weeks ago, destroying the Allenby Bridge and other important lines of communications. They also casually murdered a lot of civilian bystanders. Even worse, there has been the kidnapping of British officers in an attempt to blackmail our government. These are dark days. Evil people are moving in

Palestine. The people *we* freed from Nazi oppression now use that freedom to attack their liberators."

He pauses and his audience, a steaming semblance of sandy shirts and shorts, is held in breathless silence as he moves tensely up and down before us. Each one watches his movements, all of which are silhouetted against the evening sunlight, and we share his anger. Long windows, richly curtained in red and blue with gold tasselled edging, frame a block of yellow light which streams onto dark blue carpet and burns there, as hot as the Major's sense of injustice.

"The British Government has accepted the role of peacemaker and will not be bullied by a campaign of murder by *either side*. We have taken on a heavy responsibility here and will discharge it even-handedly and with honour. It is our duty to maintain peace while others seek a just settlement for this troubled land."

The Major stops and looks directly at me, as though he believes I'm the only man with power to stop the Zionist terrorist gangs. I know their names as well as any man: Palmach, Lehi, Irgun and Stern gang. All of them are intent on murder. I squirm in my seat, I don't want any power, I don't want to stop terrorists. I only want to go home.

"We'll therefore be engaging the Jewish terrorists directly tomorrow morning, carrying out a raid we have code-named Operation Agatha. The leaders of these thugs and murders will be interned so that everyone else here can live in peace, to the benefit of all communities in this land." He looks up with yet another pause to emphasise the drama in his words. It works; I'm impressed and breathing in the tension in the room.

"Operation Agatha will consist of a move, co-ordinated between the military and police forces of the Mandate, to arrest a large number of known terrorists. Our part in this will start tomorrow in the area of the city adjoining the Italian hospital. Each of you will be allocated to a task force and that force will visit an address at precisely 04.15 am tomorrow morning. Your officer will have the name of the person or people to be arrested at that address. This will take the leaders of the Jewish uprising out of circulation and placate the Arabs who are also threatening to start their own campaigns of murder. Those arrested will be taken to the internment camp at Rafiah and held there to be interrogated."

A few of the Officers ask questions, which are not really questions. They all find a way of supporting Major and saying what a great idea Operation Agatha is. Most of all they are saying how reasonable and balanced British Government has been in offering to partition Palestine to accommodate both Jews and Arabs before the British leave. Apparently, the Government is allowing in Jewish refugees but not as fast as they would like. So that's why they are trying to murder us.

I agree with the bit about the British leaving. For heaven's sake let's get out of this lunatic asylum.

*

The Old City is cooler at 04.00 am. It's silent and completely dark as we drive through: a curfew has been imposed and all of the power cut off. There's not even any moon to guide us, just a pale orange glow from my headlights. It's just enough once I'm adjusted to it, if I take it easy. I'm steering the first of two lorries, with Lieutenant Humphreys and an unfamiliar police officer alongside me. Every one of us carries a rifle. Mine rests against the door while my mates are holding theirs up, ready to return fire if we're attacked.

We've moved past several mosques and synagogues and have reached our destination, a block of stone houses on Prophet's Street near to the Old City, they appear to be a uniform dark grey or even black after I stop and turn off my headlights. Windows are covered with steel shutters and there's no sign of life. I pull up where I'm told, right outside the building. The handbrake squeals, an awkward interruption to the silence. Everyone glares at me.

Ten soldiers, including me and the officers, descend from my lorry. We take guard at the front door while those on the second lorry disappear round the back. The anonymous police officer goes to the house and switches on his flashlight to illuminate the front door before hammering on it. He calls loudly for it to be opened. There is no response. He calls again, even louder. Still no response.

Our anxiety is climbing and we constantly look around, to spot movement. Our rifles point outwards and upwards; covering as many windows and corners as we can. There's a lot of twitching curtains all around the square. I expect a burst of machine gun fire to hit us from any direction at any moment. The silence is intimidating.

Captain Humphreys, who appears to be in charge, calls on Fido and me to smash the door down with the butts of our rifles. The first few blows land heavily and wood splinters, before we hear bolts being undone from the inside. The door swings open to reveal a plump middle-aged man in his night shirt, blinking furiously as the flashlight picks him out.

"Rabbi Eschman?" the officer asks.

"Yes. Who wants me?"

"I am Sergeant Joseph of the Jerusalem Police Force. I have a warrant for your detention to assist the investigation into your alleged role as a leader of the insurgents. You need to get dressed quickly as you're coming with us."

"This is nonsense, you are making a ludicrous error. If you consult your superior officers they will tell you to leave me alone. I am a senior member of the Jewish Agency executive and demand respect. Now go away and leave my family and I to sleep in peace."

He attempts to close the door but a police officer already has his foot inside and pushes his way in. "There's no need for any further consultations. They've all been completed long ago. I've the warrant for your arrest right here in my hand and you're coming with us."

The bearded man backs off, sits down on a chair in the hall and refuses to move. Fido and me are told to pick up that chair and carry him into our lorry. He's quite a fat old guy; being a senior member of Jewish Agency must involve eating a lot of dinners. It's a big effort for two scrawny, underfed soldiers to lift him into back of the vehicle and he struggles all the way, so eventually we just tip him off the chair and he sprawls onto the floor of the lorry. Then we pick up his legs and shove them in after him. At last, there's something to amuse the Tommies who're already clambering back onto the truck, surrounding and jostling him into the far corner. He gets lots of prods and has good reason to look scared. His display of resistance fizzles out and he slinks into a back corner, nursing his injuries and looking away from us, pulling his night shirt up around him and avoiding eye contact.

A middle-aged woman comes screaming out of the house, demanding to have her husband released. Thank goodness I'm nowhere near her, she's really hysterical. Hitting out at anyone and everyone. It doesn't achieve anything as she gets short shrift from our soldiers, two of them drag her back into house and once there, her shrieking stops. I've not heard a wailing banshee recently but that was exactly how I imagine one.

Now it's a long, silent wait while the guys from the second truck search the house under the direction of Sergeant Joseph. We don't know these blokes; they're not soldiers and we've never seen them before. Eventually they come out with a pile of documents, several rifles and some crates of ammunition and grenades. The night is punctuated by their footfall and murmured commands of our Lieutenant. Occasionally I can see people moving window shutters in nearby buildings. Maybe three or four at every window. Everything we do is being watched by this whole neighbourhood. As the faint glow of dawn reaches the eastern sky we are loaded and off to Rafiah.

As I start the Bedford the gear change jolts the vehicle slightly, thrusting my head back. Simultaneously a shot rings out and a bullet brushes my scalp, taking off my beret.

I hit the brake, look up and see my assailant instantly. He's come out from around a corner of the house. A brilliant blue flash from the muzzle of a pistol drew my eyes there and for just a second a tall slender man stands wild eyed and looking straight at me, his arm raised for a second shot. His round, white face is illuminated and I can see him very clearly. I recognise him immediately, despite his blue eyes being strangely dull in this false light.

By the look in his eyes, Jeno recognises me too. We can only stare at each other, both confused, not knowing what to do next, not certain what immediate action is right. Should I hug him as my old friend, or shoot him dead as a terrorist murderer?

The thud of boots coming from back of my lorry and out onto cobbles indicates soldiers running to catch or kill Jeno, firing wildly as they charge towards him, bullets causing a spray of chips from dark white walls and ricocheting dangerously back across the yard. I notice Eddie Rowley is especially anxious to loose off shots. Even he is too slow, too late. The pale, round face has already disappeared, although they chase around the surrounding streets, they can find no sign of him. I feel guilty for being glad that he's escaped. Does it make me a traitor? Am I supporting the enemy?

What happened to him on his journey from Belsen to Jerusalem? Did he go via Budapest? Did he visit the Charlies family and wreak revenge on them as he'd threatened? Wherever he went and whatever he did he is now here, in Jerusalem. He's also acquired a gun and become a determined, dangerous and violent man intent on murdering British soldiers.

I helped this man recover from starvation, supported him through the death of his brother and prepared him for his journey home. Now he has turned up here, where he was never expected and tried to murder me, before evaporating into the night and out of my life. For ever?

I wonder. I have the distinct feeling our paths may cross again.

British Army camp, King David Hotel

July 22nd 1946

The whole morning is taken up in reading letters, re-reading the one from Margaux and replying. The fact that she has remembered me is flattering. That she is keeping in touch is exciting. I write quickly, easily and joyfully to Margaux. Then slowly, carefully and painfully, I craft out a reply to Joe.

I haven't quite finished when there's a sharp, dull explosion. Smoke rises over the wall from Julian's Way beyond. Bizarrely, no one in the camp is particularly interested. The way we've become relaxed about explosions and shootings is a frightening thing in itself. They happen so often now. And this is just a small one.

I know that I should be disturbed by the bomb and look towards the smoke. A tirade of loud gunfire rings out, as well. There's a battle being fought in the street but I've a wall between it and me. When the shooting persists, I grab my rifle and run to the gate. I stand under its arch, unsure whether to leave cover. Of course, there's a car racing away, Scots guards still firing after it. They seem to be hitting it too and in the middle of Julian's Way lie the bleeding bodies of two Arabs. I'd expected it would be an action of Jewish terrorists but this makes just as much sense; the Arabs hate us as much as Jews. They think this land belongs to them, just as the Jews do. Both of the bodies look like Jeno.

Something else must be going on, as a group of workers have come out of their kitchen and are standing in the street, jabbering at guards. Whatever they are saying is causing a frenzy. Guards are sprinting back into hotel.

The loudest crash I've ever heard takes off a corner of King David Hotel in a colossal billow of smoke and dust and knocks me over. There's no flash but a five-storey building disappears in a shock wave, only to re-assert itself again as a pack of cards tumbling to ground. Then it disappears again into a dense cloud of dust and smoke.

The world turns black and blue with orange edges, the noise echoes around me, as savage as the wind ripping at my clothes. My eyes are working overtime but my ears take time off. Time stops but everything else moves.

I try to stand but the suction pulls me over again, batters me against the ground and rips my shirt. Stones drop from the building towering beside me, with deafening thuds and rumble along the street throwing up yet more dust. Particles of stone rain down all around us and a huge black mushroom of smoke and dust rolls away directly over our heads cutting out the sunlight. I can hear again but only the ringing in my ears.

Recovering after a minute or two of shock I sit up, shake my head, look around and see the explosion has blown the windowpanes out of nearby buildings, spewing glass into street. Cypresses and palms have been bent backward as if battered by hurricane winds, and other small trees uprooted. A whole field of tents has been flattened and many are shredded, flapping madly in the breeze. A scene of devastation. There seems to be no people, no one in sight although those tents must have been full of men. They simply lie on the ground for a while before I see a little movement in them. Is that an angry murmur? I can't tell.

The tents start to wriggle and squirm and distraught soldiers struggle their way out of the chaos of the stricken camp. A gabble of angry and anxious voices all shouting at each other accompanies their efforts but sounds are strangely dulled and echoing in my ears. I don't understand. Everyone is speaking but none of the sounds are words.

To my right, there is nowt but a muted rumble of falling masonry and a huge plume of dust and smoke still covers the remnants of that corner of the hotel. As it's a little less dense now I can make out the silhouette of the building. Suddenly and dramatically there comes a macabre, ghostly procession of British officers, wives and waiters, all streaming with blood, their hair and clothes covered in white dust tumbling out of remnants of building. Most of them are coughing, spluttering and all are very unsteady on their feet.

I can hear muffled shouts from under a pile of concrete slabs near the remains. Again, they have that strange dull and echoing tone. There are people trapped there, they need my help.

Fido acts first, I didn't even know he was here. He jumps into an opening in the debris and begins burrowing with his hands. I help by clearing those stones away as he throws them out. Within a few minutes he's formed a hole, like a tunnel into rubble but there's no means of supporting it and it immediately collapses in front of him. Another plume of dust comes billowing out and conceals him.

Amazingly, he crawls out unharmed although coughing and spluttering, covered in sediment from head to toe. A rescue worker rubs his back with liniment and then stupidly he re-enters the tunnel. I may never see him again if I don't go into help him. I hesitate but know I must go after him.

"Where do you think you're going?" Sergeant Cox bars my way. "It's enough to have one idiot risking his life without you going in too."

"I can't leave 'im in there on his own, Sarge."

"That's exactly what you're going to do, mate. One man taking reckless chances is enough. Get round the front, where you might actually do some good."

"But that's bloody ridiculous, he needs our help."

The Sergeant, Big Dicky we've always called him, is standing at the edge of the hole Fido has disappeared into. "Don't worry. I'll look after him," he says. Finally, after he's hit me and pushed me several times, I still think it's bloody ridiculous but take the hint.

At the front of the hotel, soldiers are also pulling at rubble, working like men possessed. The task is a race against time, and not until all hope of saving further lives is gone, can we relax our efforts. Deep in the wreckage we can occasionally hear shouts and grunts which encourage us to fresh exertions. It sounds like there are many people in there, obviously in pain. I join in, removing a block of stone, placing it on the other side of the street, before heaving at another block and then another. I find that can lift and carry away rocks that I'd normally have thought too heavy.

An Army ambulance arrives. Then another and another, until a throng of ambulances have thrown out a whole horde of running men and women with stretchers, blankets and bandages. Most come towards us to assist the people sat on pavement over here but some are rushing up pink marble steps, through clouds of dust still coming through front door, into hotel itself, a hundred yards from where I'm standing. Although it's not been destroyed the area around reception has been affected first by the blast and then by clouds of dust. As have all higher floors on this side of the building.

Oh God, I know someone who works in reception.

Soon the ambulance men are returning from inside the hotel. Some are carrying limp bodies which they've already placed in bags. A line of these bags is being laid near the ambulances. Others carry stretchers with bleeding and broken people, their faces uncovered. Survivors are being loaded straight into the ambulances.

My attention is attracted to one young girl with wavy, shoulder length black hair, lying on a stretcher. She wears the uniform of a receptionist, looks rather like Ava Gardner and appears to be unconscious. The medical attendants carry her into an ambulance, close the door and drive off.

I need to know where that ambulance has gone, I no longer care about anyone else.

RAF Qastina

July 23rd 1946

I've asked forty or fifty people but no one can tell me where that ambulance containing Hetty has gone. Or where any of the ambulances went. This is bloody ridiculous, I need to know. Quickly.

Even her friends, the girls on the hotel reception, have no idea, but I guess it's great that there are still girls on reception. The hotel is operating *almost* like normal, if you ignore the fact that there's a whole corner of the building missing. Everyone has dusted themselves off, closed their eyes to the problem and are joining in a pretence of normality.

Most of us worked for sixteen hours solid to get as much stone moved as we could. It still isn't clear whether there are people buried alive, but at midnight they forced us to stand down and sleep. We're supposed to be working shifts now; sixteen hours on and eight hours off.

I can't afford the time any more, there's a more urgent task. In desperation, I find Mr Hamburger, the hotel Manager. He must know. And perhaps he does. He suggests RAF Qastina as the most probable place.

Most guys are back at work this morning, so no one will notice if I take a three-ton Bedford lorry without permission. Wrong! Big Dicky has noticed. "What d'yer think yer playing at, Billy boy? No one told you to take a truck today."

"I want to visit someone who got injured in the blast, Sarge. Can't you cast a blind eye fer once? Just let me go. It's important."

"Wise up for God's sake man, you can't just ride off with a three-ton lorry. If I was going to take a military vehicle without anyone noticing I'd take one of the motorbikes over there." He nods to three parked bikes, handing me a set of keys for a BSA M20. " I might not notice if you took that."

"Thanks, Sarge."

The road to Qastina is as hot, dusty and as bumpy as the rest of Palestine. Beyond the cooler, greener plateau that holds Jerusalem, it is all like this. This is my best guess as to where she's gone, but it is just a guess. For forty anxious miles I keep hoping it's the right guess.

Riding the bike is great. It would be as much fun as I've had since I got to this burnt wreck of a country, if I could only stop thinking about where I am and what I'm doing. But each jolt reminds me that I could be wrong. Every pothole I hit says that I'm going to be court martialled if they realise I've taken the bike. Every time I reply that I don't care but that can't be right, can it? Military prison is not likely to be a lot of laughs. I do care, I'm afraid.

The hot wind blowing through my hair gives me a great feeling though and weaving around potholes is a proper challenge, requiring all of my attention. The bike is beautifully balanced and responsive, it follows the weight of my body as I swing it across the road. I'm not used to it at first but after the first few miles it starts to seem natural to wander around and move about the road, the motion is graceful and delightful. My fears and worries get lost for a while and the pleasure of moving and swaying takes over. A delicate smell of orange hangs in the hot air. I occasionally to swerve to avoid the small group of wild goats, left to wander around untended.

Eventually an airfield comes into sight, situated on an elevated spot above the coastal plain. This must be the one. It can be seen from some distance, the orange air-sock and concrete tower give it away. There seem to be surprisingly few aeroplanes for an air force base but there's plenty of tents and, better still, plenty of room to park a bike.

Down here, nearer to the sea there is more of a breeze than we get in Jerusalem but it is still hotter. There's a stark hill nearby with a row of saplings growing in dark soil. Someone must have found a way to water them, there's not much greenery anywhere else.

It's going to need a good story to get me in but I'm not good at stories, so I just go for truth. I tell the guard on the gate that my girlfriend was injured in the KDH blast and is in hospital. Well, nearly true. She "sort of" is my girlfriend. Well maybe she will be. I hope so. Any mention of the KDH creates instant sympathy and he directs me towards a large marquee besides the tower. There are nurses walking around it so I tell them who I'm looking for. One of them recognises my description, and the name: Hetty.

"Yes, you must mean Hetty Borowska. She's almost recovered and I can see her, over there." Her finger identifies the source of my dreams.

I've found her. My own little film star, looking cool and relaxed, ready for her next starring role. She's still dressed in the white blouse and black skirt from the hotel and I look at her, she looks at me. As our eyes meet she looks a little surprised but maintains her stare. Then greets me with a smile. I'm delighted she remembers me.

"Hello soldier. This is a big surprise. What are you doing here?"

"I've come to see *you*, Hetty."

"You remember my name, that's nice. What's yours?"

"I'm Billy. Don't you remember me?"

"You're the tennis player. Is that right?"

"Yeah, that's near enough." I say, with a grin.

We both smile and I sit down next to her. She sits nice and

132

close, her knees pointing across the bench as she smooths her skirt with her delicate, feminine hands and looks into my eyes, a hint of a smile playing around her lips. I catch a subtle scent of perfume and her eye contact is as strong as ever. She smiles properly at me but the dark green eyes are narrowed slightly retaining a mysterious feline menace in them. This is a woman of many moods and her true feelings are hidden.

"I saw you put into an ambulance. I knew you were hurt in the bombing and was really worried about you. How are you?"

"I am very sad and confused but unhurt apart from a bruise or two." She blinks and looks down as she speaks. Her eyes are now wide open and watery, becoming instantly more like an instant Bambi.

"What's making you sad?"

"The bomb, the people getting hurt. All the anger that people are feeling. But also, being away from Jerusalem right now. I hate that, when there is so much to do there. The soldiers brought me here when I wanted to stay in the city. But the doctor says they will let me go now."

"Why are you still here then?"

"There's no transport to get me back."

"Yes, there is. I've got a bike and I'll be going back as soon as I've seen you. You can come as well."

Her eyes light up, I'm rewarded with another smile. I hold her hand and imagine that we're a pair of angels, floating up together into golden light as I hear a heavenly host sing and play harps.

Twenty minutes later she has signed herself out of care of the Palestine Mandate and is clambering onto my pillion. I hold her hand to steady her as she climbs on. The light caress of her hand is exhilarating and I notice what tiny, feminine fingers she has. Everything about her is delicate and elegant. A brief smile is electrifying as our eyes meet. She leans towards me and places a soft kiss on my cheek.

"Thank you soldier, it's really sweet of you to come and bring me back."

Then she hitches up her skirt and sits on the seat behind me, her legs astride the bike. I try not to stare and climb on in front of her, kick the bike into action, grind through the gears and we bump our way back in the direction of Jerusalem. Her presence lights my mood; this is happiest I've been since I arrived in Palestine. I've got her company for the whole journey.

She is the perfect pillion passenger, surrendering her will to the movement of the rider and swings with the bike. Her arms are round my waist, her legs around me and she leans up against my body. When I move, she moves with me and as the bike sways she sways too, her knees pressing forward against my legs, I know she trusts me completely. We are in total harmony.

Through my thin cotton shirt, I can feel the soft warmth of her breasts pressing against my back and her face pressed flat against my shoulder. When the breeze catches her dark hair, it blows around me and gets in my eyes, her hot thighs cling around me. The bike wobbles a little as I struggle to keep my concentration on driving.

Then she adjusts her stance and stands on the footrests. Her arms draped over my shoulder, bringing her face close to my mine, her other arm closes around my chest. Her body held tight against mine, those tiny fingers gripping me tightly. I can feel her hot breath in my ear and her lips touch my neck. I feel very hot and a trickle of sweat runs down my forehead. Maybe it's heat of the sun but I don't think so.

I'm happy to say that our trip is fairly slow, because of the poor road state and traffic, especially pedestrians, so we can chat as we ride. But many pieces of our conversation are lost into the breeze, so we stop at a village to rest and converse properly. A chance to eat too. I have a ration pack that I offer to share with her, she can even have some of the tinned pilchards in tomato sauce.

She looks down her nose at it. "You want to eat that? Horrible tinned food when there are lovely fresh foods here. I will buy some from the villagers."

Hetty strides away to the low Arab buildings and disappears

inside. I look around, feeling suddenly alone and insecure in a foreign land. There are no people in sight, at the height of the midday sun they've all taken shelter. But there is activity, frenzied and busy. A swarm of flies are all around, black, blue or green. The floor is heaving with black ants, much bigger than any we have at home. They look very organised, each performing a role, distinct from that of their colleagues. Maybe the British Army looks like this, to an outside observer. The beetles, the officers and aristocrats of this miniature world, are striding around with disdain for the lowly worker ants.

A few minutes later she returns with a smile, holding flat bread, goat's cheese and some figs dipped in just a little honey. Things I've never eaten before and wouldn't have trusted, since it's all strange foreign stuff. I could never have bought it any way since I cannot communicate with the Arab villagers as she can. And, of course, I have no money, except for a single one-pound note. The food is amazingly good, really delicious. My mouth salivates and longs for more. Quite unlike anything the British Army has provided for me while I've been in this country. We sit together in the sunshine and share them. The fabulous fresh flavours fill my mouth and refresh my taste buds. Her company fills me with happiness and conversation starts so easily. I lean back before the dizziness flattens me. This is loads better than the bloody Ritz.

"How was it at Qastina? It looked well organised, but I'd never heard of the place before this morning. It's a part of Palestine I've never seen before, this country has a lot of hidden places."

"Yes, we have a very beautiful country.

The nurses and the Doctors were so lovely there; they couldn't have been nicer. I admire the way they deal with such terrible wounds and so much suffering but are always cheerful themselves."

"They're very devoted to their profession, we all admire them."

"Yes, and very hard working too. Unfortunately, the food they serve is completely inedible, you British eat such horrible stuff."

"It's stuff we like, I suppose we're used to it and it reminds us of home."

"I love Yiddish foods, partly for the same reason as you like your strange foods, but mostly I just like fresh food. Nothing than comes out of cans is ever good."

I can see we're not going to have a meeting of minds over this. It's difficult to imagine a world without Spam, corned beef or sardines in tomato sauce so I change the subject to something we do have in common. "Must've been horrible to be in that explosion yesterday."

"Yes, of course. It was very frightening and unpleasant. I thought I was in real danger, at one point I imagined that I'd be seriously hurt but, of course, that was just my imagination. The whole thing did not go to plan. Of course, the Irgun did not intend to kill people."

"You still want to defend the Irgun, after what they've done? I'm amazed."

" They are my people. None of this is aimed at you British but you must allow my people reclaim our land. This is the land that God gave to his people and we must take it back. You're in the way and need to go."

"Killing people is not the way to do it. That's bloody ridiculous."

She frowns at me. "We didn't really mean to kill people, just destroy all documents in the hotel. That stupid girl who works on reception got a warning to evacuate the hotel but she didn't pass it on."

"What'd yer mean? What stupid girl? There was a warning? What happened to the evacuation then?"

"She was idiotic, that girl, pushing in front of me to answer the phone. I was supposed to take that call. She didn't know who to tell. She just wanted to find Major Breck and tell him. Of course, I told her he was dead but she seemed not to believe me. I think she must have liked him and wanted to be the one to tell him the big story. I guess he did have some appeal to a silly girl. In the end she did listen to me and tell Mr. Hamburger but it was already much too late then."

"They're saying that there would've been even more casualties if the hotel had been evacuated because the street would've been full of people when the building collapsed onto it."

"That's just an excuse for British incompetence." She shows a flash of bad temper, her voice rising and harsh.

"Any way, he was *your* boyfriend, wasn't he? Major Breck. I saw you dancing together on the terrace."

She smirks, laughs aloud. I see her turning slowly to stare at me through the emerald glare of those predator eyes. More predator than Bambi now but she's even more beautiful when she looks straight through me, her delicate features now seem chiselled out of the same exquisite pink marble as King David Hotel, but even harder and more durable. I squirm in my seat, wanting to turn to look deep into her eyes, but feel very uncomfortable under her stare and instead I turn away to look towards the road.

Eventually she speaks in a slow, sombre tone that I've never heard before. A mocking tone. A determined tone. "Yes, soldier. How clever you are. That's exactly what he was: my boyfriend."

An awkward silence separates us. This is not how I want our trip to develop. It's suddenly become difficult and unhappy. I want to say something clever and funny to lighten tension, but nowt comes to mind and the silence persists.

"Any way, Algy actually was a nice man," her voice is strong and the words momentarily fill vacuum.

"Algy? Who's Algy?"

"Your Major Breck, of course. Don't you know his name?"

"I never knew him as Algy, that sounds like a funny name."

"Well he was Algy to me." Another long silence gathers around us. Traces of goat's cheese lingering on my taste buds seem to taste rather sour now, and I realise the honey has produced an awkward stickiness on my fingers. I rub them in the dust trying to remove the discomfort but only succeed in getting myself dirty.

"And he was very brave at the end," she adds very quietly. Almost in a whisper.

These words, spoken so softly, strike my ear like a stone flung from a slingshot. A vein on my forehead has started to throb as it did on beach in Normandy. It doesn't mean… It can't mean…

But it does mean that. It *can only* mean that.

Who is this woman? She is not who I thought she was. And there is no resemblance to Ava Gardner at all, that silly piece of fantasy seems a very long time ago.

"Soon it will be over, you English will go home and we will be free to live normal lives. The Hagannah will have control and the Jewish people will come here freely."

"But you said yourself that the Arabs will kill you all when we leave."

"Don't worry about us. They can try to kill us but we can easily defend ourselves against the Arabs, we have good funding from the United States and also many weapons stolen from your Army. Hah! The Hagannah are ready for their moment."

"But Hetty, it can't be justified, all this fighting and killing, just so you can take land that belongs to another people. They have owned this land since biblical times, don't they have some rights."

She stands up and screams at me, "It does not belong to another people. It is our land, always has been and we have been promised it by you British for many decades. We must regain our land and be a nation once again."

"But then there will be a war," I shout back feebly, still sitting down and feeling weak, timid and third class.

"Yes, there will be a war. The religion of Mohammad was founded by the sword and spread by the sword. Those who wish to leave that religion with its false teachings are threatened by the sword. They know no way other than violence. We don't choose violence but if there must be a fight then we will win. This will be a holy war; we are obeying the command of God."

"So many people will die needlessly, including many Jews. You can't want that."

"If it is necessary to create Israel, it will happen. We Jews have been oppressed for long enough. There are many among us who were at Auschwitz and Buchenwald. They suffered and now we are able to use guns ourselves. Our time has come and you cannot stand in our way."

"I know about your guns; your people have used those guns against me. I was at Belsen and I freed prisoners there. They thanked me there, not shot at me."

"You might have been there but you were not behind the bars, you were not starving, you were not sent to the gas chambers. You weren't the one suffering. Don't try to tell me how it felt." She is standing over me now, her chest heaving, staring defiantly at me, and her voice is even more shrill.

I try to calm things, using the voice of reason. "Yes. I know it must have felt appalling and it's left many who suffered very damaged. You, who were not there and not damaged, should be taking responsibility for talking sense into them, not joining their madness. Why not use democracy, to solve problem? All the people of Palestine might vote on this issue and then they can decide who represents them."

"There will be democracy when all of our people have arrived, then the true population of Israel can all have their voice heard and we will have a majority. That's why it's necessary to resist the quotas you put on migration; it distorts democracy. There was never an Arab government here. This was never an Arab state. Just a disorganised collection of confused people, wondering who will rule them next. The Ottomans or the British?

Even the British used to accept this and allowed the Jewish Executive to control immigration. It's an abomination that you took that power away from us."

But this conversation is not what I'd expected, completely against what I want to achieve with Hetty, and so I shut up. I prefer silence. It's time to leave.

*

139

The road seems a little smoother than when I was driving out from Jerusalem, I can't feel any bumps. I can feel heat though, but when I catch a glimpse in the mirror, Hetty is looking very cool. Green eyes at directed back at me, I can sense that feral cat with its prey in its sight. There are no words between us.

As we reach Har Hozvim I see the city looming above us, just ahead. Here I approach a British Army check point, security is obviously being stepped up after bomb outrage. There's quite a queue at the barrier so I stop and put bike on its stand, and take keys out of the ignition, tucking them into my shorts. I've made my decision. I've decided which side I'm on and what I must do about it.

"Just wait here a moment, Hetty, I'll ask the boys if they'll let us through a bit quicker. I'm sure they will as we're in a military vehicle."

There's no reply as I step down and walk as casually as I can towards our soldiers, calling them into cabin at roadside to talk in private. And there, in the gloomy interior of a dark building, I tell them my story. They listen in silence, trying to decide what it means and what they need to do.

Just a few minutes later they move, as silently as possible and without being seen. My bike is surrounded by soldiers, each pointing a rifle at it. But it is now empty. She knew what I'd decided to do and has beaten me to it. There's no sign of Hetty but on pillion seat lies a handwritten note on a crumpled scrap of paper:

Go home soldier. Play your tennis games in England and leave Israel to the Israelis.

Har Hozvim

July 23rd 1946

The Military Police are arriving in jeeps and are all over the scene within a few minutes. They're not gentle, friendly people. I'm bundled into the guard's cabin and am locked up while they're talking to the sentries.

The inside of this stone building is dark and musty with a tangle of spider's webs in the corners, but it looks lived in. I sit behind the table and can see that the remains of a recent meal lying on table. Clearly, they eat well, these boys, they've had bully beef and beans in tomato sauce, a rare treat these days. Most of all, in mid-afternoon, it's unusually hot in here. It's quite dark as well but small rays of orange sunshine penetrate through the shutters on the windows. I can feel beads of sweat gathering on my brow and slowly trickling down my forehead before gathering pace down my neck.

They're back. Six tall, hefty men in carefully ironed uniforms and red banded caps. Much smarter in appearance than the average soldier, we who must live in a tent, and they're certainly much larger. As they enter through the door there's a moment where each become a dark silhouette illuminated by golden sunlight before entering the dark interior. Silently, these hulks enter with their flash of light and gather around me. Finally, the door slams shut and we all need a moment for our eyes to readjust to the dim light.

When I can see again, there's no longer any of the regular soldiers who man this post, the friendly, understanding blokes I first talked to. The circle of a Sergeant-Major's chubby face stares at me out of the many white moons that steadily resolve into faces in the gloom of room. They are crowding right in on top of me, and I can feel smoky breath on my cheeks. An unpleasant smell in a very unpleasant situation. I'm seated behind the table and they all stand across it, leaning forward.

"Driver/Mechanic Atherton of the RASC, is it?" A deep harsh tone comes in a Brummie accent as his words are delivered loudly from within an inch of my face, so I feel the benefit of his spittle, spraying my cheek and forehead.

"Yes, Sergeant-Major."

"Yow're in big trouble, boy. Helping the Irgun is treason, yow could be hanged for what you've done. And now one will care wun little bit about yower death after yesterday's bombing."

"I've done nowt that's anything like treason, you've no reason to keep me here."

"Oh no, will wut about stealing a Military vehicle then, for a start? That bike isn't yowers, is it? It belongs to King George."

"I only used it for a short while, doing something kind for an injured friend."

"Ah, you're kind is yow? I dun think so, mate. Yower just a bit of a prick, if you ask me. Well, we want to know you what you've been doing 'elping an Irgun agent. Don't you know they've been bombing and killing innocent people all over Jerusalem?"

"I know it all too well. I was there yesterday, at the King David, dragging people out of the rubble. And I lost my best pal in that bloody mess. No one can call me or Fido a traitor, we did our duty and then some more."

For an instance he turns and pale light from the chinks in the shutter illuminates his face. Enough for me to see him clearly. He becomes a human being for a moment and I can no longer take him seriously as an interrogator. I laugh. Even to me it sounds like a nervous, ill-placed laugh.

And his face freezes in anger. It's not what he wants to hear, it's not part of his plan. When he speaks again, he shouts harshly. I even wonder if he's going to hit me. His face almost touching mine, I can feel his spittle spraying onto my cheeks as he splutters his words.

"So, funny is it. Wut were yow doing with that girl then, the one yow saying is an Irgun operative?"

"I've been talking to her, around hotel and gardens. I thought she'd become a friend and I liked her. Actually, I liked her a lot, so that's why I went to Qastina to see her. But our conversation on the way back told me that she isn't a real friend and can't be. She was obviously involved in murdering Major Breck."

"And how do yow know that?"

"She told me that he was very brave at the end. I thought surely those words couldn't mean she was there, that she was involved, drew him to the bar to meet him knowing that gunmen were waiting to kill him. But they couldn't mean anything else, could they? She *was* there, she *did* see him die. I'm pretty sure she pretended to be his girlfriend, just to get his trust."

"And what did she know about the bombing of the King David Hotel?

She was actually in the hotel at the time. She knew there'd been a warning, which I knew nowt about. No bugger mentioned it at the time. She seemed to think that, in some way, this justified the bombing, which is just rubbish. I imagine she'd stayed in hotel, even though she knew it was going to be bombed, as she expected to be evacuated in time. She was trying to explain the Irgun's view of bombing and blaming her fellow receptionist. But nothing she said even started to justify anything they did."

Finally, they take details of Hetty's name and as they can

find everything about her employment at hotel, no doubt they'll continue their investigation there. The interview comes to an end, I've told them everything I know and expect to leave now. But before I can move to rise and leave the Sergeant-Major barks at me again.

"Right matey. We'll be checking yow out and we'll be checking yower story too. Mean time yow've got yerself a night in the cells. This'd better all be good, for yower sake. Otherwise, yower a dead man. They hang traitors."

The two end policemen move forward and each grab one of my arms with both hands, together they lift me off my feet, high over the table and out of the door. Within seconds I'm blinking in dazzling sunshine, my eyes blinded, my feet some way off the ground.

Then I'm flung in the back of a Black Maria and am on my way to jail.

KISHLE PRISON

23RD JULY 1946

A Black Maria is not designed for luxury but I at least want to stay on the narrow seat for the short journey. I fail and end up sprawling on the floor as the van bumps over cobblestones and bounces through narrow streets. He's driving too fast. Why? Doesn't he know what it's like to be inside the van?

It's only a brief relief to arrive inside this ugly old stone building at the end of my journey, as the reception here is not hospitable either. A very tall and muscular man in a British Army uniform, another with Sergeant's stripes, charges in and drags me out of the van, taking care to smash me first against the floor, then the door lintel, off the vehicle and into the ground before pushing me inside the building.

"Get in there, yer filthy piece of shite. I've heard all what you've been upto. We know how to deal with slimy traitors here. I hope yer Jewish bint gave you a lot of pleasure, cos it's gonna cost yer now," the Sergeant barks. He grabs my arm and takes me forcibly into the Admin Office for processing. Throughout the uncomfortable, humiliating procedure he glowers disapprovingly at me. After an hour of form filling and photos, they're finished with me.

Dressed in my "new uniform" a set of dirty, old pajamas, I'm led out of the Admin Office, down a labyrinth of narrow stone passageways and into the cells. We pass groups of prisoners, huddled in darkness of the prison. Faceless, anonymous people they have no personality and no presence, it's like going past a herd of cattle or a flock of sheep.

"Keep away from this lot we're coming to now," the Sarge grunts at me. "They're the real nasty ones, the terrorists who're condemned to hang for their murders. Death row."

It's nothing to me who they are. I know none of them, I recognise none of them and care nothing about them. They're just a group of nonentities I've never met and will never see again. None of them have any role to play in my life.

One of them, a tall slender man, darts forward and pushes his face right into mine, his eyes a vivid electric blue, and spits into my face. A great glob of phlegm and saliva slides down my right cheek and falls off onto the floor. The head is screaming at me, just a few inches away. Too loud for me to hear him, too close for me to see him, it's just noise and confusion. My arms are still held by the prison officer, I'm unable to defend myself. He lands a punch on my cheek, kicks my ankles out from under me so I end up lying on the floor, looking at his boot retracting, ready to kick out.

Then the Sergeant gets help from other officers and they drag my assailant off and I can stand. I want to see who it is that attacks me, for no reason. Understand what this weird incident represents. And when I see his face, a strangely distorted face, riddled with rage, I understand it completely.

"You, you British bastard", he shouts, "you deserve to be in prison. You betrayed me and you killed my brother, poor Gyusi. What did he ever do to you, you filth?"

"Jeno. You know I did everything I could for Goosey. He was just too far gone before we liberated the camp."

"No, no, NO! You British people, you kill him and now you kill my people here, in our country. Just because we want have our own land. You, you, you…"

"Shut up you murdering trash", growls the jailer, "you'll get what you deserve."

"I'm not a criminal. This is my country, I'm fighting for its freedom. You should know the difference between a terrorist and a freedom fighter."

"I know bullshit when I hear it and you're full of it. The world'll be a better place once you've hanged."

The prison staff drag him away, still protesting, and the Sergeant grabs hold of me. "I might have guessed you'd know all the terrorists. You're one of them aren't you, you traitor. We know how to deal with you filth."

He shunts me forward, kicking out to trip me as he pushes me into a huge, dark cell. I fall full length into the darkness, the pain of hitting my head on the floor joining the bruises biting into arms, my shins and my chest. Since I decided to choose loyalty to Britain above my affection for Hetty, Britain, or at least its soldiers, seems intent on hurting me as much as it can. And we're supposed to be on the same side?

Jeno doesn't deserve to hang, he's just lost his ability to see things straight. No wonder after what he went through. The villains are the leaders of the Zionist terrorists who've filled him so full of hate ridden propaganda.

The door is shut, keys grinding discordantly in the lock and I hear his feet move away. Now I can rest, sit alone in darkness, get used to the silence, savour the damp and fusty stench of whatever has been rotting in corner for the past decade. There barely seems any air to breath. It's a large, hot room, entirely empty, with stone flags on floor and dark stone walls. After just a short while I realise it's not really silent in here at all. There are dull sounds of shuffling and scratching, the occasional distant groan of a distressed person, probably in pain and muted sound of far away, unintelligible conversations.

An arched window made of crudely shaped stones allows a little faint day light through the iron bars into the room but I know it's around the time of sunset now and that little light will soon fade. The temperature is dropping rapidly.

There's enough light to show microscopic movements in the cell. I can make out tiny, white squirming creatures moving on the floor in the gloom. Soon I find them on my skin and biting whenever they can get a hold. I squash a few in my fingers knowing it's a futile gesture. Darkness will hold several million more.

The idea takes hold of me that this is a room in which many people have suffered and perhaps died over past decades, maybe centuries. I know enough to know that long before British came here it was used for dark purposes by the Ottoman Turks. This place is filled with brooding ghosts, their anguish and suffering hanging in the air like cobwebs. It's a stillness of hidden movement, a silence of muted screams.

Then there's a sudden crash, a heavy door opening nearby. Another crump, as it's violently thrown shut again. The sound of plodding feet moving towards my cell. Getting louder, getting nearer. Keys clattering in the lock of my cell door before it opens to reveal a short, stout, bearded man dressed in an Arab dishdasha. He also had a very ancient brown belt which matches a band around his head dress. The small lamp in his hand allows me to see his oddly misaligned eyes, one looks at me and the other seems to be staring into the corner of the room, behind me. Both are fiercely black and sit either side of his crooked nose. His yellow, broken teeth seem to glow yellow in the light of his lamp. If this is the genie of the lamp, come to grant me three wishes, he's definitely in the wrong pantomime.

"Gud efening, Meester British soldier," he meows, sounding immensely pleased with himself. "I don't get many of you British inside my pretty prison. It is mostly the Jewish terrorists. So nice to make you welcome here."

"It's just a misunderstanding, I'll be out of here in a few hours."

"Ah yes, ha ha, of course you will. They all say this. But it must be a great comfort to you to think it." He smirks as he pauses to look at his grubby notebook.

"I see you are called Mr William. Let me introduce myself, I am Mohammed al-Husseini and it will be my pleasure to be looking after you here." He bows graciously and hands me a dirty blanket and a small earthenware jog containing water, still smiling. Or is it a smirk? I taste the water cautiously. It is as rank and putrid as I expect, but I drink it anyway. It's been quite a while since I had anything to eat or drink.

Our conversation is interrupted briefly by sounds of tiny, far away feet, scratching in deep recesses of the far end of my cell. "Ah, one of our leettle friends," say Mohammed, his good eye looking directly at me. "Don't worry, they are not so many, since there's nothing to eat here, as you're soon going to find out, Mr William." He laughs, a strange high-pitched shriek, which gives me benefit of second-hand garlic and half-digested spices. Now I can see his face I realise that he is looking straight at me through his one good eye, the other, misty eye, is pointing over to his right.

"It's nice to see you enjoying your work so much, Mr al-Husseini."

"Please, please do call me Mohammed, we are all friends here. But you must be rather special Mister William, you get such a large cell all for yourself. I usually put thirty of the Jewish people in here. Of course, they are very bad people, all terrorists and murderers who want to steal this country from the Arab people, who it belongs to, by violence and terrorism. Not like you fine English gentlemen."

"But they have a long history of living in this land, the Bible tells us all about it." I say remembering Hetty's impassioned argument.

"Ah, heestory. Yes, I know something about heestory. So that gives them a right to be here, does it? There was never a Jewish government here, this was never a Jewish state. But if you believe in history then give Spain and Sicily back to the Arab people, we have a right to them because of we owned them in history. And maybe we will give Britain to the Italians? After all, the Romans used to own it as part of their Roman Empire. In heestory, since that is so sacred to you."

"That's a bit of a stretch mate, the Italians have no claim on England."

"Hah. I see that you British wear two faces on heestory. Your own real heestory doesn't matter but the heestory that the Jews have imagined, does matter. So, you let them infade Arab lands with your blessing and support. I say no. No Zionism, no Jewish immigration into Palestine and no Jewish state. But we are a tolerant people, we will allow the Jews to live here, but only if they obey Islamic law, of course." He grinned a toothy grin, revealing how awful Arab dentistry is.

"Why not let people of Palestine decide by democracy, a vote?"

"Good idea Mr William, I agree. Most people here are Arab and will fote for an Islamic state. At least they will, if you damned Britishers stop all these bloody foreigners coming here. Their plan is to cheat democracy by overwhelming us with their numbers."

"I can see there's no easy solution."

"Ah but it is easy, Mr William, ferry easy. The solution is that you will stay here until your trial and then your British friends will hang you by the neck until you are dead. In the meantime, I will help you to buy a few comforts for just a small price. I am a fair man and only want a very leettle profit for myself. If you want cigarettes or coffee just let me know. I will get you anything like this, for a fair price. I am your only friend here, apart from the scorpions. Wrap yourself up in the blanket and try to sleep. We will have many more days for conversations, I know you will be for long, efen if you have not yet realised that yet. Is there any purchase you might like to make now?"

"No thank you, Mohammed."

"Then good night, Mr William."

And then, with a bow and another squinty smile, the one good eye looks at me and blinks, he blows his scented breath over me and turns to leave. The bad eye seems disinterested and looks away, unblinking as he moves away. I hear a succession of slamming and crashing of heavy doors. The faint, flickering glow of his lamp disappears as I watch on tiptoe, peering between the cobwebs covering the rusty black grille on the door.

Ramleh cemetery, Tel Aviv

July 24th 1946

This occasion is supposed to be all about Fido but the Padre is describing someone entirely different, some one called Frederick Ian Dobson. He sounds like a great guy too, although I'm not sure Fido would have liked him. Maybe a just a bit too pompous for someone with such an irreverent sense of humour as my old pal.

It seems this Dobson bloke was respected by everyone who met him, always a leader in every military mission and respected by all his friends. Nowt like Fido then, who was always irreverent, laughing and taking the piss. More important, Fido was my best mate.

All the boys here know the story by now; Fido had done pretty well, scrambling around in his hole. After Coxy had told me to leave him, Fido had pulled two people out of rubble. Two dirty and badly injured Arabs who needed a lot of help to manoeuvre their way carefully back up through fallen debris. They'd had assistance from the Sergeant in the final part of journey and he'd risked his life in the hole too. The rescued men had been waiters in La Regence restaurant in hotel basement. Fido kept tunnel up just long enough for them to escape. Then he went back in to look for others and that's when the tunnel finally collapsed.

Coxy is here too but he shouldn't be. He's off his head with grief and shock, continually breaking down in tears. He blames himself for Fido's death and is tormented by guilt over not having been hurt himself. He's told everyone about promising me that he would look after Fido and feels he let both Fido and me down.

I'm really fortunate to be here on time, in fact, to have got here at all after my little excursion to Kishle. They only just let me out in time to attend the funeral. Apparently, it was a special request from Major MacAllan, after he'd been briefed that my story had checked out. He'd even got Sergeant Cox to come and pick me up, on a motorbike. It was a certain BSA M20, of course.

Coxy was pretty edgy with me at first. He'd had a first class bollocking for letting me take the bike. From right under his nose, they said. What was he thinking of? But secretly he wasn't that mad with me at all. He admired me for getting myself an adventure, wished he could have done it. He was full of praise for my busting an Irgun cell, an important one, probably the same bastards that bombed KDH.

The Sergeant at Kishle jail wasn't pleased with me though. He's still convinced that I'm guilty of betraying my own nation. Overwhelming evidence to the contrary doesn't affect or influence his judgement in any way. My new pal Mohammed Al-Husseini was also surprised and disappointed to be losing me as well. He had me down as a likely customer for his illicit goods. I just needed that cigarette I scrounged off Coxy and a long drink of clean water from the flask on his bike. Still no breakfast.

I've a privileged seat in the front row of the chapel, being one of the coffin bearers. When I sit down it's a chance to wipe the saliva off my uniform. As we carried the coffin into the chapel a group of Jewish youths came to spit on us and call us 'Nazis'. I remember Fido's part in helping the survivors at Belsen. He knew what real Nazis were.

They're members of the Jewish Youth Movement and organised by the Zionist Council. I know nowt about them, except for the camp gossip which says they're organised just like Hitler Youth and with a similar way of thinking. We have orders to ignore them, whatever they say or do. Apparently, we mustn't provoke them to violence. A bit bloody late I say, after ninety-one people have just been murdered, including my best mate.

They dress quite differently from the Arabs, more like Europeans, which in the main they are. When they started throwing stones at Fido's coffin the Palestinian Police finally moved in to clear them away. They'd stoned the coffin bearers too, so I collected a few more bruises in the process. I'm proud to bear all of this to honour Fido's memory but it's still shit that such a wonderful, heroic guy should be treated with disrespect by this scum. We're also aware that at any moment a gunman could have appeared among them and fired off a burst from a sten gun into our funeral cortege.

I'd like to see them all rounded up and shot.

The Padre conducts mass in a solemn fashion and the ancient rites are chanted out in Latin. Everyone here understands it equally, whether they are English, Arab or Jew. That is to say, no one understands it at all. As we come out of the chapel, the sunlight hurts our eyes and I'm blinded for a moment. A crowd blinks its way out of church and onto the war cemetery. It feels unreal; I'm still a very long way from Chapel Street.

We are surrounded by the graves of those who fought the Ottoman Empire in a different war, when this was a different place. It's devoted to soldiers of the Allied forces who fell in 1914-18. There's a large white stone war memorial in the centre of the large field surrounded on all sides by a mass of identical rectangular head stones in regular straight lines. The whole place is covered in green grass which must mean it's regularly tended and watered with great care. This cemetery is a haven of quiet, a vast open space with just the occasional dark green of a tree or a large white cross. It's surrounded by industry, the cement works is particularly prominent, its towers looming over flat countryside. Outside the enclosed area there are a few minarets, punctuating the flat skyline towards Tel Aviv.

A lot of the local Arab population have attended to show respect, having heard of how of my friend died saving the Arab waiters. Some of the Arabs are Christian and come into chapel. Of course, none of Muslims have come inside but there are many waiting in silence outside to follow his coffin to the graveyard. It's a very different crowd than one that saw us enter. The crowd of Jewish youths evaporated as the Palestinians gathered. I'd never expected to feel safe surrounded by the Arabs but things keep moving on and I have to keep re-adjusting my thinking. The Zionist terrorists who bombed KDH have shown me who is wrong in this struggle. Now all I want to know is "who is right?" And no one seems to answer that question.

The Padre says a few final words of praise and lament at the graveside, a final farewell to my old pal, before we leave him here. He will spend his eternity in a faraway, foreign place, where his family will never be able to visit or remember him.

We lower Fido's coffin on straps, slowly and awkwardly, into his grave, the priest saying a final prayer. Then we each throw a handful of soil into the pit. I can see that he is lying between two other soldiers, both recently murdered. Thomas Andrews, who was killed by Arab gangsters, and James Wilkins, another victim of Zionist terrorists.

Then there is nowt left but to slowly make my way back to the camp. No tears can come from a soldier, I'm not allowed anguish, but there's no escape from the emptiness.

*

On my return to base there's a message from the Major, delivered by Dicky Cox. I've to report to him in the Hotel immediately I return from funeral. It's bound to be a consequence to my arrest and it won't be fun. Maybe they're even sending me back to prison. I drag myself reluctantly upstairs, passing reception on the way. It's not even worth a look now. Instead, I look into the bar which has its usual gang of snooty, privileged revellers.

There are guards by front door but no one has challenged me. I'm expecting it at any moment and look over my shoulder as I reach the stairs but I'm still alone and put my foot on the steps to go upstairs. Quickly, before the trouble starts. This is unknown territory, I've never got this far before, the inner area of British High command in Palestine.

Now past the first floor and onto the second. No sign of any guards here, though I'm still looking for them. My way is clear, right to the third floor as I'm directed. Now I'm completely lost, no idea how to find my Major. I need help and stop one of the impatient officers bustling past, standing in his way and saluting him sharply. He jolts to a halt and splatters me with indignation.

"What are you doing here, man? Don't you know this area is off limits to those without business here?"

"I've been called to meet Major McAllan, sir."

"Oh! Well why didn't you say so? The door on the left over there, has his name on it." Perhaps there's a faint touch of irony in his voice.

I knock and then enter, as Major's voice calls me in. I stand to attention and salute him.

"Stand at ease, Private Atherton. I have some great news for you."

"Yes, sir."

"The Military and Palestinian Police mounted a joint operation this morning, raiding the location given to the Hotel by Hesta Karolina Borowska, as her home address, the Piastow Hotel. They found a cache of arms, mostly stolen British Army rifles, and a stash of sensitive documents taken from this building. Obviously, I can't tell you anything of those, but Intelligence are very pleased to get them back. Three people were detained at the house, a middle-aged couple and a young man."

"What about Hetty? Has she been captured?"

He looks at me sideways, maybe I seem a bit too anxious to hear about her? He takes a deep breath.

"At present Miss Borowska remains at large, she wasn't in the house at the time of the operation. It'll only be a matter of time before she's picked up. And it's largely down to the information you provided. No one at the King David had suspected her for a moment. She had seemed entirely loyal and conscientious in her work, she was very popular amongst the staff. A really convincing actress.

Congratulations on your very valuable contribution. You should be mentioned in despatches for your achievement. It will, however, remain confidential here, within the base. They feel it would not be appropriate, in view of the fact that Miss Borowska is not yet in detention. I have to say that there are also some question marks over your behaviour too. Especially in the matters of going absent without leave and using a military motor bike without permission. Nevertheless, you have the gratitude of the British Army.

No one else should know about it. I know I can rely on you to keep it under your hat. None of your pals can know about these events. Well done Atherton, this is very valuable to us in the fight against terrorists. A good piece of work." He reaches out to shake my hand.

"You can return to the camp now." And I do, I make my way out of Hotel, straight out. No hesitation, no sideways glances.

Even with the bomb damage it's still a glorious and luxurious place. They've done an amazing job in cleaning out the dirt and dust. This time I can't resist a glance at the reception desk. Although the girls there are polite, charming and good looking I can't help feeling that there's a vacuum. Something exciting and wonderful has gone out of it.

I return to my dark, cool place in the grounds: a camp bed inside a four-man tent, none of whom are Chalky or Fido, in a back garden among thousands of anonymous soldiers. I can be forgotten and alone here. Which is what I need today.

There's no temptation to tell anyone about the recent events.

King David Hotel
Army camp

July 25th 1946

What has happened to me? What's happened to everyone I either liked or loved since I got to this *Holy* land?

We buried Fido yesterday and Chalky died at Easter. Jack never even made off the beach in Normandy. I'm the only one left of the jolly lads that joined up together in 1942. Hetty is on the run from the police and is probably stalking me, looking for revenge. I've no friends left in the world.

I walk around the camp, alone. No close pals to chat to, just a collection of guys I know but not well enough to want their company. The pink walls of the hotel look unwelcoming, out of bounds. The tower of the YMCA is in a foreign land, I see it every day but have never been inside. Only the gardens with the view of the tennis court and the terrace are available to me and they have no appeal. They betrayed me. They're no part of my world, which consists of just a field full of grey, dusty tents. I stop walking and look around the inside of my tent, lie back on camp bed and contemplate the dirty grey canvas above me that's enclosed my life for the past year, and shut my eyes.

Let's see if that will remove me from this miserable world.

*

It all started right back in July '42 when we met up for the first time at a training camp, just beside Tywyn in mid-Wales. It was first time I'd become Private William Atherton, 14.274.761, Royal Army Service Corps. Although it sounded a bit strange, I was delighted with my new identity. My part in the war was finally made clear after so much debate and indecision. My Dad had hated it when I joined up.

Tiny waves on the bay had glistened in the late evening sunshine as we'd walked along the sea front, my new comrades and me. We were supposed to be the men who were going to stop Adolf Hitler but he wouldn't have been trembling at sight of this bunch of half-starved mongrels, just issued with baggy clothes that should have been supplied to much larger men. No one ever got clothes that fitted them.

In the blue sky above our heads a shaky bi-plane, painted bright yellow, rattled and droned its way back to a grass strip on the RAF base next to a beach, completing the latest of many circuits and bumps. Even at this time in the evening they were training pilots. That student might not have survived long in a dog-fight; his aircraft bounced off the runway on landing and he almost turned the plane over. Then as the rickety crate settled onto the grass, we heard the engine rev up and he took off unsteadily for another lap. I wonder what has happened to him, he'll be dead by now unless he's improved dramatically.

The Irish Sea stretched away towards a horizon where flimsy white clouds drifted slowly towards us. Water rippled against shingle nearby and a faint scent of sea pinks penetrated the stench of rotting kelp. The sunshine felt uncomfortably hot on our dark, heavy uniforms. I didn't really know what hot was in those days but I've found out since.

"How long before you think we'll get to fight?" asked Jack, a tall, fresh-faced kid, just out of grammar school in Wigan.

"Maybe weeks, maybe months, but too soon for sure." Alan, who'd always been known as Chalky since his surname was White, a plumber from Northampton, replied. An ex-plumber from Northampton, since now he became a driver in the Army.

"I guess it'll be in Europe, most likely Italy, but who knows? It could be France or Holland or Norway." I said.

"Or even Bengal, to try and stop the Jap's invasion of British India. That'll happen soon." said Jack.

"How can you know about that? The newspapers don't say anything about that."

"I can read between the lines. Things are always worse than they tell us. No sane person would ever volunteer to join the Army if they knew what it was really like," Jack gave a sideways grin at us both.

"You guys are a security risk. Don't you know that walls have ears?"

"Sure mate, but there aren't any walls here and I'm hoping these seagulls are on our side."

The prospect of defeating the Third Reich had enough difficulties to keep me, Jack and Chalky occupied as we strode manfully on along the promenade towards an ugly Nissen hut which had become our home. That's where we'd met a pasty-faced boy called Fred, soon to become Fido, and our little group of four jolly boys was ready to take on Hitler. None of us would even have known where Palestine was.

*

I'd been with Jack on D-Day, just me and him together in the same lorry. It was an event I've never discussed since. But I do remember it so well that it's come to visit me many times in the middle of many nights. Nights I'd jumped up in fright, covered in sweat, still hearing his voice speaking to me from where he was lying on the beach.

"Three hours Bill. Three bleeding hours we've been under this lorry," he'd said.

"Yeah Jack, and so what? We're stuck on the beach, but we're alive. That's three hours longer than I expected to live." I'd replied.

"How long are we going to stay under here? The war'll be over by the time we stick our heads out."

"There's no point in getting out until we know it's safe, mate. We've only been in the war three hours and you've forgotten your basic bloody training already."

"It's cold, wet and in case *you've* forgotten, they're not bloody potatoes in the cart just above our heads. That's two tons of high explosive shells. We're *not safe here.*"

"It's a damn sight safer than out in the open. In Tilbury they told us the commandoes would clear all the Germans away from the beach but after the reception we've got we know that's bollocks. Those buggers never did their job."

"But it's been three hours and all quiet since then. Jerry must've gone by now."

"You stick your head out then, smart ass, if you're so bloody sure. I'm staying here."

"But it's *not safe* here. The tide's coming in and we'll drown soon."

I looked under the lorry, down the beach towards the sea and my heart sank. Those little white waves *were* closer than when we'd got off the landing craft. We'd crossed just a hundred yards before the tirade of bullets had pulled us up and we took cover. It looked a lot less now. Jack had made a good point.

I wasn't going to concede, so I just kept quiet. The craving for a cig was strong. Could I light up under the vehicle? My training said no. No one smokes around petrol or ammunition. My craving said: "Yeah, one little cig. You'll get away with that, easy."

Neither of us spoke and it started to rain again. The breeze was strong enough for spits and spats of rain to find its way into our faces, completing our misery. My pal started to shiver.

"Bugger this, I'm going to get out and have a look," said Jack as he hauled his tall, skinny body out from under our vehicle, trying to peep out. "I can't see a damn thing from here. Too many vehicles round us. Where's that tea shop they were shooting from."

Jack crawled beyond the lorry, and knelt up, pulling up the collar of his greatcoat to keep the wind out. He looked round but said nowt. Then he moved a bit further from the lorry and must've gained a view of promenade. He scrutinised it and there was no sound, no sign that Jerry was still about.

Jack was clearly relieved. "There's no one out on the beach, no one at all. No one on the promenade either. I think they've all g..."

I heard a soft wet thwack and Jack fell onto his side and lay still. I could see his face. A small red circle had appeared in centre of his forehead. His eyes, so agitated a moment ago, looked dull. His body was completely still.

'Jack, Jack. What's happened? Are you all right?" I screamed and jumped up. I banged my head against the underside of my lorry. There was no reply. A stream of black red blood had started to seep from back of Jack's head, forming a dark pool on the golden sand.

His skin took on a waxy pallor. My posh mate from Orrell had gone. All of that expensive education wasted. Ambitions and aspirations lost. Inside one short word he'd left this world.

I hid back under lorry. Damn the cold and wet, damn the rising tide, damn the high explosives. I was staying here no matter what Jack said.

Jack said nowt, but his lifeless body alongside me told me eloquently that he was dead and I was going to die too. Every sinew and every nerve in my head tightened. The temples ached. I could hardly breathe. Maybe I would just choke to death. I felt a vein on my forehead start to pulse.

It was silent except for the occasional drone of aircraft and the incessant sound of wind and waves. Time passed slowly in the cold and wet and the tide crept nearer. I crawled to the back of the Bedford and stood up behind it, facing away from promenade. All

I could see before me was a confused mass of grey ocean which constantly lapped at the beach behind my lorry. Ever closer. To the side were the other trucks that had disembarked with us. All were stopped, and their crews hiding out of sight too. A few eyes stared back at me from dark spaces.

Getting out beyond the vehicle I had the luxury of standing up, stretching my aching limbs. On the horizon ships were passing and many aircraft were buzzing across the sky. All seemed to be keeping away from this cursed spot. There was some life left in the world but it was keeping far away.

The sea had reached my feet and my boots were in the edge of the water, every wave rippling a fraction higher. The flood tide, wearing a grey uniform to show its enmity, was higher again and I could do nowt to stop it. There's no negotiation with an inanimate foe.

A distant rumbling of vehicles engines came from inland and gradually got closer. Three loud bangs shattered the quiet. Shock waves hit the air and a bitter smell of cordite drifted past. Something had happened, the stalemate was broken. I risked one eye to peer around canvas flap on corner of vehicle. A Churchill tank was moving up to the remains of a burning building. A broad white "Salon de Thé" sign was broken but still visible, protruding from the smoke and flames engulfing the ruins.

Now there was activity everywhere, not just around the tanks but all over the beach. Soldiers emerged from under and behind the vehicles around me. All of the South Lancs Regiment seemed to have spontaneously appeared and were swarming over the sand.

One, with a canvas covering marked with a red cross on a white circle, was picking up a few wounded men. Another was picking up bodies. I waved my arms to attract attention and eventually that vehicle came slowly towards me. I pointed to Jack.

"OK mate, we've gorrim now" came in a broad Lancashire accent.

"Can you do anything to 'elp him, he's my best mate?"

"Sorry pal, only God can 'elp him now. Best look after thi'sel."

I suddenly retched and fell forward. Two ambulance men grabbed me by my elbows and dragged me back up to a standing position. I didn't even know that I'd gone onto my knees. A brown patch of vomit lay dribbled down front of my uniform, the bully beef I'd eaten earlier that day had returned. That semi-digested mess offended all our nostrils and sent a feeling of shame through my quivering body. Vomit was all around my mouth. Small patches of the splatter had attached themselves to my face and around my uniform top. I staggered off to the sea to wipe if off.

"Just get back in thi lorry and gerroff t'beach. We'll look after thi mate best we can." He sounded angry.

Without thinking I nodded and turned to obey, stepped up into driving seat and found comfort in its familiarity. The engine started, first time, thank God. My vehicle roared, juddered and then lurched under the clumsiest gear change I've ever made.

Away I went across drying sand, up a slipway, onto a promenade and along the front, in direction of the Seine estuary. I'd no idea which way I should be going. No one else did either, so several vehicles followed me, probably believing I did know where I was going.

I was finally off that beach but would never see my mate Jack again. It was my fault that he died, why did I let him put his head out? I knew it was the wrong thing to do all along.

*

I still miss Jack. And as if that wasn't bad enough, I'd now seen off Chalky and Fido as well. All of them died in my presence. So, it must have been me, I'm the common factor in all of their deaths. And why am I still here in this tent in the middle of Jerusalem when they've all gone, buried in foreign fields so far away from home? It's all the wrong way around. They didn't deserve to die and I don't deserve to live.

Jaffa

August 16th 1946

"Right you 'orrible lot, get yer kit bags. You're off to the seaside for a stick of rock, a kiss me quick hat and a nice paddle in the sea."

And that's how we found out we were going on holiday, through these kind words of Sergeant Cox, good old Dicky. Cheerful banter, intended to lighten the mood and cheer us all up. He's failed, badly, that's not what I want today. I'm pissed off. Really pissed off. More pissed off than a properly pissed off person in the most pissed off part of pissed off, pigging Palestine.

And it's all because of that bloody ridiculous woman. She's in my head all the time. Thoughts of her behind her reception desk, sitting in the gardens, dancing on the terrace but most of all, swinging around behind me on the motorbike. I wish I'd never damn well met her. Never gone into the Hotel that day, not sat in the gardens in the afternoon or evening and especially, not gone to Qastina to bring her back to Jerusalem. But I did and she inhabits my thoughts all my waking moments and visits me in my dreams too. Blast her.

Now we're here; Coxy, Kenny, me and all the other blokes. Three days' rest and recuperation to be spent at the seaside, near

Jaffa. I'd rather have gone to Blackpool, Southport, New Brighton or anywhere in England.

The British Army has a camp down here, yet another mass assembly of white tents, in a place more famous for its oranges, cafes and promenade walks. It is nice and sunny though. Of course, we still have to carry our rifles with us everywhere and are banned from being alone at any time. We're made aware that terrorists are never on holiday. This is a war that constantly bubbles away below the surface.

My rifle has been my constant companion for the past four years, ever since I arrived in the training camp at Barmouth. It's been with me across Europe, all the way from Lion-sur-mer to Hannover and now on throughout Palestine and Egypt. We've been in the middle of some of the most violent and dramatic battles in history together. And at every point I've been told to look after it, as it may save my life. I have looked after it but I've only once fired it in action. I've hardly ever practised my use of it either. The few times I've been made to take a few shots on the firing range weren't reassuring. I'll never make a sniper, but then again, I don't want to.

Happy to be out of Jerusalem for a time. Ever since I gave the evidence that got Hetty's parents and brother locked up, I feel hunted. I don't imagine her as a forgiving type, but she's got strong contacts inside a murder gang and I think she might be looking for revenge. There's no evidence of a specific threat to me though, I'd waste my time asking for special protection. Sometimes I think maybe I *am* making it all up. But then every time I go outside the camp, I can feel Hetty's bright green eyes behind me. Always staring disapprovingly at me and plotting to murder me, just like Jeno.

This morning we do exactly what the Sergeant had told us to do, paddle and swim in the sea beside the old town. There's a narrow beach, below the prom, which gets just slightly wider as tide goes out, but there's not much tide. The sea is placid, just a few tiny wavelets rippling up yellow sand.

The promenade is an ancient stone structure, which looms

above us and to our right, beyond a great jumble of ragged rocks which stand out stark and black against the azure sky, is the old port. Its breakwater wraps its long finger along the coast and encloses a sliver of sea that is the ancient harbour, rather than pointing out into the blue of the Mediterranean. Behind us the ancient town stretches up into the hills. It's a tangle of twisting alleys filled with campaniles and the inevitable minarets pointing through red roofs and punctuated by palm trees around the edges of the town. The stonework, which was earlier a pale honey colour, is trying to glow orange in the dazzling sunlight. By mid-morning it's too hot for anything but a swim. Even sunbathing in deck chairs with just our shorts on is pretty uncomfortable. Our boys all want a tan but I get sunburnt too easily and keep a long-sleeved shirt on. Our rifles stay beside us on the sand.

"How d'you like it here, Kenny? Better than the King David?" Kenny Hindley's my regular pal now.

"I like the sea. Great to stand in the water with those pretty little fish moving around yer legs. They're not frightened of us at all, are they?"

"Yeah, I like little stripy ones but can't catch any, they're really quick. By God it *is* hot. I didn't think Jerusalem was cool until we got here. This is bloody ridiculous."

Soon we've got our bright pink suntans and I'm just too hot to hang around on beach any longer, I put on my shirt and persuade Kenny to look for some shade. We stroll together along the prom and then up Kikar Kedumim Street towards the Italianate campanile of St Peter's church. After a bit of a wander around the streets we come to a halt in the shady bushes of the Hapisgah gardens on top of a small mound. From this point we can look down and along the coast to the much larger, more modern city of Tel Aviv, just north of here, with straight avenues and uniformly white buildings. Jaffa is an ancient Arab town; Tel Aviv is a new Jewish town built in a modern European style. Lots of tall residential buildings overlooking the sea.

There are a few white stones in the square here with strange carvings which depict the fall of Jericho. We sit on them and take a few minutes to eat our packed lunch and drink water, Ken has a bottle of Gold Star beer. The town has fallen silent as the locals disappear for their lunch and a siesta. The town is left for mad dogs and Englishmen.

"So nice to find a peaceful place, Ken. Stunning views."

"Yeah, you're right Billy. Bit boring though, hard to imagine much happens here."

For the next hour, maybe a bit more, we join in with local tradition and snooze in the shade of palm trees. It soothes my aching head to be out of direct sunlight for a time. For a moment. Until I wonder what it would be like to have Hetty here. I can see her smiling sweetly at me, just as she did at Qastina. My head aches worse than ever.

As the market traders start to lay out their stalls again for the afternoon trade, we wake up enough to take a walk between the Arab buildings and down narrow, cobbled streets into the old town itself. When I walk into the shaded alley, it seems suddenly dark and there's a moment of blinking, when I can hardly see. High buildings above us provide shade, each with balconies to provide their dwellers with access to cooler outside air. Today, these are used for drying the family washing. Most shops have brightly striped awnings above their windows which lighten the mood.

The streets steadily fill again as more and more people return to the afternoon market. Foods include local fruits and herbs. They fill the air with their scent and partly mask the smell of the sweaty traders and something else I can't identify. It's a rich broth of scents, aromas and stinks. There's lots of glittering goods and richly coloured clothes for sale and Ken picks out a bright scarlet scarf for his sister and some red coral beads for his Mum. It's of no interest to me, I can't spend money on gifts.

Then a great burst of shouting comes from the far end of the street, where there's a police vehicle parked beside the Ottoman

Bank. I sense danger as a group of men run out from a bank. They have cloths wrapped around their mouths and are shouting loudly and waving guns. I don't know what they saying but they're hugely agitated. There's something bad happening.

Policemen follow them slowly with their hands up, keeping a safe distance but they also have side arms available. The bank robbers, if that's what they are, fire off a volley of shots and jump into a waiting car. There are bright flashes, the percussions are ear splitting and a shock runs through whole market as the traders scatter, looking for cover. Then there's a second, more frenzied and prolonged volley, now aimed a getaway car. The engine revs, gears crunch, tyres screech and it jolts forward and swerves an uncertain path along the street, nearly hitting a lamp post.

I can see bullets striking it, holes appearing in the body of the car, a wing mirror shatters. I'm staring through the smoke, already drifting away, towards the end of the street where the car drives around a corner and out of sight. It leaves several bleeding bodies lying on the pavement.

Ken and I rush to aid the police and attend to the wounded men; our rifles raised. With our uniforms and guns, we're recognised as allies. But the first two we reach are already dead, shot straight through the heart. They appear to be two of the Arab traders, mere bystanders who weren't involved as far as I can see. The shots that killed them must have been carefully aimed to achieve a quick kill. Why would anyone want to do that? It doesn't make any sense. Who were those men?

But the gunmen didn't always make a first time kill. A third man lies nearby, still alive but bleeding heavily from ragged open wounds in his chest, having difficulty breathing. As his chest heaves, he breathes out a fine spray of blood over us. I lie my rifle down, nearby. It's never been any help to me anyway.

But I can help by ripping lengths off his long desert dresses and tying it tightly around his chest to stop or slow the bleeding. This action seems horribly familiar, I did it before with Chalky, it's always been a waste of time. A hard knot of anxiety tightens in my guts.

My hands are soon covered in the blood of this anonymous victim, who stares blankly up at me as I work. Then his staring eyes fill with pain and fear. An understanding of the horror of his situation lights his eyes and vibrates through his hands. His ragged breathing still sprays red onto my uniform, as he mutters something indistinguishable. It doesn't look good for this poor sod.

But I'm not needed for long, or even wanted, as an ambulance arrives, its bells jangling. The ambulance men push me aside without a word, although they examine my work carefully. They seem satisfied enough to bundle the casualty onto a stretcher, he's loaded alongside the dead men. There's still no word for Kenny or me. They disappear into the ambulance and are driven away. A few minutes after the incident started the scene is back to normal. Just as though nowt had happened at all, if you can ignore the blood stains on the street.

Almost back to normal, except for me and a few people weeping. My hands are trembling and I feel faint. The dark blood of the dead and dying is still shiny and wet on the pavement. No one seems to be in a mood for market trading anymore and most people have simply left. Neither Ken nor I feel normal.

We can see into the bank, where frenzied tellers grab at loose notes that still fly around and stuff them into large money bags. Maybe the police had arrived in time to stop the theft. Maybe the Arab bystanders were shot out of frustration and anger or they'd tried to stop the bandits.

Even the police seem a bit lost as to what should happen next. There's a few in the bank but a group are stood on the pavement outside.

"What *has* happened here?" I ask a police sergeant.

He answers in a strong Scouse accent. "It's the Irgun at it again. Trying to finance their activities by bank raids. We'd a tip off they'd be doing summat today but we didn't know exactly where or when.

I'd a feeling they might attack either Barclay's or the Ottoman, the two banks that aren't owned by Jews. We've a good idea who's involved in this. We've got names and'll be visiting them this affy. We'll get the bastards this time."

"But why'd they shoot bystanders? What harm were they doing?"

"Search me. I guess terrorists have a grudge against anyone Brit or Arab, and wanna shoot us all. It's been going on for yonks and is just bleeding bonkers."

"Yeah, you're right. There's no stopping 'em and they'll still be killing each other in a hundred years' time. It's all just bloody ridiculous and I wanna go home."

And then for a moment I can hear Hetty's voice, praising the robbers and justifying the murders they carried out in the great cause of creating a Zionist state. Gloating about another victory over the British, with Jeno behind her waving a machine gun. It moves me to anger for a moment but then only sadness. I put my hand over my face, on the edge of tears. Ken puts an arm around me and moves me on.

Neither of us know what to do, but we're not in any mood for holiday fun. We go back to the camp to keep out of the way, sleep the rest of the afternoon in the tent and wonder how the police are getting on with raiding the suspects. I'd like to know but I never will know.

It's not the greatest holiday ever, not a stick of rock on sale anywhere. I still prefer Blackpool.

King David Hotel

Aug 24th 1946

A gale is blowing across the camp today and it's much cooler. This wasn't in any weather forecast that I know of. Tents are flapping wildly and several have collapsed. It rattles the windows of the hotel and has demolished several parasols on garden terrace. On the plus side, it's driven all the officers indoors.

The familiar sight of Dicky Cox bouncing across the field shows there is still such a thing as normality. He heads straight to me. "Get yerself upto the Major's office on the third floor Athey, he's got something to tell you."

Permission to enter the hotel is something unusual for a humble Private these days. This must be important, Major McAllan hasn't spoken to me since the Hetty incident. I've a feeling it's not going to be good news today, it never is.

With the wind at my back, I cross the camp and go up towards the terrace, passing through the palm trees in garden and upto my bench, with its view of tennis courts. There's no one playing there today. The purple flowers of the bougainvillea bushes are again fading, a reminder of this time last year. That was a happy time but it's left only painful memories. Neither Major Breck nor Hetty are around anymore. I don't miss him.

I climb the stone steps upto a deserted terrace, where no band is playing, no one is singing Vera Lynn's tunes and no one is dancing. I dodge between fallen parasols and enter the hotel. I pass reception, making a point of not looking at any of the girls. Past the bar, noticing that the tall, athletic black waiters in their tight fitting, immaculate red jackets are still serving British Officers with tea, coffee or pink gin. Mostly gin, so nowt has changed there. The gentlemen still have pith helmets besides their seats and their ladies still carry white parasols, as neatly folded as ever. There's an air of contented entitlement.

There are guards around the front door but no one challenges me and I'm on my way upstairs. No sign of any guards here, although I'm still on the lookout. My way is clear, right through to the third floor as I was directed by the Sergeant. A perfect repetition of my earlier journey, it might be easy it for a Zionist terrorist to get in here. They are masters of disguises and a simple British army uniform would be so easy.

I knock on the Major's door, and am called in. Naturally, I stand to attention and salute him. His room is small, square and very plainly decorated. Two brown book cases break the monotony of a yellowed wall, with a photograph frame containing an image of the major and his family, on top of the right hand one. He has a wife, a little older than him I think and two pretty children, very young. I can't tell if they are girls or boys.

"Ah yes, it's you Atherton, I was expecting you. Stand at ease man." He beams a broad smile and seems to be in a great mood, very upbeat.

"When you were here last, I told you that it was only a matter of time before Miss Borowska was arrested and I'm delighted to tell you that she has indeed now been detained. I wanted to tell you immediately as I know you'll be as delighted as I am by this splendid news."

My heart sinks, black despair creeping into my soul, brought about by this wonderful news. There could hardly be any worse news. But it's important to remain British and maintain a stiff upper lip throughout. He expects me to be pleased and it would be unpatriotic to express what I feel.

"Yes, sir."

"As you'd expect, she has been charged with the murder of Major Breck and will stand trial for her crime. That trial will take place at Acre gaol next month and you will have the privilege to be the main witness in that trial. I know we can rely on you to see that justice is done to Major Breck's memory and to ensure that she is hanged, just as she deserves."

This is even worse. I felt terrible for reporting her; I never wanted any harm to come to her and always believed she'd get away. I'd actually imagined that she'd be in New York by now, just as she's always wanted and her uncle had been trying to arrange.

"Thank you, sir. It's wonderful news."

"Yes indeed, wonderful. You can return to the camp now, man. But don't worry, the prosecuting counsel will *definitely* be in touch very soon."

I trudge back downstairs and straight out of the building, at speed, not noticing anyone or anything on my way out. Thoughts of Hetty have filled my consciousness and there's no room for anything else.

Major McAllan's
office, KDH

Aug 24th 1946

I knock and am called into the room. McAllan is in deep conversation with another, even taller, officer and I just catch the end of their exchange. This officer, who I don't recognise, is speaking loudly. They both make a point of ignoring me and continue as though I wasn't there.

"…our military assessments conclude that the Hagenah is capable of forcing that solution on the Arabs, if there was no British presence. And it'd need a much larger British presence than we have now, if we were to try to force an Arab state on the Jews by military means."

Then McAllan turns to me. "You can stand at ease, Atherton. This is Colonel Beresford, who is the prosecuting counsel in the military tribunal which will try Miss Borowska on the charge of conspiracy to murder Major Breck. I have lent him my office for the purpose of briefing you."

He turns to address his colleague, "And obviously this is the man we talked about, Colonel."

"Thank you, Major McAllan."

He turns to look at me. "I'm sure you're aware of the main points of the case, Private: we know for certain, given the intelligence reports now in our possession, that Hesta Borowksa has operated for some time as a member and agent of the Irgun. Unfortunately, we cannot use much of the intelligence information as evidence, it would expose our sources and place the lives of our operatives in immediate and severe danger. Their position would be recognised quickly and they'd then be promptly murdered."

"I'm sure Driver Atherton will be a great help to you, Colonel. I'll withdraw and leave you to your conversation."

Major McAllan salutes the Colonel, who returns his salute, before turning and leaving the room. The Colonel smiles as he turns to look at me, an aristocrat's smile. Rather I think, like a mediaeval Lord, about to address one of his peasants. He is certainly the officer sort: extremely tall and slim, well-groomed and with a plummy accent. I guess he's from that Eton, Oxford and the Guards line. His uniform is grander, even than Major's, with smoothly woven cloth and sharp creases. His slender, angular nose seems to have a special bit of red tint matching the patches on his lapels and I wonder if he might have a bit of a sniffle developing since he seems to be raising his nose.

"Right, Private Atherton. Let's start," he said rapidly in a business-like tone, verging on impatience.

"Obviously we're very much relying on your evidence. But before we start about Hester Borowska, what do you know about the Irgun itself?"

"I understand they're a Jewish terrorist organisation, they've undertaken a campaign of anti-British terrorism and were probably behind the bombing of King David Hotel, sir."

"Yes. Yes, indeed."

The Major stands up and paces the room, he picks up a swagger stick that had been lying on the dark wood of McAllan's mahogany desk and slaps his thigh with a robust thwack. His eyes dart around the room, but he rarely looks at me. When he does it is just for a fraction of a second.

"We all believe; actually, we know, that to be true. Irgun Zvai Leumi has carried out a series of brutal and unprovoked attacks on Arab and British people. They are a thoroughly nasty bunch of criminals lead by a devious thug named Menachem Begin and even other Jewish organisations condemn them. We need to stop them, for the sake of every one living here, Arab, Jew or Brit. That's a big part of my job as prosecutor and that's why I'm determined to see this woman hanged, whatever it takes."

"I see, sir. So, what's going to happen at the trial?"

The pacing stops, the swagger stick is laid flat on the desk. The Colonel sits down behind it and stares me straight in the eyes from just below me, as I'm stood "at ease" in front of him. He leans back in his chair and still has a lot to say.

"We are now aware that Miss Borowska has been an operative for some considerable time. Obviously, we were not aware of that at the time she was employed as a receptionist at the hotel. Nor at the time of the bombing.

She was initially engaged in stealing intelligence documents and gaining other intelligence to pass to her fellow criminals. Much of that was recovered when we raided her home and arrested her parents and brother but, of course, the information they contain was already being used by then. Her family members have since been convicted of terrorist related crimes. She was later instructed to befriend British officers and draw them into dangerous places where they could be murdered by Irgun operatives. She may even have committed the murders herself."

"How important is my evidence going to be, sir? I don't feel confident in testifying from a witness box. Actually, I'd prefer not to be involved."

He reacts badly, almost shouting at me. "It's absolutely VITAL, given that we can't use our intelligence evidence. Your testimony, about the things she told you on your motor bike trip back from RAF Qastina will be central to the case."

He jerks forward and his voice reaches a screech." It's your duty as a British soldier to aid her prosecution. She admitted to being part of the murder to you and you need to make sure the court knows that." I can see a bead of sweat appear on his brow and it's all getting very tense. I decide to co-operate as much I can.

"Yes, sir. It was very obvious that she'd been present at his last moments and that they were in some sort of romantic entanglement."

"You'll need to be very clear how you got this information. Was it just the discussion on the pillion?"

"Not quite, I'd also seen them dancing together in terrace garden, next to hotel here. Is that relevant evidence?"

"This is a Military Tribunal, so the rules are a bit different. There will be no judge or jury as you might imagine them in England. Here, there is a president and two other judges, who are all serving officers in the British Army. In this particular case they are all trained lawyers. They can accept any evidence they find relevant. Normal rules of evidence don't apply. What were her exact words that revealed that she was a murderer?"

"She told me that he was very brave at the end."

"Right, so it's obvious that she was present at the end, at his death?"

"Yes. It's obvious to me."

"That's excellent, we both know what she meant when she said those words, just stick to those words and I'll try to ensure they know what they mean. He pauses and goes silent for a moment, then turns back towards me. For the first time, he looks me in the eye. When he speaks it is a different voice, a much softer tone.

"It is, however, just possible that the court might have a little doubt about whether it completely proves she was present and involved at his death. It's just a bit too circumstantial really. Let's hope they do see the meaning of it, but just as a little precaution we might prepare a bit of a fall-back plan."

"A fall-back plan, sir? I'm not sure I know what you mean."

"A bit of reinforcement of the evidence. If I think the court is not totally convinced, I'll add one more question. I'll look you straight in the eye and ask: Did she actually say she was present in the bar when he died? You must answer 'yes', even if you don't actually remember her saying that."

I'm distracted for a moment by Major McAllan looking out at me from his photo in frame on top of bookcase. Is that a disapproving look? Can I really be hearing this? A senior British officer arranging to provide false evidence.

"But I can't say that, she never did say it."

"I hope you're as reliable as Major McAllan has suggested." He looks directly at me in silence for an excruciatingly long time. Like we are both daring the other to say something in the way of concession. And I'm not going to break first. He looks away.

"Well look, I'll try to avoid asking it but we both know she's a ruthless, murdering terrorist and we must ensure a conviction. You just have to say 'yes', that's all, nothing more. I know you understand your duty to your King and country, not to mention your pal who was killed at the bombing of the KDH. He would certainly have wanted her to face justice. Just say it for him. What?

Now, before I forget. Did you also believe that she knew about the bombing of the King David, in advance?"

"Yes sir. She said that whole thing did not go to plan. And that the Irgun did not intend to kill so many people. She certainly knew there'd been a warning and I think she'd expected that."

"Then why was she there herself? I believe she was even injured in the blast."

"Yes, sir. That *is* a bit puzzling but maybe she'd thought the warning would save most people? Maybe she underestimated the size of the blast and thought she was safe in the reception area? But you shouldn't underestimate her, she is a tough woman. I think she is prepared to take any risk for what she believes in. Definitely determined and quite courageous, I think."

"That's enough of that kind of talk, Atherton. I don't want you to sound like you admire or respect her. There's already people suggesting that you were romantically involved with her, which would undermine your credibility as a witness. We all know how she is capable of making men do her bidding and can figure out what she does to achieve it."

This time he looks straight at me with a cold stare, his eyes exuding bitterness and anger. The Colonel suddenly seems to resent my presence and the meeting is tersely and abruptly ended.

"Right. That's enough. You can go back to the camp now, Private Atherton. I'll see you at the trial, make sure you remember everything I've said." His voice is shrill and now he won't look at me at all.

I don't like him. It's Driver Atherton, not Private Atherton, by the way.

ACRE GAOL

AUG 26TH 1946

"The court will stand."

A door opens on the left of a broad, square room with uniform white walls and ceiling and three stony-faced officers enter. They bring up dust from the bare wooden boards by their tramping feet, spoiling their attempt at a dignified entrance. Around the room, armed guards suddenly snap their rifles to "present arms" and remind us how many armed men guard just one small, slender girl. All the windows are barred and beyond them I can see only the dark stone of the outer walls. I look for a way out but they all say one thing: *there is no escape.*

A tall, grey-haired officer stomps to the middle seat and sits, the other two defer to him and take the end seats. He looks up and commands us all to sit, taking care to stay grave. Perhaps even bad-tempered.

"I am Brigadier Whitby and today I will be assisted in the trial of Miss Hetty Borowski by my two distinguished colleges: Major James and Colonel Black."

In the front of the room I can see Hetty, sat beside a grey-haired old man in civilian clothing, the only man in the room not in a British Army uniform. He identifies himself as Avraham Levi, a Jewish lawyer representing Hetty. Or Hesta Karolina Borowksa, as she is described in the court papers.

On the right-hand side is my new friend Colonel Beresford and two Lieutenants who are busy shuffling papers and occasionally muttering something in the Colonel's ear. They give the impression of worker bees, hustling and buzzing around the queen.

The charges are read and then Hetty's companion stands to declare this court to be an illegal gathering of a foreign power occupying the land of Israel against the wishes of its true people. Hetty will refuse to recognise its authority he says and will not plead to charges.

Whitby seems to find it difficult not to yawn at this response. He obviously expects it, thinks it routine and predictable. He nonchalantly rules that the court will treat this as a not guilty plea and hear the evidence. Then moves on rapidly without any other comment.

"Colonel Beresford. Will you make the case for the prosecution, please?"

Beresford stands and looks around the court. Then he drones on for a while, obviously relishing an opportunity to hear his own voice and be the centre of attention. He spells out what he believes has happened in the events leading to Breck's death. He pauses occasionally to stare dramatically at Hetty when he comes to accuse her and damn her as a scheming and evil woman. My skin crawls at these words. Despite everything I know she has done I still admire and respect her, but I'm also horrified by what she did to Breck.

Well, I'm horrified most of the time. The rest of the time I remember what a prick he was. Not as big a prick as Beresford though.

The Colonel continues and slowly heads start to droop around the room, as fewer and fewer people stay concentrated on his long, pre-prepared and increasingly tedious speech delivered in a mono-tone voice. I have to concentrate hard to avoid nodding off. And soon I fail too.

Finally, he moves on to call the first witness, a Captain in Intelligence who explains what he found when he searched the Piastow Hotel, the Borowski's family home. It all sounds very convincing. Lots of documents from the British Army headquarters in the King David Hotel. They could only have got there by being stolen by Hetty; he says.

Levi puts it to the Captain that this as purely speculative and circumstantial. Although Mr and Mrs Borowski, who are the hotel owners, have been charged with possession of the arms and documents, there's no connection with their daughter. If that find included documents stolen from the King David Hotel, where she worked, it is purely a coincidence. There are so many Irgun spies working in that building, he says with a self-satisfied sneer, it could've been any of them.

The tribunal don't answer him, don't move. They all just stare at him with blank faces in a silence which seems to last a long time.

When the Chairman finally nods to Beresford, he introduces me. This is the moment of horror, that I've been dreading. I look around in panic at the doors, but they're all shut fast: *there is no escape.*

Slowly and reluctantly I stand and walk across to the witness stand, mouth the words of the oath without really knowing what I'm saying. I can only see Hetty. She appears calm, far calmer than me. Which of us is on trial?

Wearing a grey suit with a blue blouse and green beads, her hair is tied up neatly in a bun, she looks every inch like a smart business woman. Probably there are women in business in this country, it's not like England. Her eyes meet mine. I look away but then feel compelled to look back at her. She meets my eyes with a firm level gaze, no smile. But there is no escape and they swear me in as a witness.

I want to leave, to refuse to testify but Colonel is already asking me the first question. It's hard to listen, difficult to hear what he says but one thing is clear. *There is still no escape.*

"You are Driver/Mechanic William Atherton?"

"Y-y-yes, sir." I feel terribly self-conscious. Hetty's leaning forward and her bright green eyes are following my every move. And the questions will not get easier.

"I understand that you brought Miss Borowska back from RAF Qastina to Jerusalem on 24th July 1946. Please tell us of the conversation you had with Miss Borowksa then."

"We discussed the attack on the King David Hotel and a receptionist who apparently admired Major Breck. She told me that Major Breck had been her boyfriend and that he had been very brave at the end."

"What did it mean, very brave at the end?"

"I believe it must have meant that she had been present at his death."

"Could that have happened, if she had not been involved in the plot to kill him?"

There's the sound of a table moving and Hetty's companion jumps to his feet. "I object, sir. The Colonel is clearly leading the witness, who cannot possibly know from these words of any involvement."

"I agree. The objection is upheld. Colonel, you will confine yourself to asking open questions."

There is a short pause as Beresford seems to reconsider. He seems to have been thrown by the Court President's ruling.

"I believe I have already established that Miss Borowska admitted to being present at Major Breck's death and that she was directly involved in it. Your witness, Mr Levi."

"How did you hold a conversation on the back of a motorcycle, Mr Atherton?" the little man asks. He is looking through a window as he asks, giving impression that he's not really interested in my answer.

I shrugged my shoulders. "Simple. I spoke to Hetty and she replied."

"Was it easy for you both to hear each other? With the wind

created by the movement of the bike. Surely you must have missed some words."

"Most things were quite clear, maybe an odd word was lost in the breeze. Besides we stopped for a while in a village and chatted there, at some length."

"I see. And did Miss Borowska actually admit to being involved in Major Breck's death?"

"She didn't actually say that, but it was clear that she was there and she'd lured him to the place where he was killed."

"You thought it was clear? What were her actual words?"

"That he was very brave at the end."

"How does that mean she was actually there?"

"How else would she know he was brave?"

"Perhaps because she knew his character. Perhaps because she admired his courage. Perhaps because someone else had told her, Mr Atherton."

He turns to the President of the Court. "Sir, this witness's testimony is of no value. He didn't hear the conversation clearly and he doesn't know what it meant. The only thing he can tell us clearly is that she did not ever admit to being involved in The Major's death."

"I'm inclined to agree. This is all very unconvincing," said the president. "Colonel, do you have anything further evidence to add?"

Beresford stands and turns to me and looks me straight in the eye. "Did she actually say she was present in the bar when he died, Atherton?"

I return his gaze, also straight in the eye and say "No, sir."

For a moment he falters, his jaw seems to sag. Behind him Hetty and Avraham Levi exchange glances, they can hardly conceal their glee. But I give Beresford credit for his recovery, he moves on quickly with a new line of questioning. "Did Miss Borowska tell you anything about the bombing of the King David Hotel, Atherton?"

"She told me that there'd been a warning but the receptionist receiving it didn't tell the manager until too late."

"Is that all she said about the bombing?"

"She said that the Irgun had not intended to kill so many people."

"So, she knew of their intentions in advance?"

The chair shuffles again and Levi makes a further protest against Beresford leading the witness and the president agrees with him again. "Colonel, if this really is your key witness it looks like we're all wasting our time. He clearly can't place Miss Borowska at the scene of the crime. The comments about the bombing just seem like a bit of irrelevant gossip. Anything more to say? Any more witnesses to call."

Beresford glows red, hesitates and then shakes his head.

"I'll allow you an adjournment if you think it'll allow you to reconsider or clarify the evidence."

Yet another scraping of furniture signals a new objection from Mr Levi as he gains his feet. "You can't assist the prosecution, Brigadier. That will expose your own bias and that of this Tribunal."

The Brigadier is visibly irritated and raises his voice. For first time, he seems very animated with the defence counsel. "I can allow anything I choose, Mr Levi. And I'm very tired of your allegations about the legitimacy of this Tribunal. A short time in a cell for contempt of court might be a very good thing for you. You can't claim not to recognise the court and still expect a representative's privileges. An adjournment in the interests of clarifying the evidence is certainly in the interest of justice.

Now, do you want an adjournment, Beresford?"

Beresford looks at me and hesitates before he speaks, "No sir, I don't think it will change our case."

"Case dismissed then. Miss Borowska, you are free to leave."

A smile develops behind those green eyes. Hetty nods at me before she gets up, the briefest of glances, then leaves the room alongside Mr Levi. I stare at her all the way but there is not a backward glance from her. She closes the door and is gone. *Hetty has escaped.*

The three tribunal members stand and leave too, the Brigadier saying, "Come on chaps we can get an early lunch, never thought we'd be out so soon on this one."

The only people left are Colonel Beresford, his two lieutenants and myself. He is staring hard at me and looking very angry, very angry indeed. He suddenly produced that damn swagger stick and smashes it down on the table. He'd obviously been hiding it somewhere but now his pretence at being moderate and well-balanced slips. "Fuck you, Atherton. You spineless, useless, little worm. I should've guessed you'd bugger it up. And you look so bloody pleased about it too. You're in bed with that little whore, in one way or another."

"And fuck you too, Colonel. I always thought you'd cock it up with your devious and deceitful ways. They've always told me that I can never tell an officer to fuck off but I'll make an exception in your case."

I salute him stiffly and march out of room, following Hetty's example. I'm escaping too.

King David Hotel
Army camp

Sept 9th 1946

I wake to find the morning quiet and warm, as if the city never had any other weather than this calm summer. The song birds are competing with each other to sweeten the air. Beyond the wall the sound of Arab children playing in the grounds of the YMCA, carry through the atmosphere, adding a delicious seasoning to a world in harmony with itself.

The peace lasts just a moment before the great interruption commences as the band of the Irish Guards enters the town with a loud but distant fanfare before breaking into a rousing rendition of "The British Grenadiers". The breeze carries it to me in brief bursts with a few punctuating pauses.

It is an abrupt interruption to my reflections on the injustices of life in the British Army. The deep bruises on my leg, caused by the Sergeant tripping me as I arrived at Kishle stayed with me for just a week or two but have now healed. That kick has, however, remained with me as a burning grievance long after the bruises disappeared. It holds a special place in my list of wrongs, somehow larger than its real importance. I'll remember that man's face as long as I live.

Then there's Colonel Beresford and his petty, nasty complaints. Bastard! Inevitably, I was summoned to meet Major McAllan, who had given me a real hard time about swearing, being insubordinate to a superior officer.

*

He'd started the meeting in a strange way because, after saying that he'd be disciplining me for insubordination, he allowed me to sit. That's not normal, they usually keep you standing at attention, make you feel uncomfortable and at a disadvantage. He had two written witness statements from the two lieutenants who'd been present at the tribunal hearing and he handed them to me to read. They're from the officers Beresford had accompanying him. So, I was surprised that both say that Beresford had sworn at me first.

"These officers are telling the truth, sir. And they both say that Beresford provoked the situation by swearing at me. I think they're trying to point out to you that he was to blame rather than me."

"I can see there's some problem with the way he spoke to you but you should never be telling an officer to fuck off. It's a matter of respect for the rank and the social order of the British Army."

"Respect should not be taken for granted, it has to be earned, Sir. Beresford lost my respect when he told me to lie to court."

McAllan looked down at his desk and was silent for a moment. He swallowed. "All right, I can see that was a problem to you. In fact, a problem for the whole case against Borowska. It's not so surprising that it collapsed."

"I couldn't lie to Court."

"Yeah, you've made your case. But it doesn't change the fact that a terrorist murderer has escaped justice. Justice has been denied by your testimony and you can be sure this will always remain a black mark on you. No one in Authority here will ever forget this. Any chance of a promotion or an award for your efforts can be forgotten now."

"I hope they also remember that the case would never have been brought if I hadn't found out what was happening. A whole terrorist cell, including her family, were stopped. Hetty would still be taking secrets out of this building and you wouldn't even know about it."

"OK, well that's a fair point, but you still spoiled everything for yourself."

"And my reward for that was to be locked up in a filthy flea pit of a cell for a night."

He looked up at me, perhaps detecting an edge of bitterness in my voice.

"Don't get sorry for yourself and lippy, that's not how soldiers behave. A stiff upper lip, that's the British way."

There's a short silence as I can't agree with him, but know I'm not allowed to argue. Especially, when I'm facing a charge of insubordination.

"I suppose the Military Police were a bit harsh when they imprisoned you overnight at Kishle but they had good reason to check out the facts. No doubt there are plenty of people in the British army who believe in summary justice and think that if a few innocent people suffer along the way it's a price worth paying. But I don't think like that, my soldiers deserve fair treatment. I've already written to my superiors pointing out that the officer in this case was responsible for maintaining discipline, yet he started the bad language."

An interesting insight into how higher echelons operate. He'd communicated to some one sitting in the same building by writing him a letter, rather than by walking up a floor to talk to him.

"Even if you consider that I was insubordinate at the very end of the case Beresford had given me good reason."

"I certainly do consider that you were insubordinate but that's enough on the subject, Atherton. I'm taking no action. You may go and I hope never to discuss this with you ever again."

And with that I'm dismissed and he looks down at his

papers, with excessive attention. He seems very unhappy and uncomfortable. I'm not arguing though, it could have ended a lot worse for me.

Most of the officers here know that Beresford got himself into a mess with way he conducted his case. He could have got a conviction if he'd pressed the theft of Government papers. But he only thought about the murder charge as that's what would have got her hanged. I believe his attempts to blame me caused him to look even worse in the end. But that belief is based on a few nods and winks from Major McAllan. I don't really know. Outside his office McAllan is still maintaining a cold silence. No officer wants to be seen to criticise another officer in front of "the men".

Most of the guys in the tents seem to know about what happened in Acre, though I've told no one anything. Word is out that Beresford is no longer in Palestine. It seems he has been re-posted to India. I believe there's a lot of work there for a lawyer at present. It's certainly a place receiving a lot of attention in the news. His aggressive means of getting a "right" result might be more appreciated and accepted in Bombay.

My Major had to be seen to discipline me though and he's put on my record that I'd been given additional punishment duties for a fortnight. In fact, he never enforced any extra duties at all. He's a good man who believes in fair play. He just can't admit that to his fellow officers.

I feel like I'm in a sort of spiritual prison in the minds of our officers for a crime that I didn't commit. Someone that could be guilty, should be guilty of something, because blame must lie somewhere. It's the same attitude as the Military Police at Kishle. There's a suspicion that I've somehow done something bad, though there's no evidence for anything. They just know I liked Hetty. They hate what she did to Breck but as they can't get at her anymore, so I'm the best target they have.

There's no change in our general circumstances; a total lack of any news about our de-mob. It's now well over a year since the war

I had volunteered to fight ended. I'm left imprisoned in a never ending half war, that's not really started and that therefore can't really end.

*

The marching tunes reverberating around the whole of the old city bring me back to the present and also bring out lots of bearded Rabbis and long robed Imams to see what's happening. Our soldiers are good musicians, the band of the Irish Guards, they're bloody good. And so, they should be.

Every one of us knows the story of their war, we've been talking of nothing else since we heard they were coming. They had to tell us, to explain why so many of the comrades I've been with for the past year are being moved out of the camp to accommodate the new comers. They've spent the last seven years bashing up and down parade grounds in Pune, Bangalore and Calcutta, practising their marching and playing music. Officially, they were kept in reserve to provide a final defence of India if the Japanese ever reached there. Of course, no Japanese ever made it anywhere near them. This is a bunch of full-time professional soldiers that has managed to spend whole of World War Two avoiding any fighting. Most will have ten or even twenty years' service all across the old Empire and will have travelled the world, though obviously they know India best. Full time, long term, professional soldiers who've never seen a moment action throughout the largest conflict the world has ever seen. Yet they may well look down on us, a motley assembly of scruffy volunteers and conscripts.

At the front of the band is a short, stocky, muscular Sergeant-Major. He looks well fed and is dressed in a red jacket covered in a fantasy of gold braid, black trousers with a red stripe and a tall busby with a blue plume, pulled right down onto his eyes. He's throwing his mace high into the air, twisting and spinning it wildly before catching it. It's a magnificently skilful performance in perfect rhythm with the rousing beat of the drums and stirring blare of trombones and pipes. There's something about his extra confident manner that somehow spills over the line into arrogance.

The musicians' uniforms are impeccable; bright red jackets with gold piping and white webbing, black trousers and tall black busbies, each also with that blue plume. A gold shamrock infilled with green enamel shines brightly from their collars. The bass drummer has a magnificently glowing tiger skin stretched over his shoulders and across his front. The kettle drummers rattling the rhythm, then lifting their sticks in between, level with their noses like a lengthy moustache.

They've made a long procession through the centre of the Old City and across to our base at the Hotel; proud, professional soldiers, every one of them, marching through narrow streets and past exotic, old stone buildings. The traders part to allow them through and the whole town stops to stare in amazement. It's difficult to imagine what the Arabs make of this display. Their faces show total confusion. It's difficult not to laugh at their confusion but I succeed for almost a minute. No one notices me or anything I do, I'm not part of the display. I like it that way.

This market always covers the whole street and nowt can part the crowds, nowt can silence the constant buzz of conversation and argument, rattle and clatter of goods. Yet today the immoveable traders move aside to let the band pass down the centre of the street. All activity stops while they gawp at the spectacle, lining streets in silence on either side, as the band passes noisily onwards.

It's dramatic, it's rousing and it's a feast for the eyes. The most exciting thing to happen in central Jerusalem for months. No one has ever made a more dramatic entrance. But the blank looks on the Arab's face raise the only question that matters: *what the fuck is this all about?*

A rag tag parade of the tattered soldiers already here greets them in silence. We're all wearing grubby shirts, dusty shorts, with tired old boots and socks at half mast, every man folding his arms and standing with legs parts. A few are wearing their berets but most have shoved them under an epaulet on their shirt, an untidy bundle in an awkward place. We, now feeling like untrained, unclean and amateurs, line the way in silent greeting as these splendid fulltime soldiers make their spectacular and grandiose arrival.

None of us are impressed. Why should we be? We may have no musical talent but we *are* veterans of D-Day, we *have* fought our way across Europe to the steps of Berlin before we came here to contain terrorists. We've taken casualties at every point, we've all lost good friends and brave fighters and so we have our own views on what real soldiers are, who are real men, and who'd look better in a box of tin soldiers.

When the band halts and stops playing their men fall out and busy themselves in occupying a new array of clean, new and dazzlingly white tents, just a little further down the lawn from our own old, grey, dusty ones. None of us welcomes or even looks at them. We all keep our distance and our silence.

There's no means of avoiding them though, as they soon appear among us in the canteen. They seem a friendly bunch and want to chat. They have so many questions to ask. What've we been doing here? Where've we been before? What's it like in Palestine? Who are the Arabs and what are the Jews like? Is there good beer and food? And especially, what are local girls like?

One of them comes to shake my hand. "Good to meet you guys. I hear you're doing a great job in the worst of circumstances with all these terrorists about." It's the Sergeant-Major and incredibly for an Irish Guard, he actually does have an Irish accent.

"Fran Mulhearn," he introduces himself," from West Belfast."

"I'm Billy Atherton, from Lancashire."

Close up and without his mace, he seems nervous, not arrogant all. He has red blotches all around his neck and marking his face. I've heard that this can be a sign of anxiety, and it might well be in his case. He finds it difficult to look me in the eye. I know that West

Belfast is a Catholic area, so we have a connection immediately. I instantly know this about him, he may not know that we have the same religion. I've not found an instant liking for him, but certainly have a bit more sympathy.

"Yes, mate." I take my hand back and retreat to a far corner of our NAAFI with a cup of tea and a cigarette. The Guards are trying hard and two groups do not mix that badly for a while. Although they're grating on our nerves the peace holds. In fact, it's almost half an hour before the first fight breaks out. But that starts several more. I heard something said loudly about parade ground soldiers; another thing about scruffy urchins. Something nastier about cocky Paddies, an angry response about arrogant English bastards. And then it's all in for a full-scale brawl involving around fifty men.

It doesn't bode well. We're not going to get on well with the musical soldiers.

I exchange glances with the Sergeant-Major, sat at the next table, who rolls his eyes, and looks away to continue reading his book. I don't have a book, so I've no excuse for not writing to Joe. I still owe him a reply. I've been too busy doing stuff. Just can't remember what stuff it was right now.

*

Another sunny afternoon passes, another day with not much to do except wait for an order to drive back across the desert to Ismailia with yet another supply run. I've completed around ten of these trips now and not enjoyed any of them. At least there's been no repetition of the dysentery incident. They'd warned me that it might well re-occur.

I've been summoned to see a Captain Smith; someone I've never heard of. We all seem to be being called, in alphabetical order, to see him in a private room in the Army Pay Office next to the Jerusalem YMCA. A place I've never been invited to before.

This seems a funny thing and I anticipate trouble. Visits to officers have usually meant trouble.

This Smith bloke greets me in a friendly way, a suspiciously friendly way, and invites me to take a seat alongside him before launching into his spiel. "Now that the Irish Guards are here, you are no longer needed in Palestine. You're listed to be demobbed, Driver Atherton."

He pauses for a moment, amused by looking into my eyes, enjoying the amazement that he can see. I think my mouth might be open. Then he smiles.

"Here is your travel warrants for the passage home. You're travelling from Haifa to Toulon on the HMT Georgic, leaving on Monday, September 16th 1946. Then on by rail onto Paris, Calais and Aldershot where you'll be actually demobbed."

He stands up and shakes my hand vigorously. "Congratulations, on behalf of King George and His Majesty's Government I thank you for your loyal war service and wish you good luck in civilian life."

The Irish Guards have rescued me, God bless them, for the fine body of splendid men that they undoubtedly are. I love every one of them and wish them well. I hope they will enjoy their time in Palestine as much as I have but that they will stay here much, much longer. They deserve that.

It's all over. I'm going home, actually going home at long last.

An image of Joe's face appears and the prospect of going home no longer feels quite such a happy one.

Monday in Haifa

16th Sept 1946

It's a strange feeling to be lurching around in the back of a lorry; I've always expected to be driving. Now, having been driven down from Jerusalem by one of the Irish Guardsmen, I've arrived at Haifa docks along with Dicky Cox, Kenny Hindley and all of our boys. I've seen my old Bedford for the last time and have let it go without a pang of regret.

Going home is all I've wanted since I arrived. I'll get to spend time with my Mum, get to know Celi and Betty again and enjoy my time with my Dad, now we're friends again. Oh, and I'll see Joe too.

This lorry trip reminds me of the many long drives across the Sharon desert. Another time I wasn't in the driver's seat. I think of the early morning raids on Jewish houses in the old city too.

It was difficult to walk past a certain BSA M20 as I left, the best memory of my entire time in Palestine. Moving this bike on roads to Qastina and the sway of our bodies on it. Hot bodies, clinging together. Though even that memory is tinged with a sour taste. I wonder where she is now, what she's doing? Does she remember me? Stupid question, I know I've never even crossed her mind.

The sack in my hands holds the whole of my life. All clothes I have and everything else I possess, all stuffed into a single kit bag. I started with very little and I've now got even less. But it's here, with me now. This is all my life has added up to so far, unless the memories of dead pals are worth something.

Of all the strange feelings the weirdest is being without a rifle, taken away for the first time since 1942, and I guess I'll never have one ever again. Being without a gun seems unfamiliar, reminding me of a new vulnerability but perhaps it's a good thing to be without a gun? It won't be needed any more once we're out of Palestinian waters.

We're dumped off the lorry, abandoned at the side of a dock. Our impatient driver leaves immediately and without ceremony, our last contact with Jerusalem disappearing out of the dock gates in a plume of dust. Then he goes around the corner and is lost to sight. The supervisor runs across to hustle us into a little out of the way space, so we won't obstruct the workings of the harbour. We're hiding in a patch of shade under the outer wall. Some men formed a card school and played for pennies all day. I've only got a few shillings left and I'm keen to keep them.

The old white stone docks stand out in stark contrast to the deep blue of the water and the paler hue of a vast open sky, from which an impossibly bright sun is pouring searing heat onto anyone caught out in the open. This dockside holds a few old cranes, not really man enough to handle the work that's waiting for them and they need a lot of attention to keep them going. Men in white overalls are running from one to the other, carrying bags of spanners and oil cans. Always shouting loudly, with or at each other.

Everywhere there is movement and everyone seems to have a job to do and knows where to go, what to do. It reminds me of bustling Liverpool, though much smaller, much hotter and a great deal dustier. My small group of soldiers without rifles, newly arrived and confused are different. There's no place for them in my memory of Liverpool.

We just sit still in our grubby, little refuge. Requests for information are greeted either by Arabic blank looks or foul abuse in English. We're expected to know where and what our place is without any communication and without interrupting any of the busy workers.

Beneath my feet, amid the grime of the dock flooring, a large beetle is hunting. A glorious blue green sheen on its shell. I remember another beetle with a similar blue green sheen from another place, another time. A memory that makes me shudder, a place I'd rather forget. I crush the beetle beneath my boot.

Two long jetties made from blackened, steel beams define a central area to this port. Beyond them is much older seawall, in familiar white stone, that stretches along the coast to a narrow entrance to Haifa port and then to the open sea beyond. Moored alongside the left-hand quay is HMT Georgic, that name plainly visible in white letters against its darker hull. A low, regular and entirely grey hull, with groups of life boats hanging from its side, clustered tightly around a single funnel. A pleasing and elegant vessel with a huge red flag falling from its stern and rippling in the soft, hot breeze. Georgic is a large vessel as I'd expect for an Ocean liner but a great deal smaller and less fancy than the Mauretania II which I saw passing through Ismailia. I'd have much preferred that, playing deck quoits with some pretty ladies in elegant dresses.

Behind us and beyond the port area is the city itself, stretching across a low range of hills that border its coast. Most buildings seem modern and the road network is laid out along straight lines parallel to the coast. A grand white building with a long flight of red steps and a red dome stands out midway up the hill, no doubt a shrine to some important local dignitary. It's surrounded by the only patch of greenery visible, mostly decorative palm trees. We know from the earlier part of our journey that this appearance of grand modernity is not the whole story. There are large areas of older, humbler buildings on the outskirts of town, where the Arab population have their homes. Those are less grand.

We're within sight of Georgic but not wanted anywhere near it. We're just cargo to be stored somewhere, so we can be loaded quickly when our time comes. They'd have preferred it if we had come boxed up in neat wooden crates. Best to be out of sight and especially out of the hot sun. Further groups of soldiers keep coming all day and are also parked around and then outside the docks, wherever they can be put without restricting dock work or obstructing vehicles. There's no longer any shade left for the newcomers who must just bake in the sun.

While the loading of vessels continues, no one takes any interest in us, we're left alone. But finally, the cranes stand still and the drivers who brought goods to be loaded can all drive away. Any labourers left on the quay look around, to find that they too are in need of shade, though none is now available. The Arab workers seem to have their own place to disappear into but the British dockers who were supervising their work, jostle to join us in the shade of the dock wall.

The sailors on Georgic are waving, apparently beckoning us on board. But our Dock supervisor is angry if we move, even to stretch aching limbs. A tall, gaunt man with brown leathered skin that speaks of too many years exposed to the Haifa sun. He wears a blue overall with a small gold badge sown onto its lapel to tells us he is in charge.

"Can't you men sit still? There's enough to worry about, without you gerrin' in the way all the time."

Cargo is supposed to remain in its place before it's loaded. At least until the crates of oranges lying around the dock are all craned into the hold of the MV Per Johannsson, which will carry them to Europe. Copenhagen, I guess, since that's where it's registered.

But when the job's complete he seems to mellow and is much more inclined to chat, the stress that was his distinctive hallmark has disappeared from his eyes. He wears a glistening sheen of sweat as a badge of honour, since it distinguishes him from us soldiers, who've spent the afternoon hiding in the shade, fighting off mosquitoes and playing cards.

"You blokes going home, are you? I guess your war is finally finished."

He starts a conversation with me, in which we compare our experiences since 1939. I've seen a lot more countries than he has and a great deal more combat. As a competition to see who's got involved in the most historic moment it doesn't last long. He has to acknowledge that he can't beat D-day or Belsen. Maybe not the bombing of the King David Hotel either. Anyway, I'm very happy to shut up and listen to his tales instead. I don't want to remember any of those occasions.

He's seen an enormous number of bedraggled and bewildered refugees coming in through this port in the past ten years but the rate has really increased recently. So many of the War's most pathetic victims. The refugee ships that have come here were incredibly overcrowded, there is rarely insufficient water or food, sanitary facilities are always wholly inadequate. Many have sunk at sea before they even got here, with the loss of everyone on board. My new pal has a lot of sympathy with the Jews and has little time for either the Arabs or Ernest Bevin.

The worst event and perhaps the most dramatic, he'd experienced was the Patria incident which took place right here in November 1940 behind the dock where our Danish friends are now moored. Two ships, the Milos and Pacific, both carrying illegal immigrants had been guided into Haifa by the Royal Navy, and their passengers were being transferred to the Patria, with the intention of shipping them on to the Mauritius. Suddenly an enormous explosion had ripped a hole in the ship's hull, causing it to sink in a matter of minutes. Many of the refugees were rescued by British and Arab boats but it killed 267 people, mostly Jews, but also a few of the British crew, and injured hundreds more. It turned out that this was a bomb planted by Zionist terrorists, intended to assist the refugees stay in Palestine by immobilising the ship's engine. They weren't that clever in their use of explosives back then but they've learnt a lot more since, they've had a lot of practise.

Bizarrely and ridiculously, the Irgun had blamed the British for their brutal, criminal and incompetent actions. The same sort of bloody ridiculous nonsense we'd heard in respect of their terrorist action at the King David. On that occasion the Haganah had ridiculed the attempts to shift the blame, as it was carried out by a different Zionist group. There's always some else to blame and the Brits are the soft option in Palestine.

Having told me his story the Dock supervisor turns to me. "Now I've told you my story. It's your turn, no more excuses. I want to know about what it was like in Normandy."

"I never speak about it; those things are best forgotten. Especially those landings on the beach."

"Yeah, I can imagine they are painful memories. Forget the landings then and tell me about what happened next. A battle for the town of Caen I think."

I remember Caen well, too well. All of those memories come flooding back, uninvited.

*

I was bounced out of troubled sleep by an intense noise and peered out of my cab to see a flight of single-engine planes pass overhead. The aggressive roar of aero engines diminished as they passed through the sun, low to the east. They were attacking Caen with rockets launched from under their wings. First time I'd seen this; there's always new methods of destruction in a war.

I looked around, aware of snipers; those hidden eyes which follow every movement with the intention of killing me. I could die at any moment and many did. Remember Jack.

The crump of shells exploding nearby rocked my trusty Bedford. I was hit with the jarring effect of the shock waves, throwing me to the ground. More bruises, blast it. The Germans in the woods couldn't see us and were probably sending over the occasional shot to disturb us. Shells seemed to land anywhere with no obvious pattern, killing a few more of the black and white speckled cattle so common here. Their corpses littered the fields everywhere in Normandy. That scent of burning cordite and seared flesh drifting on the breeze became familiar.

The seats in the cab of my lorry were a damned uncomfortable bed and gave me a disturbed night. No need, the anxiety alone could have done that; I constantly woke and tried to settle. I was hungry, tired and frightened. There was nothing for breakfast; just a mouthful of water from my can.

The grey walls of the mediaeval town were visible a couple of miles or so away and the Germans were still there, hanging onto the old city. The green of the fields seemed darker than yesterday when we'd arrived off the long narrow road that follows the river up from the coast several miles away. The countryside was mostly rolling hills and fields interrupted by the occasional apple orchard. The rustic charm of the stone-built barns was immense and quite different to anything I've seen in England. If I was here as a tourist I'd have been impressed with Normandy, but this was not the perfect holiday.

The mood in our field was pretty miserable until Sergeant James had a bright idea, no wonder he wore the stripes. A stocky man with a handle bar moustache and two decades of service in the British Army, mostly in India, he had a lot to say and said it loudly. During his time on the sub-continent he seemed to have acquired the look of a bull elephant. With small ears and a red face.

Now he wanted action. He pointed at me and the guys next to me: Jim and Bertie.

"Right you three plonkers, take your lorries and get back to the beachhead to pick up supplies. First priority is petrol, after that food. We've enough ammo here to fight three wars, we're just going to starve to death."

He reminded me of my brother; always pushing me around. Why should I have taken orders from this fat bastard? Jim and Bertie had already scrambled for their vehicles but I wasn't moving.

I strode over to the Sergeant and stood in front of him staring eyeball to eyeball. Of course, I was smaller than him but just as aggressive. Nothing was said.

Then I remembered why I should take orders from him. I couldn't defy a sergeant in war time, not even an ugly one. So, I turned away, leaving the bastard in confusion, strode quickly over to my vehicle and drove off in the direction of the coast. We were off. No breakfast; no chance to wash; no cheery good wishes from the Sergeant. Obviously, we had no maps and little idea where to go.

The road was being shelled steadily but inaccurately from a low ridge in the wood on the far side of this little river. They were landing in a field beside the road, throwing up plumes of smoke and soil. I went past that point at some speed, bumping over the potholed road. The two blokes behind me seemed keen to keep up as well, so much of the journey was completed rapidly. The story I'd been told before we set off about Panzer tanks counter attacking encouraged me to get as far away as possible, as quick as possible.

I passed through a lot of evidence of battle, smashed and abandoned tanks and guns. Encouragingly they all seemed to be German. 'Achtung Minen' skull and cross bone signs leant on their sides or lay on the ground.

Eventually I found the tanks that I'd been warned about, but they're heading towards Caen. We'd expected the Panzers to be pushing towards the coast to attack the landing beaches. I slowed right down, considering a U-turn. Maybe I was going the wrong way? Maybe I was going straight into the German lines? Without a map who can tell?

By now they were near enough for me to see that they were not Panzers but a group of Cromwells trundling up along the lane to reinforce our group at Caen. Maybe we were winning the bloody war after all? Who could tell?

Just along the road I came to a cross roads and slowed down. Red capped MPs were frantically marshalling the traffic. One waving vigorously, pistol in hand, to get us through. I arrived at the

T-junction at the same time as a Canadian armoured car, crossing in front of me. A different MP had been waving him through too.

Braking late and swerving I almost miss him but still caught the back of his vehicle, spinning it onto its roof and into the ditch beyond the lane. I braked, stopped, looked in horror. There were going to be casualties in that car. A vein throbbed in my forehead.

The Police were looking at the front of my truck. Apparently, there's not much damage to my vehicle. They wave me on, shouting "Get going. You're blocking the frigging road. There's no time for stopping and staring; don't you know there's a bloody war on."

"What about the poor sods in that car?"

"Bugger off, it's up to us to sort 'em out."

"But surely, they need help, they're going to be hurt and I did it. I 'ave to help."

"You can help them by getting out of the bloody way. Do your own job."

"Where can we get the supplies then?"

"There's a dump just north of Bayeux. That way. Drive."

So, I did. Behind me the MPs were waving their pistols at Jim and Bertie. They got through the junction too. The MP's were very committed to waving people through. Everything had to happen quickly. At any price.

*

The Quartermaster at the supply base near Bayeux was the most important man in Normandy, he told me so himself. He decided who got what and anyone who argued with him got bugger all. The yard was a frenzy of activity. Petrol fumes filled the air and there was a constant noise of machinery and chatter. Lorries coming up from the beach appeared all of the time, bringing in supplies, but there even more were waiting to load. Cases and cans piled up all over, as a hundred men in khaki loaded, unloaded, stacked or just moved around for no obvious reason. They all looked busy.

This depot was already established but the place wasn't secure and an occasional shell fell nearby. Everyone knew the Germans were close but the Royal Navy was just offshore and could fire over our heads into German positions. There was a steady series of reminders as we heard shells whistling above us to land a few miles away with an occasional spectacular flash, boom and then a tremor shook the ground. Occasionally we could see the dark shapes passing over us. Bonfire night had nothing to compare with this.

Although he was fierce and under pressure, the Quartermaster was a good guy and listened to us. We came from the front and got priority to fill with petrol. There were several extra jerry cans too. Then he let us load up with individual 24-hour ration boxes. The prize items were tins of spam and bars of chocolate. You couldn't get these at home. We also managed to get hold of a case of Senior Service cigs, much better than the Woodbines we normally got. After that he told us to bugger off, we'd pushed our luck as far as it could go.

I was pretty happy to bugger off, knowing I'd be greeted like a returning hero at camp. A mile along the road though I pulled up against the roadside onto a side track, near a small village. The others followed so we could open up the cases, taking two of the 24-hour boxes each. We didn't move again until we have eaten everything in the first and thrown away the case. The second got hidden in the cab for emergencies along with my share of the cigs.

An old lady appeared, walking out from a barn outside the hamlet. She shuffled along to look towards a shattered house, not much more than a pile of rubble. She didn't look at all happy and comes across to tell Bertie in broken English.

"You Anglais. What are you doing here, causing all this trouble? You 'ave broken my 'ouse. Why do you need make your war here? Allez, allez! Vite, vite!" She waves her hands at us, trying to wave us off.

Bertie laughs. "You silly old crone, we've liberated you."

"Well stop it. Stop it now. We don't want to be liberated. Here was no trouble with the Allemands. They were very polite peoples, no bombing, no 'ouses burnt."

"Tough shit, you're being bloody liberated, whether you like it or not."

She glowed red, turning with a grunt, to the barn where a group of small children had appeared. She fussed them back inside like a brooding hen with her chicks and was gone.

Suddenly I remembered the road accident and the anxiety hit me. I started to shake and sniffle. Or maybe it was a reaction to what had happened yesterday on the beach. I felt very queasy and instantly sat down on the floor, legs apart, head drooping. Both my mates put their arms around me, dragged me up.

"That bloody collision with the Canadians. What were those dick'ead MPs doing?"

"We saw everything that happened mate, there's no way you could've avoided that, it's the police who caused the whole frigging thing. They're pumped up to get everyone through fast and don't take any care. I bet there's ten bloody accidents a day there with those buggers."

"Yeah, guess you're right. I couldn't have done anything differently."

"Make sure you slow down when we go back, 'ave a look at what's on the cross roads no matter how much they wave you through."

After a smoke I was ready to go, no one got long to recover in Normandy. This time I let Bertie go ahead. He could struggle along without a map.

The return journey was slower and calmer. When we got back to Caen a swarm of soldiers appeared, the rations were unloaded within a few minutes. They went rapidly out of sight and then everyone disappeared again. I wasn't a returning hero, no one even said thanks.

*

For much of the day I was occupied in driving back and to. Down to Ouistreham, and then returning to Caen, my lorry full of newly arrived soldiers. Troops were still coming ashore where we come up the previous day. I got a weird bunch of new arrivals, a particularly noisy and colourful of men in skirts. The 51st Highland Division, the Black Watch, were keen to demonstrate what they didn't wear under their kilts. So, this passes as humour in Scotland?

When I finally returned to our field near to Caen there was a new Army around us. It included the Cromwells that frightened us on the road to Bayeux. The 7th Armoured Division, better known as the Desert Rats, so naturally Normandy greeted their arrival from the desert with another shower of rain. They were all gathering for an attack on Caen, our first major target in France.

Our field was a tiny haven of peace surrounded by the sounds, sights and smells of war. Everywhere around us we could hear cannon and rifle fire. I could see a lot of the action as I looked towards Caen. Smoke was drifting across from a village beside the river in the valley just north of the city. I could see panzers firing on our infantry, who must have been taking heavy casualties. Houses jumped around in a shower of bricks and tiles as explosions ripped them apart.

Then the air was shattered by the thunder of aircraft engines overhead, a group of USAAF Flying Fortresses aimed at the point I was watching. The whole village was suddenly torn asunder by a line of huge blooms of fire and smoke, a devastating new level of destruction. Even here, a couple of miles away, I was deafened by the blast. Panzer tanks flew through the air and landed at crazy angles. The village our infantry was defending had disappeared. Friend and foe alike were just gone; to be replaced by a mass of smoke, dust and flame. Lone bricks continued to fall around me for several seconds.

None of it felt real, I'd no feelings for the dying men. Just relief that it didn't affect me.

The aircraft turned away, task completed, reached the clouds and were lost. The sound of engines was lost too in another wave of artillery fire. What the hell was happening to me? I didn't know what to feel any more. I'd watched thousands of men die but felt nothing, just numb. Was it really happening, or was it just a game to watch from a hillside?

The memory of Jack's death came back. He mattered. The accident with the armoured car came back to me. That mattered. I started to tremble again and knew I should be dead already. I really should have felt frightened but somehow, I'd lost the ability to be afraid.

Looking away from Caen there was another confused and confusing war. The tanks of the Desert Rats were pulling out and going back along the road they'd come along. I'd no idea why. It took twenty minutes for them to pass; then I saw the last of them disappear from sight.

From up here I could see Sergeant James inspecting the front of my lorry, his trunk sniffing around the dented grill. His ears looked even tinier; they'd shrunk into the side of his head. This was not a good sign. Damage from the accident was superficial but very obvious. The radiator and bumper looked as though they'd been twisted to the left, scratches all over them. He turned, could obviously see me and strode purposely towards me, his huge feet pounding the earth.

"Hey you, Atherton. What the bloody hell have you done with my lorry? I gave you that to look after and now look at the damn thing. What kind of care is that, your horrible little man?"

There was a minor accident Sarge. No one's fault."

"No one's fault! No one's bloody fault? It's your fault, you moron; you were driving it."

"The redcaps waved me through. I went into the junction under their guidance. They got it wrong, and tried to get us all through too fast. That's how I hit the Canadians. Bertie and Jim saw it all."

"Oh, they did, did they? And will they tell me this isn't your lorry, the one given to *you* to look after? Actually, it's not bloody yours, it belongs to the King; he left you in charge of it and anything that happens to it is your responsibility. Don't give me this horseshit about not your fault. You're on a charge, Private Atherton. See the Captain later."

He turned and strode away, shoulders set back, his chest stuck out and his arms swinging in an exaggerated military march.

The drone of yet more aero engines announced the arrival of a second wave of Flying Fortresses. These targeted the town itself, running directly over the ancient castle, dropping sticks of bombs into the old town. The ancient stone masons would have been proud of their work if they could have seen how it withstood modern bombs. The castle seems impervious and the thunderous explosions only chip pieces off its stubborn walls which fall into the tangle of masonry which was once the homes of the citizens.

I wanted to see the castle and the town crumble, as easily as the village had. I wanted the enemy to be destroyed and to see our side win. Quickly and easily; but it was not happening like that. Those stupid bloody masons. This was going to be a long war.

No one had anything to eat and the Sergeant had another bright idea. He points at me and the guys next to me, Jim and Bertie.

"Right you 'orrible lot. Off you go, back to the supply depot and no bloody damage to my lorries this time. Not you Atherton, you're seeing the Captain." A happy smile crosses his scarlet face.

"But what about my witnesses? You're sending 'em to Bayeux."

"Bollocks to witnesses, you little oik. You damaged that lorry. You're guilty as charged. Go and see the Captain, NOW."

The sergeant smiled as he politely pushed me into the tent where I saw a very bored Captain. He cut my story short. He didn't say if I am guilty or not, just decided I'll dig latrines for the next five days. As I left the tent, Sergeant James was sat outside, looking across from his bivouac and gave me a cheery wave. He loved this and made quite a pantomime of it. He must have intended to continue this for some time.

There was the rising scream of an incoming shell and the explosion threw me onto my back. Flame and soil were flung about around in equal measures in a blue-black flash. I was half buried this time; smoke filled my lungs and stung my eyes. It took minutes to scramble the earth away, frantically digging with my hands, so I could haul my battered body away from the pile of smoking earth. The mud sticking to my body, had a strange red tint to it.

Just for an instant my brother Joe's face appeared in the smoke and mist but when it cleared there was just a crater. No trace of Joe, the Sergeant or his tent.

I never did dig any latrines, no one ever mentioned it again.

*

The Dock Supervisor stares at me. A worried look on his face.

I guess I must have some kind of dreamy vacant look on my face as I remembered all of those incidents. Maybe I got too agitated as I explained it. Either way, it seems to have disturbed him, he must think I'm some kind of loony.

He stands up, says a quick good bye and goes off as fast as he can. I take a deep breath and sit back against the wall, looking past the Georgic, away into the open sea.

*

The completion of dock work, which gave my new ex-friend the chance to chat, has also made it possible for us to board the Georgic. The process of embarkation has begun for several thousand tatty and exhausted soldiers waiting around the dock area, each with a single kit bag over his shoulder.

We're formed up in neat ranks in the bright sunlight, before being allowed on the ship. A large formation of men, several thousand strong. We shuffle forward, slowly but relentlessly, the front line being peeled off in turn. I can see it getting nearer to my turn. I walk through the steel rails embracing the wooden stairway and onto the ship via a tiny hatch in the side. I can take my place on board the liner, arriving in a claustrophobic hallway, with staircases up and down. Ken and I, inseparable now, are sent down into the lower decks. It takes hours and everyone waits impatiently, grumbling all the while. We take consolation in complaining about the stupidity and incompetence of officers.

The heat of the day is starting to moderate and despite the delays our mood is now noticeably upbeat. No more worries about Jewish gunmen, no further concerns on Arab gangsters. My time in this place is finished, thank God.

Goodbye Holy Land, it really is time to leave.

HMT Georgic

Sept 16th 1946

Slowly the gap between the Georgic and the jetty opens up. First a tiny glimpse of dark, muddy water but then great swirls of water as the hull of the Georgic edges away from the jetty. More sideways movement than forwards until a throaty rumble signals the next stage and we start to produce a small bow wave as we surge forward. Then, much more smoothly, we gather speed towards the narrow harbour exit.

"We're on our way home, Kenny." We both look away from the side of the ship, to see lights of Haifa sliding away behind us into the dark of the night.

What do yer think of this posh boat then, mate?"

"I like the cabin, loads better than the tent we've been living in for the last year. The canteen is nicer too. Best of it is we're on our way home."

"Yeah, I'm surprised we get beds, thought it'd just be a hammock." Our beds on board consist of iron bed frames, one on top and one below, and canvas is stretched across these iron frames to form each bed.

"Four to a cabin is all right too, not too crowded. The worst thing about it is the bloody engine noise, we must be right on top of it. That tannoy system that keeps everyone informed is really annoying. The opening words never vary, 'D'yer hear there, d'yer hear there.'"

"Depends who yer've got in wiv yer, though. There's a load of guys down the corridor who're just trying to get as much beer down their necks as they can, in the shortest time possible. They could be well be trouble tonight."

"I'm not too fond of the shitty out of tune croaking, burrat least it's all been good humoured so far."

"Yeah, no point in trying to sleep fer another hour or two, let's go and gerra cup of tea in the canteen. Keep out the way until they pass out."

The warm breeze kisses our cheeks and then, as the ship reaches the breakwater, the first movement in the water causing the deck to surge up and lift us momentarily before dropping us softly into the next lifting wave. I think about being on our way home, the thing I've been longing for over the last eighteen months. I see Joe's face and the prospect of going home doesn't feel so comfortable.

The ship accelerates as it reaches the open sea and the engine noise increases. Even the gulls sound excited, maybe they're going home too.

*

A bored waiter directs us to the tea urn, full of dark brown, stewed tea that we pour for ourselves. His service is only for the Officers. The tea tastes like rusty nails mixed with sour cabbage water, perhaps a delicate hint of diesel too. Even the condensed milk can't disguise it. He's happy to chat though, telling us all about the ship. I think he's made this speech a few times, sounds like it's been well-rehearsed.

"The Georgic was the last ship built for the White Star line before it got taken over by Cunard. She was completed in Belfast in

1931. She's already had an eventful war, as we were totally trashed out in 1941 in Egypt, after an attack by German bombers. There was a blast in a store of ammunition, smashing up the stern. The ship settled at the bottom of the shallow water and was left to burn out. They patched her up later, managed to refloat her and got her to India for emergency repairs.

In January, 1943 she left Bombay for Belfast for a complete refit. And after December 1944, her exterior was altered considerably, with the forward funnel removed and foremast shortened to a stump. Georgic resumed service as a troop transport, carrying out military duties around the Middle East and India."

Not sure any of that makes me feel better. Let's hope they fixed it properly.

The time passes slowly. Very little to do and the noise from the drunkards below decks is getting worse. Time to stroll around the decks, Haifa is just a glow of orange light on the horizon now. Further along the coast more lights mark the position of larger towns. Maybe Tel Aviv? Maybe places I've never even heard of? Out at sea red, green and white lights twinkle as solitary markers of ships passing us in the night.

The boat rocks gently from side to side but also forwards and back. The waves seem larger now we're in deep ocean. When we reach the stern, we can look down we can see the propellers, as they occasionally lift clear of the water before plunging back under. The sound of ch-ch-ch-ch-ch when the rear of the boat lifts to reveal the turning prop, changes to wer-wer-wer-wer-wer when the blades go back down under the water churning it into a white froth.

The two props stir up a swirling mass of water, pushing against itself to wriggle away from the blades. Two long white lines stretch away from the stern towards the horizon, maybe even to the horizon perhaps beyond, pointing back to Palestine. That country has been my whole life in the past year or so, but I'll never see it again. I strain to see it beyond the edge of the earth. There's nothing there.

I expect to see something that represents it, that says what the country is. It should be loud explosions and smoke, rifle cracks with bullets zinging and ricocheting. But there's none of that. Instead I can see Fido. Then Fido and Chalky. Looking at me. No expressions on their faces, just looking at me. I've no idea what they want to say, what they want to express. But it makes me feels bad, a sick feeling in my stomach.

If I look back at my life to see what I've done that's worth doing, what I've had that's worth owning it doesn't seem to add upto much for a thirty-year-old man. All I own is in my kitbag, washed out clothes, mostly old underwear, a shaver and a badly frayed toothbrush.

The best thing I've ever "owned" was the friendship of those guys. It was precious, vibrant and wonderful, valuable beyond measure and it's gone. I lost it. It was my job to look after them and I failed. I look back at those guys to see them again, one last time and there's nothing there. I guess that's what I got left now. Nothing.

Who am I? When I first left England that question was easy. "I'm Billy Atherton." But now that answer is not enough. Who is Billy Atherton, what is he, what has he achieved? And I have no answer, my identity started to die with Jack, on the beach at Lion sur Mer and I suppose it finally expired with Fido, in the tunnel at the KDH.

Where can I find Billy Atherton now? Is there any Billy left out there? Is this a new one? Perhaps it's just the body, the empty shell of the old one while his soul has stayed behind, beyond the horizon, at the other end of those two white lines. And what does the future hold for Billy? When I try to imagine that I'm looking into a void. No images come to me, just a huge blank emptiness. I feel afraid.

Eventually the drunken row, from downstairs, declines to a constant mutter and only now do I realise that it's been noisy all the time. Some of them have been playing cards all night with the hammocks swinging over their heads and they're carrying on. I take to my bed and sleep an exhausted but deeply unsatisfying sleep.

*

In the morning there's very little to do after breakfast, except drink more tea and wait while the ship ploughs westwards towards Toulon. The sky remains blue and sunny, the never changing sea stretches out before us, behind us and to all sides. It has few features, save an occasional distance vessel, heading in the opposite direction.

The officers organise a boat drill after breakfast, in case of an emergency. They have us jog marching around the decks and announce that we'll be doing this twice a day until we arrive in France. It must be amusing for them! After that there's just sunbathing, that's the most popular pastime, now the beer's run out. There are prone, red bodies of toasted soldiers all over the place.

Somewhere north of Alexandria

Early morning, Sept 17th 1946

It is hot, hot and hotter in here. Unnaturally and strangely hot, my body is streaming with sweat and my skin tingling. There is a noise, like low conversation or insects, perhaps a bluebottle banging its head against the window pane trying to get out. It's as hot as Hell. I'd expected the temperature to fall during the night, but I seem to have set on fire. My skin is burning and bubbling, the sweat dripping down my face and rolling down my back. My head aches as though a man with a hammer is pounding the inside of my skull. And my knees ache. Most of all my intestines are bubbling and gurgling.

I can just about stagger to the latrines before it starts. As bad as before and just as painful but this time I can't blame the pies. First the diarrhoea, then I retch. Vivid colours, orange and yellow, soft and slimy. It oozes from my body, taking my strength with it. I sit there for hours. Well, it seems like hours, as the internal tempest blows itself out, noisily and messily. Until there's nowt left inside me. Then there's that horrid smell infecting every bit of my nostrils.

I try to drink water from the tap but I can't take much of it. It tastes salty.

Afterwards I stumble through claustrophobic corridors and then crawl along the splintered boarding towards my bunk. There is no daylight here, only the nicotine-stained glow of a naked bulb. No one passing me in the walkways seems concerned, they think I'm either drunk or seasick. And there are many others who are seasick. They get no sympathy either, just laughter.

Everything is painted grey.

Did I mention that it's hot?

Once in my bed I try to rest, sleep it off, but no sleep comes. I'm too hot and too restless to find any peace. I'm weak and my body seems not only sweaty but weirdly slimy, wrapped in the sticky blanket. Then there's still that smell, maybe not quite so strong now.

Although the door hasn't opened, a beautiful lady, dressed in the uniform of a receptionist at the King David Hotel, looks down at me. How did she get in here? I recognise that white blouse and black skirt and her black hair. It's wonderful to hear that soft, lilting voice again.

"Hello, soldier."

"Hello, Hetty."

"You remember my name, that's nice. What's yours?"

"Billy. And I'm very pleased to see you." I say, fully aware that my grin and the glow in my cheeks have already given her a clue about my reaction. I try to look into her eyes rather than at the sublime body. But it isn't Hetty after all, it's Ava Gardner, the real Ava Gardner. A true film star has come here to meet me, all the way from Hollywood. Looking at me and talking to me. But not for long. She's impatient and takes my hand to pull me up. Her tiny hands are now much larger, so strong that I cannot resist her and the delicate, feminine fingers now have become hooks instead of the polished nails I remember from the gardens of King David.

"Come on Billy, I'm taking you out." Ava says, using Hetty's voice. These actresses are wonderfully convincing, I could easily believe it is Hetty.

She pulls me through the door of the cabin and out onto

the busy streets of Jerusalem. The sudden emergence into bright sunlight dazzles my eyes. We're hurrying along past the stalls of the street market. I spot my brother, Joe, buying some dates from an Arab trader and turn to greet him. But Ava tugs me back impatiently. Joe looks towards me and smiles, a knowing smile, as though he knows what is happening to me and approves of it. I think I heard a chortle.

"What are we doing here Ava? I thought you'd be in New York by now."

"Why are you calling me Ava when you know my name is Hetty, don't you know it's very annoying when someone forgets your name, soldier. It's as though you don't think I'm important enough to be worth the effort."

"Sorry, Hetty. I'll get it right now."

"Come on soldier. We don't have time to dawdle." She sounds very like Hetty but much more driven, no patience at all. Just bustle.

And she takes me towards a bar on the Cotton Merchant's Market, running up the hill near the Blue Mosque. Just near the spot where Chalky died. The man walking down the hill towards me looks like him, exactly like. And he smiles at me too, Chalky's familiar grin, as he recognises me and he comes over to take my hand.

"Good to see you, Billy."

I want to chat with him, find out what's he's been doing since he died, but Hetty knows what we must do and that we must do it straight away. She plunges into a small, grubby bar towing me with her. The interior is dark and smells of old food, musty and yet still sweet and spicy. She does not hesitate in this tiny room and goes straight through thin, dirty curtains with a faded red and orange pattern, which brush easily aside, into the private area at the back of the building. An even darker room with brown stained walls, just a bedraggled cloth hanging in the one window.

And here's another familiar friendly face. It's Jeno, sitting on one of the four mahogany chairs and dressed as an Arab. He is nervily spinning a Webley revolver on the table in front of him. It rumbles as he turns the wobbly Webley, the heavy metal of its cartridge cylinder rasping irregularly against the wood.

Of course, he recognises me instantly and jumps to his feet. His face is one big, glorious smile, his bright blue eyes lighting up the room with the brilliance. And he stands, his arms open wide to give me a huge hug.

"Ah! Hello Mister Billy. I been wait you come. Nice see you at here. We still the big friends, aren't we? You helped me so much in the Germany, saved my life, set me free. I been travelling since then and I now the fight to free my country."

Despite the incidents at Rafiah and Kishle he's the pal I left behind in Germany once more. I forgive him for shooting at me, kicking and punching me and feel the same affection for him as at Belsen. I give him that big hug but he reacts very badly to it and pushes me away, down into one of the chairs. I feel exhausted after the dash through the town and need the rest.

"What happened to you? You all horrid, slimy and stinky? Get away from me."

He pushes me away and brushes down his garments, smearing the slime further across his clothes and looks confused. I try not to laugh.

Ava shouts at him. No, it isn't Ava any more. Now it's definitely Hetty and she looks very agitated. A red flush on her cheeks and her arms waving wildly in the air.

"Come on Jeno, get on with it. We don't have time for this. If you're not quick the British soldiers will realise he's gone. I've been arrested and been put on trial once before because of this bastard, I'm not going through that again. Just shoot him now and finish it."

Jeno picks up the gun and points it towards my head. I try to stand to take it off him but my legs are too weak and I fall back into the seat. Hetty laughs. I turn to look at her.

"But I helped you, allowed you to escape the court, Hetty. I helped you too, at Belsen, Jeno. Why are you planning to kill me?"

"Friendship and gratitude don't matter, my duty to my country comes above everything. All British soldiers must die or go home and play tennis."

"But it's the British who allowed the Jewish people to come here and protected you from the Arabs who wanted to kill you. Anyway, I'm going home, I'm on the ship."

"You stop Jewish people coming to Israel where we belong. You should have gone home before and left this holy land to God's chosen people. And you didn't go, so now we must kill you." And with those words my friend Jeno looks me in the eyes and raises the pistol to my head. A steely look, that incorporates dull blue eyes and tight lips, has taken him over. His eyes are dull and blank as though he's hypnotised and doesn't recognise me anymore. His finger tightens on the trigger and his blue eyes stare directly at me, manic and uncontrolled.

I see the danger and make a run for it. Dashing for the door but a small, stainless-steel spoon, marked SHEFFIELD STEEL gets caught up in the laces of my shoes and I sprawl headlong into the next room. I find myself lying in darkness on the floor of a cool room. It is the cell at Kishle prison. Mohammed al-Husseini is looking down on me, one eye looking directly at me and the other looking over my shoulder, perhaps to see if Jeno is following.

"Ah! Meester Billy, you want heestory. I bring you heestory." And he directs my attention, with his outstretched arm to a very large and muscular Roman Centurion looming over me from his side. Behind the Centurion I hear the crunch of another 99 Roman soldiers all marching on the spot. Then they all start to march forward towards me.

But I'm not waiting for them. In a flash I'm off again but fall over in the darkness of the cell. A flight of B 17 Flying Fortresses drone past, very low, dropping a cluster of Hershey chocolate bars onto Margaux's mother who is grabbing all she can. Then she turns to throw the chocolate bars at my head, shouting "kurt, kurt, kurt".

Two hands grip my arms, another two grip my legs as I'm hauled out of my bunk and a loud voice I've never heard before invades my hearing. I can just see it's a man with a grey beard wearing a grubby naval uniform of some sort through sweat that's pouring down my face and filling my eyes. It is so hot; my eyes are boiling over.

"Get the dirty little beggar on the stretcher and don't touch anything. Don't touch nuffink, or else make sure you wash it off. Wash yourself completely using disinfectant, including all your clothes."

And I'm lying, confused and bruised, on a stretcher being carried away down the walkways inside the HMT Georgic. Neither Ava Gardner nor Hetty Borowska are here anymore. Maybe Jeno is but, if so, he's hidden away, perhaps frightened off by the bulky stretcher carriers who are bouncing me towards… towards… well, somewhere. I don't know where they will take me. I just know they are making a point of hitting the walls as often as they can on their way through the many doorways, all painted grey.

And it is still very hot.

The journey is surprisingly long, several miles I would say. No wonder they eventually slow down and bang the stretcher a little less against the narrow, metal walls. All of it in silence, no one has anything to say; only heavy breathing.

We arrive somewhere and then stop. My stretcher is put on the floor as they open the door and they enter slowly and cautiously, though with a final bump of the stretcher against the doorway. It seems to be a small hospital ward. Or maybe a mortuary, since the whole room is filled with the corpses of German soldiers in their Wehrmacht uniforms, their hands wired behind their backs and a single gunshot wound on the right side of their foreheads. And they're all lying on bales of bloodstained hay, a bit curious for a hospital ward.

No one else seems to notice them but it's immediately obvious that no one is eating boiled eggs. Not one, not a single boiled egg in sight. That really tells you something, doesn't it? Clearly, my carriers know all about that and they move smartly past the Germans as though it's quite normal to have a room full of dead boys wearing grey. They have a point. Grey is certainly normal on this ship. I think they're consciously ignoring the bodies, pretending not to notice them, as they take me through another, even smaller door into a tiny room at the back.

The white beard speaks loudly to his companion. "He can be left in isolation here; we'll all be safer. Now get back to his bedding and dump it into the sea. Then get out of those clothes and get washed as quick as you can. We're all at risk of infection from the bug right now."

The steel door clangs tightly behind them, locking with a dull thud and leaving me alone, lying on a new bunk. Cleaner at the moment. And the tiny room is entirely grey, pale grey though, not as dark the German uniforms, which are the greyest grey ever. Maybe that's why they've locked me in here, to keep the Germans out? That would be a good thing but it's still really hot in here, a prickly heat that runs all over my skin, needs more ventilation.

At least it has its own latrine for me to sit for an hour or two as my body drains out. There's a sink with a for washing your hands. Some drinking water too. It's luxurious, everything I need, except something to cool me down. I try pouring water over my head but that doesn't work well.

Then the door opens and a snowman enters. It's really quite surprising to see a snowman in this heat but then it's been a funny sort of a day altogether.

"Hello, I'm Doctor Richardson. Billy, isn't it? Let's see what we can do to make you more comfortable."

Slowly he comes into focus through my boiling eyes and he's not a real snowman at all. No carrot for his nose, no coal for his eyes and no funny hat. He's more like a doctor dressed in white gown and trousers. With white gloves and a white hat, only his eyes uncovered, except that he even wears plastic goggles over them. He's even carrying a syringe. I suppose it must be some sort of game they play to keep themselves entertained during a long voyage. Good to see they've got a sense of fun.

Jack, Chalky and Fido will be happy to join in with some snowballs when they arrive. It can't be long now before they get here.

The lights are going out. Who turned the lights out?

And it feels really hot.

Somewhere near Crete

Sept 20th 1946

The medical staff have been wonderfully caring. They risk infection every time they enter my little cell to look after me. I've had several doses of penicillin and some salts and they're constantly pressing me to drink water. It seems to be working. Less time sat on the khazi and even a little bit of normal, dreamless sleep. The sweats have become less frequent and the ache in my knees has declined there, though it has now moved into my elbows. But the grey walls have moved closer and this room has become even smaller.

Chalky and Fido came last night and they brought Jack with them too. So nice to see them all again, I've seen nowt at all of any of them since they died. They all seem to be in good form and looking well, straight of limb, true of eye, steady and aglow. It seems that they are not growing old, as we that are left grow old. Surprisingly, none of them blame me for their deaths at all. On the downside, none of them have gone to Heaven yet. Apparently, there's been a mix up in their transfer papers and they're going to have to wait it out for a while. They seem confident that they will be going up rather than down though, as soon as they have their rail warrants.

I suggested that they join with us and go to Aldershot for their demob but that didn't seem to go down well. None of them are expecting a demob. Not now, not ever. They'll be a part of the British Army for ever.

Soon I'm fit enough to join Kenny for a walk around the decks. He's my only pal, a lot of other men have started to regard me as a bit of a loony and some are happy to tell me so. They have good reason to think I'm not functioning as well as I should. And maybe it is my fault.

The sea breeze ripples our hair softly as we stroll around the promenade deck, rips up the white horses, riding over the sea on either side. A full circuit around the ship six times gets our temperature up and it's already a warm day. And then we sit on one of the benches and stare out to sea.

I offer Kenny the 239th Senior Service, take the 240th for myself and throw away the last packet. Ken produces a box of Bryant and May matches and we light up.

"Do you have any plans for when you get home, Ken."

"Yes. I've got a couple of options. I can go back to working down the pit or I can go work for my brother in his pub in Tyldesley."

"Wow! That's so close to me. I thought you were from Manchester."

"Well, the family home is in Eccles and I was a miner at Agecroft but Jim moved to Tyldesley when he bought the Cart and Horses."

"How did you get into the Army then. I thought mining was a reserved occupation."

"I volunteered in May 1942."

"Wow, that's amazing. I joined in July '42. Just at the point the war started to turn in our favour, Monty had just won the Battle of El Alamein. My folks thought I was mad though, had no chance of getting though alive. But you joined earlier, when we'd had nothing but defeat after defeat."

"Well, that was sort of the point. It was desperate then. We seemed to have no chance of stopping the Germans but someone had to go and try. Even if it had all been in vain, at least I'd have died knowing I'd done all I could. My country needed me."

"You're a brave man, Ken Hindley. I admire your strength of mind."

"You too, Billy. It was hardly any different, just a few months later."

"Thanks, pal. At least there was some glimmer of hope in July. Do you regret it now, or do you still think it was the right thing to do?"

"I regret a whole lotta things about the war, but not joining up. I still know that I had to do my bit."

"I think that too. But I have regrets, mostly I regret going to Palestine. That was shit."

Kenny smiled. "Yeah, I can see why you think that."

"So, what will you do now, Bill?"

"I dunno, Ken. That's my big problem. I don't have any job to go back to."

A lovely, pleasant day on the Mediterranean Sea, just the way I'd imagined it would be all the way from Haifa to Toulon. Is this the start of peaceful times, or is it just the calm before the storm?

Toulon

Sept 22nd 1946

In the pale half-light, just before dawn, a faint smudge appears on the northern horizon. It describes the limit of the Mediterranean Sea, like a long straight line drawn by a very hard pencil. Maybe a 4H, the faintest of greys. But as the times passes and the light gets stronger it transforms into an HB line and soon that becomes a firm 2B. We're approaching Europe, closer to home. Still far from home but a degree or two less foreign than Palestine.

In the gentle breeze a shifting sea leaves the ship uncertain whether to pitch left or right, so it tentatively tries first one and then the other. The caramel shades of the decking heave, compress my legs, start to move my ankles towards my knees and then drop them. The last of the night's breeze chills my face. Everything is motion; steady, regular and normal.

As we approach, a red light is winking at us from the sea, then joined by a sister green one. The Georgic passes between the siblings and the rows of red brothers and green sisters stretch ahead of us, showing us the way in. Orange daylight illuminates a dark green sea contrasting with a pale blue sky, Picasso would have been delighted. We approach a hilly, mostly white land with many patches of dark green across it. A few buildings huddle low against the hillside, pretty white houses with red tiled rooves in isolated groups. I'm surprised, I expected a large city.

We pass a large chalky headland and spot a rugged, hilly coast that was previously hidden, passing into a large sheltered inner bay. And as we enter, bright sunshine comes through, lighting and warming it, as though to welcome us. It feels good but it is not home. Just a less threatening foreign land.

The roar of the engines dies away, making me notice that there'd been a roar. Immediately behind the boat the white-water calms and the two white lines that stretch to the horizon drop away, first a flurry of bubbles, then just a line of swirling water. Those white lines were my final link back to Palestine and have now detached from the ship. When I look up, over the horizon to the east, there are no faces looking at me anymore. I've seen the last of Fido and Chalky and the feeling of relief is swiftly followed by overwhelming shame. I've survived the war and left my friends behind in a foreign grave.

The morning must be getting late as Kenny appears to stand alongside me on the deck, offers me a cig and we both smoke our way into Europe. No words, just a nod and then our movement is synchronised into comradeship, as we both leave over the rail. I look tentatively towards Ken. He's alive. One of my pals is coming home with me.

The rugged, hilly coast gives way to a naval military complex, which encompasses a vast part of town, a city within a city, stretching some eight miles west along the harbour front. This is more like my expectation. A number of small naval vessels, complete with red, white and blue tricolours, are moored up and a host of men in naval uniforms, move along the dockside. But the Georgic ignores the naval base, carries on, not slowing, not arriving and apparently still with somewhere to go.

We're easing into the port, past the wreckage of several ships that still show above the surface. Whatever wrecked them also blew up several of the cranes on the dockside. They still stand in ruins, although new cranes are running alongside them.

I can look beyond the water now, north into the mainland, towards Central and even Northern France. I remember my last arrival in France, in Normandy, where I left Jack lying on the beach. As I look towards the horizon the little grey fluffy clouds seem to look back at me, the top of Jack's head appearing among them, peeping over the horizon.

A moment passes. Maybe two.

This is strange, Kenny is grabbing at me, looking down at me, holding me tight. He looks very alarmed, agitated. Something seems to have frightened him.

"Don't worry Mate. I've got you; it's going to be all right, you'll be fine."

But he's wrong, it isn't fine. My chest is heaving as I gasp for air. I'm lying on the deck, despite not having moved here. It's all strange and confusing.

Worst of all there's a group of guys gathered around me, staring and looking confused and well, sad. Most of all they're curious and asking Kenny what's wrong with me. Very sensibly he ignores them. Less sensibly, he sticks his face right into mine and stares into my eyes.

"Don't cry Billy, it'll all be OK. No need to cry."

I pull away from him, shocked. First at his intrusion into my personal space, secondly at his bad breath and body odour. His brown eyes peer straight into mine from close range and I can examine the tiny stubble rising from his neck through his short back and sides. Then as I realise what he is saying, I'm a bit confused. No, not confused; indignant. What is he saying about me? I don't cry, I never cry, I'm a soldier and soldiers don't cry. I decided that long ago.

"No worries mate, it's all right, it's fine for a man to cry, they say it's good for you."

I'm not crying. Why can't he see that? Doesn't he know how bloody annoying he's become?

"Don't be daft, Kenny. I'm not crying. That's bloody ridiculous."

I ignore him. Turn away and maintain a dignified silence, trying to stop the spasms that are passing through my chest and wiping away the wetness that has inexplicably appeared around my eyes and run across my cheeks. This is all pretty weird.

I stand up, Kenny and a few of the soldiers, helping me towards a swaying upright position. I've drawn quite a crowd of gawping, open mouthed men. Bet they don't know how stupid they look from down here. I resist the urge to shout at them. Keep quiet, just wriggling enough to get back on my feet.

"OK guys. I'm fine now. Thanks for your help."

I stagger off awkwardly down the deck, sweeping along a curved line, Kenny struggling along behind, still trying to offer me a hand. I'm still ignoring him.

Over to the right of the boat Jack's face is now fully visible above the horizon, he's watching me in silent rebuke and must have seen everything. I guess he's satisfied to see my discomfort, retribution for leaving his body on the beach and driving off, never to return. I didn't even go to his funeral. If there even was one.

Beneath me the quay has drawn close up to the side of the ship, now just creeping along and it's clear we'll hit it if we don't stop soon. We do stop and we're in France, ready for the next step and I just wanna get off. The ship is in port, the voyage has ended, let me off. For God's sake, let me off! I've had enough of this friggin' boat.

*

The ship's passengers are silent but trembling with anticipation, a muddled, expectant mass of shaking khaki. We've responded to the call to gather at our muster stations. Ours is inside the saloon, a dull place with brown décor, a bar that sold no beer, an orchestra pit where no music was played and a dance floor that wasn't danced on. I wonder who designed this. He was optimistic about the end of a war that has dragged on for years but some day he may prove right and this space will be used for the amusement of the wealthy cruise passengers he intended it for. For now, it is fitted out with rows of crudely worked benches and long tables where we've eaten our meals. Will the privileged upper classes also get to sample the delights of corned beef hash, spam fritters and whale steaks? I've eaten every scrap that's been put in front of me but it's never been enough.

I'm so tired, need to rest before any action, no matter how slow. I sit back on a green leather couch, heavily stained into an interesting patchwork of black, green and brown with spilt beer or tea. It looks familiar. It's the seat from the George and Dragon in Leigh where I last sat with Don.

I'll soon be back there. Maybe with Don. I might become a draughtsman at Callender's Cables alongside him. My Dad got him that job, so he must be able to get me in that Company too. But maybe not. Old Joseph Atherton is not a fraction of the man he once was and he's no longer a Grand Knight. Don may have used up the last of the privileges and favours he could dispense in his days of glory.

So, what does await me when I get home? No job, no money and nothing to do or look forward to. I might have Don as my pal, but last time we met I was pissed off with him. He's had a bad war and if our visit to Liverpool is anything to go by, he's picked up some pretty nasty attitudes too. I didn't like him anymore.

And Leigh itself? I used to be really proud to belong to my little town and its lively people. But compared with Jerusalem, Hannover and Antwerp, it's not the most exciting. Mile upon mile of cotton mills, coal mines and terraced houses. And Lancashire weather as well. Do I want to go back to spend the rest of my life in dark cloud and rain? Really?

The voice of a smiling, confident Sergeant Cox cuts through the depressing thoughts as he addresses his men in his usual uppity manner.

"Right, you 'orrible lot. Listen up, this is what's gonna happen." He holds up a bunch of brown paper docs in his right hand.

"Rail warrants for the Froggy railway, all the way to Paris and then on to Dover. Then another lot to Aldershot where you'll get your lovely demob suit. If you're really lucky, some of you might even get one the right size. OK, just kidding, no one will get that lucky.

I've got the docs, so you need to stay with me or they'll probably guillotine the lot of you. Yer heads may be ugly but you're better off keeping them on yer shoulders. Make sure you got everything; we're never coming back. Now, everybody ready?"

Coxy looks around, to be greeted by the sullen silence of an unsmiling squad of weary, uncertain soldiers. His cheerful manner has found no admirers, and certainly no imitators, this morning. Quite right too, I bloody hate cheerful people.

"Right then," he said happily, "We're off. Pick up yer kitbags and follow me."

*

Emerging from the side of the ship into bright sunlight leaves me dazed. The gangplank sways vigorously under the tramp of hobnailed boots. It's a pleasure to get onto land until I find that it seems to be moving. My sea legs can't cope with solid ground.

Coxy forms his platoon up in ranks behind the other platoons and off we go, quick marching into this strange unfamiliar town. The Georgic is behind us now. I hope whoever's at the front knows where we're going.

As we go towards the dock gates, we pass a large group of British troops. They're slouching around, rifles across their shoulders, in the shade of the black walls of the port of Toulon and seem to be waiting for something. They must be getting onto the Georgic. The realisation dawns on me that we're leaving Palestine to go home, but for someone else the nightmare is just about to begin. They look as though they know.

The depressed, miserable looks on their faces is almost enough to cheer me up, as we turn our backs on them and go off towards a distant smear of acrid black smoke rising from a white tiled building into a blue, cloudless sky. Its pungent smell already reaching us in the soft, warm breeze. It has to be the railway station.

Onwards.

GARE DE LYON, PARIS

24TH SEPTEMBER 1946

I've arrived in the city of love in the company of thirty dirty, smelly and grumpy English soldiers. One of the world's finest cities but none of them wanna be here, just a passing through place. It may be my imagination, but I think they've marked their arrival by reducing the amount of farting and burping which was such a characteristic of the train journey. Perhaps it's a mark of respect to this gorgeous town.

This is my first sight of it. Despite passing through France in 1944, I'd seen nothing of this famous city. Thank goodness we've finally arrived, at the Gare de Lyon. That was the longest train trip ever, I'd never realised just what a huge country France is. It's big. We left Toulon just after dawn and it's now dark as we complete the journey. Most of us tried to sleep during the day and most failed.

I'd still got the company of Kenny, life is not all bad. "Not long before we're back in Blighty, Billy boy," Ken says with a grin. "It'll be great to get back to civvie street."

"Will it, Ken? I don't know. I don't know anything about what it'll be like. What I remember of civvie life before the war wasn't that great. At least the Army's provided an interesting and changing life and we always got clothed and fed properly. Heaven only knows what lies ahead of us."

"Yeah, but you'll be with your family again."

I think of Joe and flinch.

"Yeah, damn it. That's what worries me most. We've all got along great while we were two thousand miles apart, it was never that happy when we lived together."

The thought of living back at 179 Chapel Street is crap. Lots of time with my Dad, discussing the morality of the methods of the Knights of St Columba, lots of time to chat with Joe about who should be supporting my parents. No doubt they will both be great at telling me how I've got it all wrong. None of that gives me a warm feeling.

Beyond that, no chance of meeting Hetty. That might be a good thing. No chance of meeting a sweet and fascinating young Margaux, if I go home. "If" might be the biggest word.

Thank goodness there was a group of mates together on the train. I'd never have managed alone in a foreign country, few speak any English here. The officers were a big help, for once, as one of them seems to speak very fluent French, and he got us something to eat. Not that it was very good, just some sweet tasting breads and a bottle of water. Funny stuff they eat in this country but at least it's better than the oily yellow paste we had in Jerusalem.

We've clunked our way across hundreds of miles of countryside and then finally through many rows of humble houses with red tiled rooves. So many lush green fields, hundreds of pale brown and white cows and funny conical hills. Everywhere people working the land.

All the way through France thoughts about returning home have haunted me. It's time to make decisions. I can just go home and live with my parents again. A nice safe option but amazingly dull after the excitement and dangers of the past two and a half years. Maybe that's my fate? Doing my duty is the whole story of my life so far, to the Army and to my parents. There's been few brief spells when I've been doing something that I want. The last time I made a really big decision for myself was in July 1942 when I volunteered. Before then, and since, someone else has made all the decisions for me. I've also done the right thing by my parents, sending them all of my wages.

While I've been away, Joe will have taken the opportunity to persuade Dad to change the house will again. Whatever argument I make now will be useless. The only option will be to hold a grudge against Joe for his part in the deception. It's pointless but I already know that's going to happen.

There's been adventure in the past few years but I didn't choose it and enjoyed it even less. Now times are changing, I've left Palestine for ever. The British Army will be a thing of the past. All I have left is a short journey to Aldershot to be demobbed. The life I had before the war has gone too. When the family business went bust my job went with it. What is there to go home for?

Is this the time for a big adventure? The chance to take an outrageous decision. I could search out the one person who has always shown me real affection. A few thoughts occur to me, a crude plan is forming in my head. Do I have the courage to carry it out? Probably not.

Eventually we're passing the grand old buildings of the inner city. I'm pretty impressed with it. A distant glimpse of the Eiffel Tower, it's like being in Blackpool. The only building I recognise; it appears above the black tiled roofs and disappears behind the covered platform as we draw into the station. The other buildings look nearly as fancy as Liverpool did in 1939.

"Right, you 'orrible lot. Every one off the train and form up on the platform."

The huddle of the khaki clad transforms into neat static lines, just as we've done so often before. Coxy leads the way, a comforting figure. A bit of a bighead at times but he's been alongside me for some time and he's helped me a bit. Soon he and all these blokes'll be gone for ever. Will I miss them? Maybe see I'll Kenny, maybe even Coxy but that's it.

On the platform we're hidden by steam and smoke. A big, bright green engine with brass fittings, at the front is still hissing and gurgling as we march along the platform past it, through the barriers and into the main concourse. The stench of burning coal infiltrates nostrils and bites into the back of our throats. Acidic but it's still a good smell, friendly and familiar in a strange and unfamiliar place.

Out in the street the sunshine of the Riviera has given way to grey cloud and drizzle. Astonishingly cool too, I've not felt this cold for a couple of years. Not since the freezing January of 1945 I spent in Molenhoek, following the rapid thrust up from Antwerp. We'd been waiting for the chance to break out across the German plain. Persistent Luftwaffe bombing and the flooded ground had held us up. There was also a story about some big battle the Yanks were fighting over to the east, causing our long wait.

At the front of the station a convoy of lorries are waiting for us, the French gendarmerie are taking us across town. Their drivers say nowt to us, just an occasional grunt or a nod. They're smoking something with a strong smell of roasted camel droppings. Whatever it is, it's not for me!

Our boys file quietly and obediently into the back of these quirky old vehicles. Exhaustion's given way to a quiet thrill of excitement and anticipation. We're on our way home. When the wagons are moving, there's an amazing and fascinating city to see, we only get glimpses of it beyond the canvas cover. Soon the boys are peeling it off and braving the light evening rain. Whether the cover stays on or off, we can always tell that we're travelling over cobbled streets.

At the Gare de Nord we are dumped outside the station under the command of a young and confused 2nd Lieutenant. As soon as we're off the lorries they leave, without a second glance. They disappear into the Parisian traffic. There's a lot of advice for Lieutenant Palmer from the locals, but he's not a French speaker and ignores them. Bleary eyed taxi drivers stare at us for a moment but soon lose interest, just another band of lost souls making their way home after the war. This process is not new to these Froggies but it's completely new to our little band of Tommies though. We're finally nearing the end of a war that's run over its time. Palmer seems to be taking advice from Sergeant Cox, who then points to a sign above one of the platforms and cries out to us.

"Right boys, this way for the train to Calais, then straight on to Blighty!"

Every one streams forward. Everyone except me. I'm at the back, then I'm going off in the opposite direction, to the ticket office. At the window of billeterie I peer in and say my only words of French, the ones I've been practising all the way across the length of the Med. In fact, ever since I acquired the French dictionary and phrase book from the Jerusalem branch of the YMCA.

"Un billet simple a l'Amiens, s'il vous plait, Monsieur."

A firm hand grabs my shoulder.

"Come on Athey, what the bloody hell are you doing? There's a train to catch."

It's my friendly Sergeant, chivvying me along.

"I'm not going home, Coxy. There's nowt for me there. I've got to get to Amiens and see someone I left there in 1944. I just hope she's waiting for me. Either way, I just need to know."

"You know this isn't allowed, its desertion."

"Don't be bloody ridiculous, I've done my stint with the invasion of Europe, and more than my stint with Palestine too. Now the Army is finished with me and it's time I got a bit of life for myself. I'm going and I'm going right now."

I turn back to the ticket clerk. "Quel quai pour Amiens, Monsieur?"

"Nombre huit, Monsieur, il depart a dix minutes."

"Au revoir Coxy, mi owd pal. I'm off to find the bright new tomorrow I've always dreamt of!" He shakes my hand warmly and looks me in the eye. After all this time together and so many adventures, we'll never see each other ever again.

"Say goodbye and good luck to Kenny for me."

Finally, we break the eye contact and hug each for several seconds.

"Bonne chance, mon brave!" Coxy says as he turns his back on me to go back to join the Calais train. And strides away, purposefully.

"Adieu, Coxy, adieu."

179 Chapel Street, Leigh

6th April 1947

Another day, another funeral. I should be an expert in funerals, having attended so many in both Palestine and England. My expertise may have competition though, as funerals have been very popular all through this decade.

Maybe a thousand people gather around the graveside today, my father was well known and widely respected in this parish. They'd turned out in numbers for his funeral a few weeks ago and now they turn out for his widow too. We'd all wondered, as we'd helped my Mum to struggle to Dad's graveside, how long before her turn? We knew it was not going to be long, maybe a year, I remember thinking but it was just a few weeks.

First, we gather at our house, then all go together to St Joe's for the requiem mass at eleven o'clock and out to the cemetery on Manc Road, where our ancestors already lie. The priest wears black vestments with a golden cross to read final prayers before we lower Mum into the ground. The same hole we put our Dad into so recently, his coffin's been exposed by the Council workmen. A dark, deep hole cut into the sodden, green grass in a flat low field lined with poplar trees and an undisturbed view across to Winter

Hill in the mid-distance. A large mound of sodden clay by the side, waiting to return to the earth and cover my mother's grave. The stench of mouldering earth and sad, wet grass fills our nostrils.

Each of us in turn, throw a single white rose into the ground, all coming to rest on top of the coffin. It's unlikely to help her, but I like it. She's with my Dad again now, which might or might not please her.

Looking round at the mourners, I decide that St Joe's has the edge over Palestine for solemnity, especially since the choir turned out for a high mass. The chant of "Requiem Eternam" was particularly rousing, echoing into the high vaulted ceiling and around the many, brightly coloured statues and huge paintings depicting the stations of the cross. The altar, lit with many large candles, had a crucified Jesus dangling on a cross suspended from the ceiling on gilded chains above it. It made me cry, my parents are gone for ever and now we're the last of the Athertons.

This ceremony is quite a contrast to Fido and Chalky's burials at Ramleh. Not just the weather but more the way we're all dressed, no military uniforms, just uniformly black. No groups of hostile youngsters spitting and throwing stones either.

As usual, I've a privileged place, carrying the coffin and afterwards a seat in the front row. I seem to have a close connection with the dead. It's an important landmark and all seven of us are collected to support each other, a unity we never showed while they were alive.

That unity doesn't last long. It thrives in the spring sunshine that covers us for that lingering moment at the graveside, but fades as the clouds returned. We have just that brief moment of silence, with our heads lowered, before the cawing of a group of rooks disturbs our peace and we all look up at the darkening sky. They circle around, searching for the way forward, but never finding it, go sideways.

The moment of calm reflection has passed and we each move back to ordinary life.

*

The reading of the will sees an end to any goodwill, as it was always going to. I know, we all know, that the house is promised to me, but we also all know that Joe campaigned to get Dad to change his mind, to break his promise and leave it in equal portions. Joe has won, he was close enough to stay in my father's ear, while I was far away fulfilling the bargain. Of course, there is only the house which has any value in the will.

The drab old parlour looks as brown and dour as ever and fits my mood perfectly. Through the corners of my eye I notice the glances towards me, occasionally a stare. They are trying to judge my mood, waiting my reaction. I deliberately stay silent, sipping at my tea, looking at no one letting the silence be sufficient. Nash is scratching his nose, Celi is wiping tears from the corners of her eyes. Joe looks happier than he should on such a day, a flicker of a smile playing around the edges of his mouth. Some thoughts are running in his head, perhaps he's taking strength from the company of his wife and daughter or maybe he feels that he's achieved a victory over his upstart younger brother.

This is the second time we have gathered here, with similar thoughts on a similar occasion. We might have been told the content of the will after my Dad's death but maybe the idea never occurred to Mum, or she preferred to delay the moment until she'd gone. She must have known what was in the will and perhaps felt aggrieved. I understood that. It's normal for a widow to inherit the matrimonial home, Dad knew she'd only a short time left.

She'd looked relaxed when she got back here after his burial, wearing her old blue slippers and wrapped in blankets. It was not a calm, happy relaxation more like a collapse into an exhausted sleep. She was with us but we all knew she would not be for much longer.

This room is full of ghosts, memories from my youth and early adulthood, recalled with mixed emotions. Affection for my parents and for Celia, my youngest sister, we were the best of playmates, the great outpouring of joy when I came back here alive, against all of their expectations. First in '45 and then again for Christmas '46, though that second was coloured by confusion and curiosity. Particularly by my late arrival, they knew that I'd been officially demobbed but didn't appear for a week. It was only when I did return, that they found out I'd been in France.

My trip to Amiens was the subject of a lot of questions. Not especially hostile but completely confused. What would have attracted me to such a place? None of us had any contacts with that place, or so they thought.

Perhaps it's a funny thing that I spend so much time thinking of Hetty, when once I'd thought that it would be Margaux who would become my dream girl. Not anymore, not since my visit to Amiens.

A pair of clear blue eyes met mine across the space of the back parlour. I don't blink, I don't look away. But neither does my sister, Celi. Cecelia, my favourite sister. There'd been a strong bond between us, once. Her brown hair hangs onto her shoulder, her lips part into a soft sweet smile. Is she one of the schemers too? I can't believe it; she has always been my ally. The only one left today, since Betty and Vinty have left the party early.

Since I'd got home the old bond has only been noticeable by its absence. She only has eyes for her fiancé, Harry Daniels, now. So, it's a shock to find her staring so intensely at me now. I won't back down, though her stare is provocative, aggressive. And she's certainly challenging me, like she's somehow turned into Hetty.

Whatever's happened she's never the one to back off. She's over by my side in an instance, sitting next to me and asks the difficult questions that they all want to ask, but no one else has the balls to put to me. She straightens her skirt and looks me directly in the eye.

"What the hell did happen after you which made you late in returning? Where were you? What were you doing?"

"Why should I tell you, it's private, it's personal. I can have private things, you know."

"Yeah, but this one is eating you. You've changed into a dull, miserable little man. If you don't let me in, there'll soon be nothing left of the laughing friendly Billy that we all used to love. Where were you in that week you were supposed to come home."

"I went to Picardy."

"What? Picardy? Where even is it for God's sake? France or Belgium, I guess. Why the hell would you go there?"

"To see Margaux." She's won. I look away, I can't keep up the eye contact.

There was a little laugh from the space above my head. "Look up, look at me. Oh, you've gone red, how sweet!" The giggle intensifies until she turns to hold her hands over her mouth. Then she looks up, deliberately and consciously straightens her features to disguise her amusement.

"Right, Billy Atherton." She turns her knees to position her body directly in front of me and looks directly at me, "I need to hear everything about… Picardy."

"Well," I said. Then stop and think.

"It was late in the evening, Celi.

I'd approached the house with a strong feeling of foreboding, a knot developed deep inside my guts that twisted and moved as I'd walked towards their home. It'd been a bright sunny day but now it was bitterly cold and even the slight breeze cut through my greatcoat.

Finding the farm house had been a major task, my memory of Amiens was pretty sketchy. The town looked very different today from late September of two years previous, but they'd been busy rebuilding shelled out houses for some time. I'd navigated mostly from remembering their house was east of the River Somme, I could see the impressive tower of the mediaeval Cathedrale Notre Dame in the distance, standing over the rubble which was what remained of the town, it was a miracle that it alone had survived. Margaux and her family lived close to the British cemetery from the first War.

The best thing about Picardy was the food, they seem to have some special way of adding extra flavour to everything. They even have a way of making eggs delicious, I never thought I'd be eating them there. Of all places the places in the world, that part of France should have been the last place in the world where I could eat eggs. But Margaux made them into a custard pie with burnt toffee on the top, really delicious. When I got back, I tried to show Mum how to make them. But the flavour we achieved was more like soggy cardboard, perhaps the recipe doesn't suit powdered egg. And it took up a whole week's ration of both egg and sugar."

"Well Billy, you should've known better. My Mum was a lovely, caring person but cooking was never the best of her skills."

"The worst thing was living with her parents. They were shocked by my appearance and obviously hadn't known that I was still in contact with Margaux. They clearly remembered me though. I was a strong association with a terrible time; the destruction of their home and their own injuries. Her father still walked with a limp, a severe handicap for a man who made his living from the land.

I was dismayed by the crude and simple nature of their house too. Picturesque stone walls on the outside, bare stone on the inside, the roof covered by metal panels, badly in need of repair or, better still, replacement."

"Yes, I see. You're painting a lovely picture but you've still not told me anything about the girl, that's what I really want to know." She leant forward and took my hand. "Let's get to the interesting bit, love."

"Well, Margaux was overjoyed. She'd never really expected that I'd visit her, much less understand we could have anything of a life together. "Ah, Billy. You 'ave com to see me!" she blurted out and rushed to hug me the moment I entered the house. My memory had played tricks on me, she was even prettier, though a bit smaller than I remembered but she really was such a sweet little thing. I was completely charmed. The sentiment was divine for a moment but her English was so fractured that a dreadful realisation came to me. *I was going to have to learn French.*

I guess it was really always doomed from that moment."

"Don't be silly, Billy. Love conquers all."

"Not sure this was really true love, Celi.

One evening, there came a knock at the door. When Pierre, her Dad, answered it a tall, blonde man stood in the frame of the door. Every one shot to their feet in a frenzy and shouted – Kurt, Kurt. He spoke to them in a language that was not French. They all replied in the same language, that was not English.

He shouted something, angry and aggressive, pointing a finger at me. They all looked at me and mumbled something in reply. Margaux sat down and started to cry.

It was too awkward for me, so I went outside, sat on a tree stump and looked around at the tranquil scenery. A blackbird was singing from the nearby bush. I lit a cigarette, having scrounged a packet of Gitanes, a bit of an acquired taste.

After a few minutes the teary Margaux came and sat next to me. "Sorry about all thees, Billy," She sobbed and looked down at her feet, taking a minute to settle.

"I know Kurt from German Army is here. He was my friend then and he said we would be for ever, but he went when your British Army come. After that nothing from him. Nothing since 1944. I thought him dead. After that, you were my pal by pen."

"Well now you must decide, Margaux. You can only have one boy friend."

She sobbed some more after this and I felt sorry for her, held her head on my knee and stayed silent with her for ten minutes. After that we held hands and walked back to the house. I opened the door and we went in to face her family. All of them turned their heads to look at me, I only noticed the German. There was silence. He looked at me, I looked at him.

One of us was going to have to go. Either me or the six-foot, blonde, blue-eyed Prussian. Which one would Margaux choose? Would I survive the Prussian's anger?

That night we were both sent to sleep in the hay in the old

barn, which lay close to the farm cottage. A large, rickety, wooden building that had been there for a century or more. Kurt said nothing to me, took a place on the far side. I couldn't see him but the whole night was filled with his restless sounds, which changed frequently. Initially heavy, rasping breathing which descended into snorts and snores. Then he started muttering to himself, there was the sound of violent rustling and turning in the straw. Although I understood none of his words, it was obvious that he was involved in a bitter argument with his dream.

I was puzzled by everything that was happening here. Who was Kurt and why had he come here, especially how had his arrival coincided with my own? Was it somehow connected with me?

Finally, I realised and when I did it was so obvious. I'd come back to the place where those German soldiers had been found executed. They'd followed me around in my sleep before, but here they were so much more powerful. Kurt was one of them, but here he had the power to walk around and look like he was alive in a normal way. Now he could reach me in the day time and in my real world. The dead Germans had decided that their fate was all my fault and he had been sent here to punish me. It all made sense.

The next day he'd have made sure we had boiled eggs for breakfast. He'll be able to sit there devouring his and mocking the way they frighten me. He might even bring all of that unit with him, staring at me over their boiled eggs with a waxy pallor. I'll not be able to face him."

"You do know that there's no such thing as ghosts, Billy. You were brought up as a good Catholic boy. You can't accept these superstitions."

"But I was there. I saw it all, Celi. You must believe that everyone has a soul. You were brought up as a good Catholic girl, so you must believe there's a moment after death when the soul leaves the body. I was there at that moment for these men and it's given them an attachment to me. Where does religion become superstition anyway? If it's supernatural we can't really know where the boundaries are.

So, early that morning, just as the first rays of sunlight hit, I gathered up my few belongings and walked into Amiens, to the gare to catch a train and get on my way home. I wrote to Margaux to thank her for their hospitality after I got home, but sadly, I haven't heard from her again."

Celi held my hand, "Oh, sorry, love. You really have suffered, haven't you? The British Army has given you back to us very damaged."

"No, Celi. I'm the one that survived through it all; alive, unhurt and uninjured."

"You may be alive, my sweet little brother, you may still have your body unharmed but you're certainly not uninjured. I'm really gonna have to keep an eye on you."

LATER THAT DAY

The flames of the fire light the dank room and its red light play in the shadows on the ceiling. The coal crackles in the hearth and occasionally spits tiny ruby red embers onto the rug before it, which now has an array of blackened wool forming a pattern on the front edge.

Around the room my family sit in silent comfort. The active part of the funeral and subsequent wake having finished, no one wants to be seen to leave first. There are the seven siblings of course, plus Joe's wife Agnes and daughter and Celi's fiancé Harry, an uncomfortably small space for such a large group. It reminds me of the time we had crammed in here in September '39 to listen to Neville Chamberlain's speech crackling its way to us through the radio set, which is still sitting on the shelf above our heads.

*

"This morning the British Ambassador in Berlin handed the German Government a final Note stating that, unless we heard from them by 11 o'clock that they were prepared at once to withdraw their troops from Poland, a state of war would exist between us.

I have to tell you now that no such undertaking has been received, and that consequently this country is at war with Germany."

The Prime Minister's words had spun around in my head several times before they sank down into a deep pool of black emotions. I'd felt dizzy; it was the worst possible news. Great Britain was at war with Germany. Again, after all of the slaughter last time. I felt frightened; this time it would be my generation that must shoulder the burden; this time I would be doing the fighting. It was my turn to die.

It was mid-morning and the whole family had gathered in the front room office to hear the broadcast. My father leant over slowly, turned off the radio and we all had watched him in silence.

*

It was a long time ago now and seemed even further back. The entire span of the war separated these times: the slaughter had again been terrible, but I'd shouldered the burden and done the fighting. Even more than that, the whole Palestine thing that had never been in the plan. Although it had been my turn to die, I'd failed to do so. My parents had now both gone and we'd to find new lives, new roles without them at the centre of our world.

There might not be any conversation but there's a lot of thought. I look around the room at the huge personalities that occupy so little space. Joe, the eldest and always identifies himself as our leader. Gertie, his accomplice and Ignatius, who we always call Nash. They are the senior group, the older ones who always hold themselves just a little distant from our junior group. They consider themselves the clever, capable ones.

Then there's me. A lot younger than the clever, capable ones but still older than Betty, Celi and Vinty, the young ones. I wonder what'd happened between Nash's birth and my own? No doubt there'd been a story to that but I'd never asked for it and it's far too late now.

Looking round the room my eyes meet Celi's. Again. Something is stirring behind those brown eyes and it's all about me. Now I know how a chaffinch feels when it's spotted by a sparrow hawk. I need a bush to hide in. Too late, here comes the hawk. Grabbing me by the hand Celi drags me in to the kitchen, where Joe is smoking a Park Drive.

"Right, you two. We're going to have it out right now. We'll settle all this here."

"Settle what?"

All this bickering between the two of you. It has to stop. It serves no purpose and helps no one. Besides underneath it all, you're still brothers, you're even quite like each other. You're both digging in your heels and are just both too stupid to back down. Well, I'm not having it anymore."

"Oh, you're not? Well actually Celi, it's none of your business."

"I say it is my business. It's all of our business if we're a family. And I say we all need you both to see a bit of sense, shake hands and be friends again, like sensible grown-ups."

"Oh! So, you think it's as simple as that do you? It can just be forgotten and swept away, as though nothing had ever happened."

"Yes. For a start, nothing actually did ever happen."

"That's not true, I never got what I was promised. That's all I ever wanted, what was promised. All because Joe worked away behind my back to get it off me. He's held a grudge against me, ever since I joined up."

"Billy! You're seeing something that isn't even there. I don't care about the house and I've never spoke to Dad about it. If he changed his will it was because he chose to. I've never suggested that to him."

"I think Joe's telling you the truth, Billy. To be honest with you, we all thought that it wasn't right for the family inheritance to go to just one of us. I'll admit that I've said that to Dad. I don't think he'd really thought it through when he made that promise. It was just an honest mistake. He realised that later but I guess he was too

253

embarrassed to say that to you. Or maybe he's just been too ill since you came back from the Army.

I don't think you should bear Dad a grudge over that. Especially where he is now."

There is a silence as we all glower at each other, Celi with her arms folded, determined to stare us both out. Then Joe speaks: "If it means that much to you, I'll give up my share so you and all the others can get a bit more. Agnes and I have already bought our house."

This is not part of the plan, it doesn't fit. Joe can't have spent the whole war scheming against me only to give it up so easily. Something's wrong with this. It would make him a completely different person than the one I've known all these years.

Then Joe laughs. I laugh, just a bit of a laugh. And Celi laughs out loud.

We all hug and Joe and I shake hands. The war is over.

After the war

A letter had arrived for me. It was waiting for me on my return and added a new level to the mystery for Celi. A letter with an American stamp and New York post mark. What could have brought that here, who could I possibly know there? It had been difficult for her to understand about Amiens, but at least they knew I'd been there. But New York? It was impossible for me to have been there, ridiculous to think that I'd know anyone from that far off place.

To add to the curiosity of my little sister, I was reluctant to explain it. This was not like her own Billy, once so open and honest. That Billy had not returned from the war. Naturally, she resented the change and wondered why. Suspicions clouded our friendship.

I'm sure Celi has gossiped about it with Vince and Betty. I saw them whispering together and make a comment before all their eyes turned to me. They discussed it in darkened places, the corner of rooms and in the corridor. If I moved, they scuttled away, like mice looking for a place to hide.

Nothing was said to me, I was left to feel it drifting in the air. A mist of curtailed whispers and hidden glances. Joe brushed it aside, as though it was just not important enough to deserve his attention. I never saw his hand move with a dismissive shrug of contempt but I was conscious of a haughty manner. A shrug of the shoulders here, a swivel of the hips there. I've lived in the cauldron of suppressed feelings and emotions that makes up an Army camp and know how to read body language.

I wasn't reticent just about foreign contacts, I'd very little to say about my adventures in either Europe or Palestine. Those times were gone, only painful memories remained. I'd no desire to revisit any of it, let alone share it. "War is an abomination," was all I wanted to say about my war time experiences. "Let that be enough explanation."

When I sat down in this room and opened the letter that had held pride of place on the mantelpiece, I felt their eyes following me. Their questions didn't need to be spoken, they wandered unsaid in the air around me, coloured by disappointment that I was so indifferent to their burning need to know.

The answer, had they known it, said that nothing was happening. It'd all happened and finished much earlier, the letter was an amazing and unexpected afterthought. A rich and full flavoured taste of those distant events of years ago. It has the power to pitch me back into a dream of something that might have been. Back onto the seat of a motor cycle roaring across the Promised Land, in the company of an angel. I can still feel the soft touch of her breasts pushing against my back as we bumped over the rocky road to Jerusalem, the heat of the sun burning my arms and the dust stinging my eyes.

She was never mine but was the object of my hopes for a moment; the woman whose company I worked so hard to earn and enjoy. I'd had that company for just a few hours, the memory still has the power to raise joy in my soul and even a bitter sweet, forlorn and futile hope. But only for a heartbeat. Each time the hope rises I only need to glance around this sullen room for them to be brought crashing back down to earth.

My family have become used to that far-away look, knowing

I've left the room and gone back in time to events that I'll never share. It would confuse them and make them realise that they don't know me at all. They're right to be concerned. I know myself that I'm drifting off to a land I left behind, spending my time in a dream: reliving my first meeting with Hetty at the reception, walking through the gardens to sit on the bench as the fat officers played tennis, or watching Hetty and Breck dancing to Chattanooga Choo Choo, as the swing band plays on the terrace.

Gertie and Nash know that I see them conspiring in corners. So, they move out of sight, so their schemes are invisible to me. Or so they think. But I know, I know for certain that they are still sneering at me, judging me.

I'm not sure how she got my address, that was the first mystery. The second was why she was interested enough to write at all. I always thought of my overseas service as being a different world, not connected in anyway with dreary Lancashire, but she managed to find a way to penetrate my inner world, reach into the other side of my life, from thousands of miles away. It does seem that the Zionists have easy access to every piece of information the British military holds. I don't know whether to be horrified and frightened, or shrug my shoulders and laugh. It's hard not to admire their ingenuity and efficiency.

This letter is a prized possession, reminding me of someone I'll never see again, never hear from again. I won't share it, no one else has read it and no one ever will. I carry that letter everywhere, in my wallet. It never helps me to read it, over and over again, but I do it any way.

I've got it now in my breast pocket. Here it is:

179 Chapel St.,
Leigh,
Lancs
Great Britain

13th Nov 1946

Dear Billy,

Yes, I always knew your name. It was just fun to tease you by pretending I didn't. I was fond of you, in my own way. You were a sweet boy, chatting to me in the hotel and garden. You were always trying to impress me and you really succeeded when you turned up on the motorbike to rescue me. We had fun riding across the land back to the city and I loved our meal together, under palm trees and in the sun.

I'm pleased and a little surprised that you got out alive. Now you can enjoy being at home, something I will never know. I'm not even sure what that word really means. I had to leave my childhood home, I remember so little of Piastow, and move to a new home far away in Jerusalem. As you know that home was also taken away when I had to flee the country. So now America is my new home. I got what I asked for, my uncle got me an entry visa to the USA and after a while I'll be able to apply for citizenship.

I'm working for the Zionist mission, they think I'm some sort of hero here, for my actions against the British. You must think that's funny as you know how much I messed up in Jerusalem. My family are still in prison there and that hurts more than anything.

I know you didn't really want to be there and hope you're happy to be in your cold, wet country. It was always better to leave lovely, sunny Israel to the lovely, sunny Israelis. We deserve it, it's our land. You British deserve only to own your own country, nowhere else. You should celebrate having been in Israel at the time of our emergence as a new nation. This is important to the whole world, real history in the making.

Thank you for standing up for me in the court, I was very frightened and expected to be hanged. Sorry about Algy, he was quite nice, just got himself in the wrong place and I had my duty to perform.

I hope you enjoy your tennis and have a good life, you're better than any of your horrid officers.

Good luck and goodbye for ever,
Hetty

Also by the Author

VIKING VOICES
THE SWORD OF AMLETH

Chapter One

THE BATTLE OF DYFLINN

Even in the midst of a siege it is a lovely feeling to wake up lying alongside your new bride.

Lovely, but this time it is also tinged with a bitter sense of anxiety, so there is not too much of our happy laughter together today. Aud puts her head on my shoulder, too sleepy to speak while we lie side by side together, our naked skin touching sensually under the warm skins that cover us. We feel safe and comfortable here but we are also very conscious of how dangerous and how cold it is beyond these skins.

I am Amleth, Amleth Eriksson, and a proud young warrior of the Lochlain of Dyflinn, the Norse people who founded this town long ago. Alongside me is my darling wife, the tall, blonde and very beautiful Aud Gerdsdottar. I am looking into her eyes but am not very comforted by the anxiety I can see etched on her face today.